By MARK DAVID CAMPBELL

Tiramisu After Midnight

Published by DREAMSPINNER PRESS
www.dreamspinnerpress.com

Mark David Campbell

Tiramisu After Midnight

Published by
DREAMSPINNER PRESS

5032 Capital Circle SW, Suite 2, PMB# 279, Tallahassee, FL 32305-7886 USA
www.dreamspinnerpress.com

Tiramisu After Midnight
© 2020 Mark David Campbell

Cover Art
© 2020 Tiferet Design
http://www.tiferetdesign.com/
Cover content is for illustrative purposes only and any person depicted on the cover is a model.

Trade Paperback ISBN: 978-1-64405-824-4
Digital ISBN: 978-1-64405-823-7
Library of Congress Control Number: 2019957868
Trade Paperback published June 2020
v. 1.0

Printed in the United States of America

Dedicated to my husband, who else?

ACKNOWLEDGMENTS

THANK YOU to Nancy Feyen, Robert Morley, Andrea Elizabeth Smith, and the members of the Milano English Language Writers' Group, for their encouragement, criticism, and guidance. Thanks to the Onondaga Historical Association for their suggestions about Syracuse, New York, and Eleonor Shannon for her advice on wine. Also, thank you to my other friends, Markus Dolderer and Debra Pecoraro, who read and commented on various versions of the manuscript. Finally, thank you to my friends and family at Lago Maggiore and especially to my husband, Piero Salvioni, for his recipes.

PART ONE

CHAPTER ONE

ENRICO WALKED into the bedroom, unpinned his plastic name tag, and placed it on the dresser. "I can't believe it's only June and I'm already sweating like a pig."

"Global warming," Fabrizio said without looking up from his computer. "How was work?"

"We've got a German tour group coming in this afternoon." Enrico undid the knot of his tie and unbuttoned his shirt. "Oh, and Ottavio and his new best friend Massimo entertained me with a set of jokes." Enrico sneered. "Today it was gays and Arabs; yesterday it was gays and women."

"Why don't you just tell them to go put it in their ass?" Fabrizio continued to stare at his screen.

"Because if I let them see I'm upset, it just eggs them on." Enrico took off his white shirt, held it up, sniffed it, and scrunched up his nose. "Italy is full of guys like them. And there's not a thing I can do about that." Enrico tossed his shirt into the laundry basket and plunked down onto the bed.

Fabrizio looked up from his screen. "Sooner or later you're going to have to stand up to them."

"Well, now is not the time," Enrico said. "By the way, have you paid the garbage tax yet?"

Fabrizio shook his head. "No, not yet. We barely had enough to cover the gas and electricity."

"Well, it'll just have to wait until we get paid next week." Enrico shrugged.

"We need to find something better than the Sunshine Inn." Fabrizio looked back at his screen. "It rains here half the time anyway."

It had only been a year since the boys had graduated from college in the hospitality and restaurant service program. Afterward, they both got jobs at the Sunshine Inn, the small local hotel in Castelveccana, the village just over the hill from their house, on the shore of Lago Maggiore in Northern Italy. During the May to October tourist season, Fabrizio, who was good at accounting, did the books, and Enrico, who spoke English and German quite well, worked at reception. During the fall and winter months, when there were no tourists, they helped their friend Angelo clean and maintain the gardens and grounds of the grand villas for the rich people from Milan who summered at the lake. And even if Fabrizio longed for new horizons, Enrico never wanted to venture too far from his lakeside home. Besides, Papà was not well and they couldn't abandon him or Tata.

"Listen, I just came home to change into a fresh shirt. Massimo has a football game at seven, so Ottavio told me I have to cover his shift." Enrico stood up and walked into the bathroom. "I've got a splitting headache." He rubbed his temples.

"Why do you always have to cover for Massimo?" Fabrizio already knew the answer to that question.

"Guess." Enrico spit out the word as he came out of the bathroom holding a glass of water with a painkiller fizzing inside.

"Phone Ottavio and tell him you can't come in—you're sick."

"And who's going to receive the twelve Germans arriving at six?" Enrico sat down on the bed. "I know it's just a job for you, but when Luca retires, I'm next in line for a promotion." Enrico threw back the glass of water. "Yuck." He stuck out his tongue. "But Ottavio is going make me grovel for it first."

"Look, you stay here. I'll cover for you." Fabrizio opened the closet and took out a white shirt and black tie. "You owe me, *fratellino*." Fabrizio always liked to remind Enrico that he was the eldest, sometimes just to taunt him, but mostly because Fabrizio felt it was his responsibility to protect his brother, even if they'd been born only four minutes apart.

"Yes, yes, I owe you," Enrico said as he flopped backward onto the bed.

"Here, do my tie." Fabrizio bent over and Enrico sat up again and looped his tie, knotted it, and pulled it straight.

"Take my name tag. Remember, you're supposed to be me. And please, whatever you do, don't say anything to make Ottavio angry," Enrico moaned.

Fabrizio pinned Enrico's name tag on his shirt. "Give me the scooter license, just in case."

Enrico threw his brother his wallet and Fabrizio stuffed it into his back pocket. Even if he was the oldest, Fabrizio still hadn't got his motorbike license yet. Maybe he was nervous about taking the exam or just too lazy. One thing was for sure, since they were rarely apart, Fabrizio really didn't need his own license. It had always been like that between them. They shared most things: socks, underwear and clothes, toys and books, and even homework assignments. Besides, they only had one scooter, so why would they both need a license?

Papà had bought the blue Vespa scooter back in 1982, before the boys were born, but after he became ill it remained sitting in the garage under a tarp. On the day the boys turned eighteen, they wheeled it out into the light of day. They sprayed it with the garden hose and lathered it down with dish detergent. Then they wiped it clean, rinsed and dried it, changed the plugs and oil, and filled the gas tank. It took about twenty sharp pumps of the starter pedal before the gas made its way into the engine.

"See, I told you. These Vespas are indestructible!" Enrico said loudly above the idling engine.

"Let's call her Angelina," Fabrizio said.

"Why Angelina?" Enrico revved the accelerator.

"Because its wide back end reminds me of Angelina down at Bar Happy." He cupped both hands and jiggled them.

"You're a pig, you know?" Enrico sneered.

"I know." Fabrizio grinned. "But whatever you do, don't tell her we named our scooter in her honor."

That was five years ago, and ever since then, both summer and winter, Angelina had faithfully served the boys as their only means of transportation.

Fabrizio rushed out of the bedroom and down the stairs, darted outside across the terrace and down the steps to where Angelina was sitting in the gravel driveway. He slipped his helmet on, straddled the bike, and with a sharp jerk popped it off its kickstand and pumped the accelerator with his full weight. The motor sprang to life, roaring like a demonic popcorn maker and belching out a cloud of blue smoke.

Fabrizio gunned the accelerator, sending fumes and a spray of gravel out behind. He steered up the drive, out the gate, and onto the pavement. Angelina made a low throaty growl as it labored up the steep hill toward the church in second gear. At the crest of the hill, Fabrizio shifted into third and Angelina's growl rose a note. He sped past the church steps, under the arched passageway between the buildings, and down the other side of the hill. Shifting into fourth, he flew down the hill past the stop sign at the foot of the street and zoomed out onto the southbound lane of the Lago Maggiore provincial road, which ran from Laveno along the eastern shore of the lake north to Luino and the border with Switzerland.

Swooping sharply around the curve, he turned down the street into the village of Castelveccana nestled in the bay below. Angelina puttered softly as Fabrizio eased off the accelerator and glided past the row of old wooden boats that were pulled up and fastened along the edge of the sloping break wall of the harbor like seals lazing in the late-afternoon sun; while moored to floating buoys out in the bay, shiny white fiberglass sailboats and speedboats bobbed up and down like horses waiting at the gate for a race to start.

He glided up to a planter filled with a red flowering oleander bush in front of the newly renovated four-story art deco Sunshine Inn, which sat directly across the street from the port. With a sharp yank, he pulled Angelina up onto its kickstand and flicked off the engine. He slipped off the seat, readjusted his pants, which had bunched up around his crotch, and hung his helmet on the handlebar. Checking himself in the mirror, he smoothed his thick black hair back, then strolled up the steps and in through the front door.

"Hi, Fabrizio," Lucia chirped as she looked up from her screen at the reception desk. "I thought Enrico was coming in."

"He's got a headache, so he asked me to cover for him."

"You're such a sweet brother." Lucia kissed him on each cheek.

"And I'm not fattening either, so I wouldn't ruin your diet." Fabrizio put on his best sexy smile.

Lucia gave him a mock shove. "I'll be sure to mention that to my husband."

"Ah, why are all the beautiful women married?" Fabrizio pouted.

Lucia rolled her eyes. "Hey, did you hear?"

"Hear what?"

"Ottavio just promoted Massimo to head receptionist." Lucia shook her head.

"What?"

She let out a long breath. "I know, it was supposed to be Enrico's promotion." She patted Fabrizio's arm. "I tried to reason with him, but he's always had it out for Enrico."

Fabrizio felt his face burn and he began to sweat. "I want to hear this for myself." He turned and marched toward Ottavio's office.

"I wouldn't if I were you. He's in one of his moods," she called after him as she packed up her purse.

Ottavio was sitting at his desk, the buttons of his shirt straining to hold in his belly.

"Is it true that you made Massimo head receptionist?" Fabrizio stepped through the doorway.

Ottavio leaned back in his chair and locked his hands behind his head, making no attempt to hide the image of the bare-breasted woman on his screen. "Yes, as a matter of fact I did. Do you have a problem with that, Enrico?"

Fabrizio knew Ottavio could never tell the difference between him and his brother, and as he often did, Fabrizio just answered as if he were Enrico. "I've worked here for four summers—longer than anyone on reception. I'm always on time. I work every holiday, and I cover for the others when they're sick. And I've put in a lot of overtime I've never been paid for."

"My decision is not based on performance. I made my decision based on potential. Now get out of here. I'm busy." Ottavio unlocked his fingers, sat forward, and looked back at his virtual girlfriend and leered.

Fabrizio's heart was thumping. He put his knuckles on the end of Ottavio's desk and leaned forward. "Last August when you went away on your honeymoon and we were short-staffed, I took over your responsibilities, plus your wife's shifts on the front desk. I've already proven I can do the job and more."

Ottavio looked up. "Who do you think you are to question me? I'm the hotel manager here, not you."

"Massimo only just started this May." Fabrizio stood upright and shot out his open palms. "And in that short time, he's managed to piss off everybody in the kitchen by helping himself to the food, and also the cleaning staff after he used one of the guest rooms for a little tryst and left it in a state of disaster."

"Those are minor things I can overlook." Ottavio shrugged. "Hey…." He snorted out a laugh. "He's a hot-blooded Italian male."

Fabrizio continued. "Not to mention, he's often late, continually messes up the reservations, watches the football game, and ignores the guests."

"I can make allowances for Massimo." Ottavio leaned back and tucked in his shirt. "He's a football star and knows how the chain of command works. I chose him because I want a real leader who the staff respects."

"Nobody can stand working with him and, as far as I can see, you're the only one who has any respect for him."

Ottavio stood up promptly, sending his chair rolling back against the wall. "Oh, you think anyone respects you? That's a laugh!" Ottavio jabbed his finger at Fabrizio. "Who's going to take orders from a little *frocio* like you?"

Bile rose up in the back of Fabrizio's throat. He squeezed his fists tight. He wanted to smash Ottavio in the face, but Ottavio held all the cards; his brother would lose his job and he would end up in court. He was trembling as he turned to leave.

"You're fired! And tell your brother Fabrizio to stay away from my wife. If he dances with her again, he'll regret it."

Fabrizio stopped and turned back. "I am Fabrizio, dickhead! And as far as your wife goes, she's the one who asked me to dance. Told me her husband couldn't keep up the rhythm."

"Get out of here and take your *frocio* brother's things with you. You're both fired!"

ENRICO LOOKED up from his book and frowned as Fabrizio walked into the room. "Why are you back already?"

"I had a little talk with Ottavio about your promotion." Fabrizio avoided Enrico's eyes.

"You did what!" Enrico pushed himself upright in bed.

"Eh, all I did was point out how dedicated and responsible you are."

"I hope you didn't say anything to piss him off." Enrico stared suspiciously at his brother.

"I must have." Fabrizio shook his head. "Because he fired both of us."

"What!" Enrico launched his hardcover book directly at Fabrizio's head. The corner of the book caught Fabrizio's eyebrow with a dull thud, splitting it open. A trickle of blood ran down the side of his face. Enrico looked in horror at what he'd done. He leaped out of bed and over to his brother. "Oh shit! Sorry, sorry. Are you all right?"

"*Porca puttana*! You could've taken my eye out." Fabrizio was holding the side of his face.

"I wasn't thinking." Enrico was trembling. "It just happened."

"Get me a towel. I'm bleeding like a statue of the Virgin," Fabrizio said.

Enrico returned with a washcloth. He took Fabrizio's hand from his face, dabbed at his eye, and examined the wound. "You're going to need stitches."

"Ottavio gave your job to Massimo," Fabrizio said. "I was trying to stick up for you."

"Screw Ottavio! It's just that I hoped the hotel would lead to something more stable for us. Come on. We'd better go to the outpatients." Enrico headed out the room with Fabrizio following, holding the cloth against the side of his face.

"Angelo could use our help now that Omar's gone," Fabrizio said as they hurried down the stairs.

Enrico grabbed the second helmet that was sitting by the door. "What happened to Omar?" Enrico put on his helmet.

"Couldn't get his papers." Fabrizio pulled the sides of his helmet out as wide as he could and carefully slipped it on so as not to touch his wound. "He said he'd had enough of the Italian *cazzate* and was going to Germany to find a factory job." Fabrizio delicately tucked the blood-spotted washcloth under the edge of the helmet. "Hey, why don't we go to Germany too? They say there's lots of work there, and since we're EU citizens, we'd be legal."

Enrico straddled Angelina and pumped the starter pedal with his foot.

"Or we could even travel and see the world!" Fabrizio said above the roar of the engine.

"We can't leave Tata alone to look after Papà." Enrico revved the engine.

Fabrizio let out a breath. "Yeah, I know. It was just a thought." He braced himself on Enrico's shoulders, swung his leg over, and straddled the seat behind, gripping his brother's waist.

Enrico gunned the accelerator and they sped down the driveway, leaving a cloud of blue smoke and a spray of gravel behind them.

Fabrizio leaned close to his brother's ear and shouted above the growl of Angelina, "Turn right! Let's go to Laveno instead."

"But the hospital in Luino is closer."

"Yeah, but Chiara should be on shift in Laveno. You know, the one with the big tits." He sat back, then leaned in close again. "But don't tell her how it really happened. Say… I don't know…. Tell her I got into a fight. No, better! Tell her I crashed during a Formula 1 test run."

CHAPTER TWO

TYPICAL OF northern New York State in late June, the evening of their graduation from Syracuse Central High was clear and cool. An hour before the ceremony Jessy, Owen, and Maggie met at their usual hiding spot at the far end of the parking lot behind the old oak tree.

"So, are you ready, Mr. Valedictorian?" Jessy said.

"I'd be scared shitless if I had to give the speech." Maggie sat down on the exposed root of the oak.

"I am. I put on a ton of deodorant, but my hands are sweating like clams." Owen rubbed his hands on the side of his jeans and sat down beside Maggie.

"Well, I have a little something that will calm you down." Jessy took out a joint, stuck it in his mouth, and lit it.

"Wow! I can't believe I made it through." Maggie nudged Owen with her shoulder. "But what's going to happen to the Terrible Trio now?"

The Terrible Trio was the name they had given themselves, but their trio was anything but terrible. With his *GQ* looks, swimmer's physique, and goofy sense of humor, every boy since grade school had vied to be Jessy's best friend and every girl longed to be paraded on his arm. While Jessy was an American dream, Owen, with his rusty hair, freckles, and nervous eye-twitch, was basically a nerd, the top of his class and on the yearbook committee. But Jessy and Owen had a kind of symbiosis. It was as if Jessy were the yin and Owen the yang, or maybe even Batman and Robin. Whether it could be attributed to oriental mysticism, comic books, or simply two boys who completed each other, you rarely met one without the other.

Maggie, on the other hand, hiding within her long black hair and baggy black clothes, was the girl who nobody had ever noticed. At least until that day the boys adopted her, and from then on, if Jessy and Owen were the dynamic duo, then she was Catwoman.

Owen looked up at Jessy. "We've still got the summer together." His hand was trembling as Jessy handed him the joint.

"So, what are you going to say tonight?" Jessy said.

He had offered to help Owen with his speech, and surely with Jessy's gift at turning a phrase it would have been great, but Owen had wanted to do it on his own. Perhaps Owen was asserting his independence, or maybe he needed to say something very personal without the guidance and protection of Jessy.

"You know, the usual shit. The future is ours, blah, blah, blah. Be true to yourself, blah, blah, blah." Owen took a long toke.

"Wouldn't it be cool to, like, tell them the real truth?" Maggie said. "Man, they'd have a collective shit hemorrhage!"

"This is your last chance to come clean and tell them all," Jessy said with a lyrical taunt.

"Ha, I've managed to stay just below radar all these years, and I'm sure as shit not going to blow it now." Owen scoffed.

Of course there had already been gossip about Owen, but his best friend was Jessy, the most popular guy in school and an athlete. Who could possibly believe that Jessy was best friends with a fairy boy?

"Besides," Owen added, "we still have to live here, and Syracuse is not that big."

"Hey, did you talk to your mom about college yet?" Maggie looked up at Owen.

"Yeah, she said my dad won't pay for my tuition, but as long as I'm still living at home and still going to school, he has to continue to pay child support." Owen scowled. "And she wants to make him pay as long as possible." Owen took a short toke. "It's only three hundred dollars a month, but with my tuition waiver and a part-time job, I should be able to swing it."

"Man, everything has a price tag, doesn't it?" Jessy frowned.

"Yup, and according to the state of New York, I'm worth ten dollars a day." Owen plunked down beside Maggie and handed her the joint."

"Well, my only prospect is Dad's real estate agency." Maggie held the joint in her fingers.

"What's wrong with that?" Jessy said.

"Nothing, I guess." Maggie sighed. "It's just, it's like my whole future has already been mapped out before I've even had a chance to taste life and see the world. How long will it be before I become just like Pathetic Patty? I can get really fat and start to wear neon polyester pants and collect Hello Kitty and manga cult figurines, and check my

Facebook every ten minutes in case someone has given me a like for some stupid cat picture I posted?"

"Hey, are you going to take a drag, or are you just planning to hold on to it while you live out your Patty paranoia?" Jessy asked.

Maggie pinched the joint delicately between her forefinger and thumb and took a long toke. Holding it in her lungs, she passed the joint back to Jessy. "Have you made up your mind yet?"

"Yeah, you've got that swimming scholarship," Owen said, doing his best to hide the panic in his voice at the thought of Jessy leaving for Michigan State.

Jessy's chest expanded like a cobra's hood as he drew in the smoke. "The high school swim team is one thing," he squeaked out as he held the smoke in his lungs. "But I'm hardly big league, and the truth is I don't want to be just another chlorine rat who winds up coaching a bunch of pimply backed adolescents." Jessy released his cloud and passed the joint to Owen.

Owen took a toke, trying to appear nonchalant and not let on how relieved he was.

"But I am seriously thinking about circus school in Montreal," Jessy added.

Owen coughed out his puff. "Circus school?" he said as he gasped for air between coughs. "But Montreal is like a foreign country!"

"Yeah, or maybe creative writing here at Syracuse U." Jessy thumped Owen on the back.

"What would you write about?" Maggie took the joint from Owen.

"I don't know. Us, maybe," Jessy said.

"Us?" Owen said.

"Yeah, you and me and Maggie, the Terrible Trio," Jessy said.

"Speaking of us, I want to ask you two something." Maggie held the joint to her lips and took a drag.

"Yes, it's true. Jessy did have sex in the showers with that guy from Jefferson High after the swim meet," Owen said.

Maggie shook her head and waved her hands in the air, then blew out the smoke. "I already know that. And he also fooled around with Keven Simpson under the bleachers during band practice."

"Wait a minute!" Owen turned to Jessy. "You had sex with Keven Simpson and didn't tell me?"

Jessy put on his innocent little bad-boy face. "Well, it wasn't really sex. I just let him play my trombone."

Owen frowned. "And you told Maggie but didn't share with me?"

"I told you." Jessy hunched his shoulders. "Didn't I?"

"No, asshole. You didn't." Owen swallowed the rising lump in his throat. If only there were some way to make Jessy understand how much he loved him and that he was willing to risk everything for him.

Jessy plunked down beside Owen and reached over and hugged his neck. "Well, it was no biggie. Sorry."

Maggie looked at Jessy, then back at Owen.

Of course anyone could see Owen was hopelessly in love with his best friend and, oddly, for a boy like Jessy, whom the world seemed ready to welcome with open arms, he needed Owen's adoration most of all. But would Jessy ever completely reciprocate his love?

"Excuse me for interrupting the hug-fest, but can we return to my question?"

"Yes, dear." Jessy released Owen and sat up straight. "Vaginal dryness, clitoral orgasm, blow job techniques—what do you want to know about?"

"No, idiot!" Maggie handed the tiny nub of a joint over to Jessy. "I want to know why you two asked me to come for coffee with you that first time—seriously."

"Seriously?" Jessy sucked in air and the remains of the smoke.

"Yes. Why me?" Maggie said.

"Simple," Jessy said.

"'Cause you are, well, Maggie." Owen held out his hands.

Maggie cocked her head and furrowed her brow.

"We thought about asking Anna Lester." Jessy held up the nub and examined it. Then with a flick, he sent it sailing through the air. "But she always wears those push-up torpedo bras."

"And she's about as interesting as hemorrhoids," Owen added.

"Oh, my aunt got those!" Maggie piped up. "One was about the size of my little finger." She held up her finger.

Owen grabbed his head. "Ahh!"

"Well it was!" Maggie said. "I saw it!"

"Oh, the horror!" Jessy moaned. "I'm not even going to ask."

"Thanks for the visuals," Owen said and covered his face. "I'll never be able to look your aunt in the eyes again."

"And now you know why we love you." Jessy laughed.

"What other girl in school could discuss blow jobs, smoke weed, and tell us about her aunt's hemorrhoids in the same conversation?" Owen beamed.

"Hey! We better get inside," Jessy said as he jumped to his feet.

"After all, you have a big speech to give," Maggie said to Owen as Jessy pulled her up.

Jessy bowed toward Owen, who was still seated on the ground. "Oh, great one, we await you to impart your words of truth and wisdom upon us." Jessy reached out and took Owen's hands, pulled him to his feet, and wrapped him in his arms. "I hope you know how proud I am of you," Jessy said staring deep into Owen's eyes.

Owen, unable to look away, unable to run, tried to smile, but his lips began to quiver and his eye twitched. Jessy clasped the back of Owen's head and pressed their foreheads together. "Go in there and knock 'em off their feet." Then Jessy kissed him on the lips.

Owen's head spun and he felt that all too familiar roll in the pit of his stomach. He knew it wasn't nervousness over the speech he was about to give. It was, as always, Jessy.

"C'mon, you two." Maggie tugged at Jessy's arm. "We're going to be late."

The high school gym floor was covered with thick plastic sheets to protect the wooden basketball court and filled with stackable chairs. Parents, all vying to get the best view and camera angle, chatted with one another and pointed to their children on the stage dressed in rented black robes and sandwich-board hats. Owen stood at the podium in front of the row of graduates and looked out at the audience. His mother, in her cream dress, white pearls, and clutch purse, and his sister, in a yellow dress and patent leather shoes, were poised in the front row. His mother gave him a nod of approval and held up her phone.

Owen started his speech in the usual way by thanking his mother and sister, friends and teachers. Just as he had said, he talked about the horizons that lay ahead. But when he reached the part about being true to yourself and those who are important to you, what Jessy said back at the oak tree about this being his last chance to come clean in front of everyone, suddenly resounded in his head. His heart pounded. He cleared his throat and said, "And now for my truth...."

Not that he had planned to do it. It just came out. Like a fart in church, the word *gay* seemed to echo throughout the room, followed by an uneasy silence. After years of hiding from that dreaded label in the security of Jessy's shadow, there he stood on center stage in the school gym, making his declaration out loud for all to hear.

For the first time in his life Jessy was speechless, but Maggie, who had never called attention to herself during her entire high school career, stepped onto center stage and burst out with a hoot, waving her arms in the air. Jessy followed her cue, bouncing around the stage like a big rubber ball. He picked Owen up from behind, lifted him off his feet, and yelled, "That's my boy!"

His classmates on the stage behind him clapped and cheered and one by one, with the measured spirit of political correctness, parents throughout the room clapped along. Even the principal, who had refused to allow him to bring Jessy as his date to the prom, clapped. While their classmates and some of the teachers crowded around him, Owen caught a flash of his mother clutching his sister by her hand as they quickly made their escape out the doors of the gymnasium.

After the ceremony, he and Jessy walked back to Owen's house together. Jessy stood in the street as Owen sauntered down the walkway, past the *Make America Great Again* sign on the front lawn, up to the front door of his house where the red, white, and blue hung listlessly over the portico. There on the stoop was Owen's suitcase with a bible resting on top.

Owen imagined his mother sitting inside on the sofa with a cup of herbal tea to calm her nerves. He looked up at his little sister peeking out through the second-floor window. He waved, but she didn't wave back. He looked back down at his suitcase. Sticking out from the bible like a bookmarker were some bills—three hundred dollars—the exact amount of his child support for the month of June. He opened the bible. Just as he expected, Genesis, Chapter 18—Sodom and Gomorrah. She didn't need to tell him to his face he was out, cut off, and his plans for university were gone. He took the bills, clapped the bible shut, and tossed it on the stoop.

As he trudged back down the walkway trailing his suitcase, its plastic wheels sounding like a miniature train, he remembered watching his father through his bedroom window doing the same almost ten years ago, and he felt that deep sadness once again.

Still standing there in the street waiting was Jessy.

"Left or right side of the bed?" Jessy said as he threw his arm over Owen's shoulder.

CHAPTER THREE

"C'MON OVER here and take a look at this." Fabrizio leaned forward and fiddled with the keys of his laptop as Enrico walked into their bedroom.

"Let me get changed first." Enrico took off his jeans and slipped on a pair of sweats.

"I had to make a website for my online business course." Fabrizio clicked the mouse and pulled up a home page with a wallpaper picture of the lake in the background, the title *Lago B&B* in red-white-and-green-striped letters across the top banner, and a row of thumbnail photos of the house across the lower part of the screen.

Enrico was now standing behind with his hands resting on his brother's shoulders.

Fabrizio clicked on the first thumbnail and it expanded and filled the screen.

"Wow, where'd you get the photo of the house?" Enrico said as he stared at the image of their eighteenth-century three-story faux-brick villa, with its terra-cotta-tiled roof, nestled amidst the *tulia* trees and northern palms like a giant hen in the roost. The tower, where the boys had their bedroom, stood majestically against the blue Alpino sky. Just under the eaves of the tile roof, the yellow band inscribed with zodiac designs circumscribed the villa, and every window was flanked by wooden shutters. Red, pink, and yellow roses filled the garden like the colored paper children throw during Carnival.

"They're all yours. I just photoshopped them a bit." Fabrizio turned and looked at his brother.

Enrico studied the other photos. "A bit? We look like a regal villa. The only thing that's real is Papà's rose garden."

"You know with a little cash the old place could look like this again," Fabrizio said.

The house had originally been their grandmother's. After her death, Francesca, their older half sister, got a luxurious apartment in Milan and the boys got the house at the lake. But since the boys were babies at the time, Francesca took over managing the combined estates and had done so ever since.

"I wish we could fix it up, but Francesca said any leftover money in the inheritance fund is almost gone, and so if we don't figure out something soon, we could lose everything," Enrico said.

"That's why everyone calls me the brains of the family." Fabrizio jabbed his brother with his elbow.

"Everyone calls you something, but it's definitely not the brains of the family." Enrico bent over and bit his brother lightly on his shoulder.

"Well, they're going to start after our B&B is a big success."

"What B&B?"

"Ours. Here at the house," Fabrizio said.

Enrico wrinkled his brow. "You know, a B&B is not a bad idea. If we moved downstairs to the back of the house with Tata and Papà and fixed up the four bedrooms upstairs and the two in the tower, I'll bet we could make it work."

"And if we refinished the garden cottage and made an apartment over the boathouse, we could fill this place every summer with rich American and German tourists," Fabrizio said.

"And you could service those lonely women travelers looking for a young Italian stallion," Enrico said with a sarcastic tone.

"You know, that's not a bad idea. I could be a gigolo." Fabrizio beamed. "And you could do the guys."

"I'm not becoming a prostitute."

"Not a prostitute." Fabrizio held up his palms. "An escort. That's completely different."

"How's that different?" Enrico snapped.

Fabrizio ignored him. "Oh! And don't forget, Tata is the greatest cook this side of the Alps."

"Yeah, but how are we going get a bunch of rich Americans and Germans, word of mouth?"

"No, *cretino*, with our webpage." Fabrizio held out his hand toward the screen.

"Well, we've got a long way to go before the old house looks anything like what's on that webpage." Enrico shrugged. "So we're back to the main problem. Money."

"Look, if we get a few guests, we can start to earn extra money and fix the place up. You know it's true; you always go in assfirst while I come at something face-on."

"We'll need to work out a proper business plan and everything. Let's talk with Francesca and see what she says." Enrico kneaded his brother's shoulders.

"You're right, and if we're going into business, it's time we separate our part of the inheritance from hers." Fabrizio turned back to his screen. "Come on, let's celebrate with some porn." Fabrizio pulled up YouPorn.

"Forget it." Enrico plunked down on the bed behind Fabrizio. "Besides I'm not into hetero porn." He picked up his book and began reading.

Fabrizio fiddled with the keys. "Here's one. It's an ancient Roman orgy with both guys and women doing it. Look, there's even a donkey." Fabrizio leaned back in his chair and began rubbing his crotch.

"How can you get hard to that?" Enrico glanced up. "It's so fake and the guys are really ugly."

"Yeah, but the donkey's pretty hot," Fabrizio taunted.

"You know sometimes it frightens me to think that we share identical genetic material," Enrico said without looking up from his book.

"Hey, you remember when we were kids, we used to watch porn together all the time," Fabrizio said with his eyes fixed on the screen. "You used to fantasize about Dario at the boatyard."

"What about you!" Enrico looked over the top of his book and sneered at his brother. "You had the hots for Signora Bianchi!"

"Still do. I'm thinking about her right now, bent over the sofa with her tits dangling, wearing nothing but a garter," he said in a low raspy tone.

"Yuck! She's old enough to be our mother." Enrico tossed his book down onto the bed.

"Yeah, but I'm imagining her husband hiding in the closet watching me fuck her." Fabrizio slipped his hand down the front of his sweatpants.

"You're a freak, you know that, don't you?" Enrico got up from the bed.

"When did you become such a prude?" Fabrizio briefly glanced over as his brother marched toward the door. "Hey, where are you going?"

"I'm leaving you and Signora Bianchi to finish your business alone!"

"Don't forget her husband watching in the closet." Fabrizio grinned.

"Whatever," Enrico said. "I'm hungry and Tata said she left a pan of tiramisu in the fridge."

"Save some for me. I'll be down in about ten minutes." Fabrizio repositioned himself in the chair but kept his eyes fixed on the screen and his hand buried deep inside his underwear.

As he was partway out the door Enrico heard Fabrizio say in a throaty whisper, "Oh yeah! Come on, Signora Bianchi. Take it baby. Yeah, yeah!"

"And don't get anything disgusting on the computer!" Enrico barked.

"Hey, like you said, it's all the same genetic material!" Fabrizio called back.

Enrico shook his head and continued down the stairs to the kitchen.

Chapter Four

JESSY'S PARENTS had always considered Owen one of the family and hardly took notice when he moved into Jessy's room for the summer. If Jessy's parents were disappointed when he declined the swimming scholarship at Michigan State, they never let on. Or if they were relieved when he also turned down circus school in Montreal, they never let on either.

"Do you know what chlorine does to my hair?" Jessy said to Owen and Maggie as they hung out in the park down at the waterfront. "As for circus school? Love the outfits—hate the elephant poo. Besides, who needs the bearded lady and the dog-faced boy when I have the two of you?" That irrepressible smile spread across Jessy's face. "So, it's Syracuse U and the creative writing program for me. Besides, how could I abandon you? You'd be lost without me."

Owen's heart just about exploded out of his chest with the news. Jessy would stay with him for a little while longer.

"Just promise us you won't wind up being a creepy English teacher like Mr. Scrivenor," Maggie said.

Jessy flung his arms open wide. "*Ney, but to live in the rank sweat of an enseamed bed, stew'd in corruption, honeying and making love over a nasty sty,*" he said, reciting one of his favorite lines from *Hamlet*.

"I can see we're too late. The transformation has already taken place." Maggie sneered. "Pig Boy!"

"*I am the one, Mr. Tun, that comes to tell you your daughter,* Maggie, *has fallen in with the beast with two backs.*" Owen rolled out a bastardized quote from *Othello*.

"*Oh, get thee to a nunnery!*" Maggie, quoting Hamlet, gave Owen a mock shove.

That summer, while Jessy worked at the pool as usual, Owen's after-school job at Party Harty's Party Supplies and Balloons became a full-time job and Maggie got a desk in her father's office next to Pathetic Patty and her collection of manga figurines. By September they had saved up enough for first and last month's rent on a two-bedroom ground-floor apartment in a dilapidated two-story clapboard house in downtown Syracuse. Maggie took the small room and Jessy and Owen shared the larger one.

While the leaves turned burgundy, orange, and yellow, Jessy was immersed in classes at Syracuse U and Owen and Maggie were learning what life after high school, on minimum wage, eight hours a day, six days a week, was really like. As the days grew shorter, cold rain stripped any remaining leaves from the branches and everything outside appeared dead—except maybe the famous Christmas tree in Clinton Square. With the new year, bitter Canadian winds swept across Lake Ontario, covering everything in snow and ice. In the evenings, while Jessy was at the library, or swim practice, or out with friends, Owen and Maggie, wearing pile pajamas and woolen socks, took refuge in the kitchen with plastic containers of Ichiban shrimp-flavored instant noodles or under a blanket on the sofa in front of the TV.

"Eat up, our show's on in five." Owen looked across their chipped linoleum kitchen table at Maggie.

"Honey, if we don't do something soon, our lives will go from dreary to downright dreadful." She slurped up a noodle. "Are these the bold new horizons you talked about in your valedictorian speech?" Maggie watched Owen chase a noodle around with his fork.

Owen stuck the noodle in his mouth, then stabbed a dehydrated onion and held it up. "I feel like this onion. Limp and soggy, laying in the bottom of a plastic cup just waiting for someone to eat me." Owen popped the onion into his mouth, chewed and swallowed. "There, I'm all gone."

"Another evening of fine dining?" Jessy said as he strolled into the kitchen. "Well, wet noodles, I have fantastic news that's going to change your lives forever!"

"Does Ichiban have a new flavor?" Maggie brooded.

"No, better!" Jessy tossed his books onto the kitchen counter.

"Coke has just brought out a new, new Coca-Cola that tastes exactly like the old new Coca-Cola?" Owen pined.

"No, not quite that earth-shattering, but I have a great idea." Jessy took the fork from Maggie's hand, scooped up some noodles, and popped them into his mouth.

Owen furrowed his brow and looked at Maggie, who grit her teeth. Jessy often had grand ideas, like when he decided they should sell

T-shirts at Pride last year. Ever since that disaster the word T-shirt had been taboo. Jessy opened the fridge, pulled out the milk container, and took a big swig directly from the carton.

"Ahh, gross!" Maggie said.

"I don't want to know what's been in his mouth over the past twenty-four hours." Owen curled his lip.

"Or who," Maggie added.

Jessy bent over and planted a big wet milky kiss on Owen's lips.

"Bluk!" Owen pulled his head back with a contrived look of disgust and wiped his mouth.

Jessy grinned while Maggie just rolled her eyes and shoveled another fork-load of noodles into her mouth. "So, what's your great idea?" Maggie said with her mouth half-full of noodles.

"It's simple! With your experience and connections, the two of you could put together something really great," Jessy said in his usual optimistic tone.

Owen and Maggie looked at each other, then at Jessy.

"Are you kidding me? I work in a balloon store," Owen said. "I'm just one step away from a birthday party clown." He pointed at Maggie. "And she's been taken hostage in her father's real estate office by manga figurines."

"You can spend the rest of your lives eating freeze-dried noodles and lamenting the disappearance of classic Coke, or you can get up off your butts and do something." Jessy's tone was now serious.

"Like what?" Owen said.

"Like special event organizers." Jessy held up his palms.

"You mean, like wedding receptions and parties and stuff?" Owen said.

"Yeah, like that," Jessy said.

"We live in Syracuse—land of tailgate parties and backyard barbeques, not New York City!" Owen threw his hands in the air. "Who wants a special events organizer?"

"I organized my thirteenth birthday party and it was a disaster. Nobody came! Not even my sister." Maggie moaned.

"What could we possibly put together?" Owen said.

"You've already put together a number of special events," Jessy said. "What about Joe Spenser's birthday party at the skating rink, the Henderson's twentieth anniversary on the riverboat? Oh, and let's not forget how Maggie found that amazing horse ranch for Julia and Lena's wedding." Jessy dashed out of the room, leaving Maggie and Owen still sitting at the kitchen table in front of their empty Ichiban noodle containers.

Maggie and Owen looked at each other and hunched their shoulders. "We were just doing some favors for some friends. No biggie," Owen said.

"Special events?" Maggie snorted.

CHAPTER FIVE

IT WAS only May, but spring had come early to the lake this year. Fabrizio wrapped his arms around his brother's waist and squeezed his legs tight against his hips. After a winter of gardening with Angelo, their bodies were lean and their muscles were hard. Enrico torqued Angelina's throttle and the two boys, like two kayakers riding the surf, sailed south down the lakeside road along the shoreline beneath the *platani* trees, leaning and bracing as if they were one and the same. They flew through the gallery and down the hill into the town of Laveno. They raced past the church and rounded the curve by the now-quiet Old Milano Pub. Enrico cruised along the street, dodging a woman having an animated conversation on her cell phone while she stepped mindlessly into the crosswalk. They zipped past the boats moored in the harbor, coasted up to the lamppost near the ferry ramp in front of the station, and sputtered to a stop. Fabrizio climbed off the back, removed his helmet, and fluffed his hair while Enrico jerked Angelina up onto its kickstand.

At the end of the parking lot, a man in his midforties, with silver hair and designer sunglasses, stood beside a new blue Lancia and watched them, while a woman on the other side of the car with a large Gucci purse slung over her shoulder opened the rear passenger door and extracted a ten-year-old boy by his arm. The boy squirmed and jerked from her grip as she steered him away from the car. The man walked up to her, and the three of them, looking straight ahead, marched across the piazza. Fabrizio stared at his brother, who turned and hung his helmet on the steering bar of the bike as if he hadn't noticed them. Fabrizio hung his helmet on the other side of the bar, not breaking his stare.

Up ahead the man was saying something to his wife. She stopped and propped one hand on her out-thrust hip while firmly gripping the child's hand with her other. The man turned and rushed back to the car with his keys jingling between his fingers. He opened the door and leaned in. A moment later, he stood up with his cell phone in his hand, waved to his wife, and started back toward her. But this time, as if drawn by some magnetic force, his path took a decided bend toward the boys.

As he neared, he slid his glasses down the bridge of his nose. "I'll call you later, Enrico," he whispered and winked. Then he trotted up to his wife and child.

Fabrizio breathed in deeply and exhaled loudly. "Why?"

Enrico held out his hands. "I know he's an idiot but what chance do I have to find someone other than a Grindr hookup?"

"He's an old married idiot. You deserve better than him." Fabrizio rolled his eyes.

"I know. Come on." Enrico shrugged and stuffed the keys in his pocket.

The ferry from Verbania, the city on the other side of the lake, had just docked, and a group of university students rushed up the ramp, across the platform. They joined the other students already waiting to catch the 7:00 a.m. train for Milano, as they did every morning, starting with the shrinking days of autumn, all through the cool drizzle of winter, until the long glorious days of spring returned. Enrico and Fabrizio might have been part of the flock, studying business at Bocconi University, or computer science at State University, or even fine arts at the Brera Institute, but Papà was on disability with a small pension, and according to their half sister, Francesca, their grandmother hadn't left them enough money for university. They had to work.

Fabrizio stood in line behind the trail of students shuffling into the station through the double wooden doors toward the one working automated ticket machine.

Enrico nudged up to his brother. "Come on, we'll have to get the tickets from the newsstand or we'll miss the train." They jaunted back out the door, over to the newsstand, and pressed up behind the cluster of students in front of the kiosk buying tickets, cell phone cards, and cigarettes.

With their tickets in hand, the two boys rushed out onto the platform to join the students boarding the train.

Two hours later they stepped off the train at Cadorna station in Milan. The distinctive odor of diesel and dog poo hung in the smoggy air. For most of the year, Milan was a car-clogged chaos of stressed-out people always in a hurry, all trying to scale the social ladder one designer label at a time. It was hard to believe that in little more than a month the city would feel semideserted. With school out, those privileged Milanese housewives and their children would retreat to the west coast towns of

Liguria and the Costa Smeralda in Sardinia, or along the east coast's wide, flat beaches of Rimini on the murky Adriatic Sea, for three months of tennis and sailing lessons for the kids, and yoga, tanning, cards, and gossip for their mothers. On Friday evenings, their husbands would hop into their Mercedes and Audis and motor westward, or into their Fiats and Škodas and drive eastward, to join their seaside families. As for less privileged working men and women without a vacation home, they would remain at their desks and on assembly lines during the weekdays and hang out in the parks and public swimming pools during the weekends, dreaming of *Ferragosto*, that most venerated of Italian holidays in mid-August, when they, too, would inch bumper to bumper along the highway on their way to spend three weeks on a beach under a rented umbrella, leaving the city to the Latino and Filipino immigrants.

Enrico grabbed his brother's arm and steered him over to the outdoor coffee bar beside the station. "Two coffees." He held up two fingers to the barman.

Fabrizio took out a cigarette from his pack, lit it, took a drag, then passed it to his brother before taking out another for himself.

After throwing back their coffee and snuffing out their cigarettes, they walked out to the piazza in front of the fiberglass sculpture of the large needle with its rainbow-colored thread, a nod to the fashion industry even though everybody knew that the clothes designed in Milan were actually sewn in sweatshops in Naples or China. They stopped at the street corner, keeping their heads pointing straight ahead so as not to appear like tourists or countryfolk from the south new to the city, even if their eyes darted back and forth at the unfamiliar sites. A giant double-decker bus full of Chinese tourists belched out diesel fumes as it growled past. Along with the flow of office men in black and dark gray business suits and shiny black shoes and office women in impossibly high stilettos, tight skirts, and low-cut blouses, all talking on their cell phones, the boys crossed the street and the tram track. Fortunately, their sister, Francesca's apartment was just off Via Dante, one of Milan's better addresses, close to Cadorna station and easy to reach.

"It certainly sounds like you've thought about this quite a bit," their sister said after Fabrizio and Enrico had outlined their idea to start a B&B. "And you know I want to support you in every way I can. After all, you're my only family." Francesca lounged elegantly on the velvet sofa with a crystal wineglass in her hand. Her forehead was as smooth and immobile as marble, and her glossy red lips protruded outward like a goldfish's. The maid came in and placed a tray of little sandwiches on the art deco coffee table and retreated back to the kitchen.

"So, we're back to the same old problem," Enrico said as he reached for a sandwich.

"Money." Fabrizio placed his wineglass on the table and reached for a sandwich too.

"I hate to say it, but as you know there's not much left in the inheritance fund. From my side, the Italian stock market has not been doing well and my investments are all tied up right now." She clicked her tongue. "That old house is so large it would take a small fortune to fix it up."

"We're not looking to restructure it, just fix it up enough to host guests," Fabrizio said.

"We estimate about twenty thousand should get us started," Enrico added.

Francesca took a sip of her prosecco. "Have you considered Pietro's proposal?" Francesca's husband, Pietro, like many architects, specialized in converting those lofty old Italian villas into modern apartments. "He knows some interested investors. He said he could easily design four independent units and you could use your share of the sales to purchase something much more manageable." Francesca looked at the boys.

"We can't sell the house," Fabrizio said with a tone of panic.

"We have Papà and Tata to think about," Enrico said. "And where would we all go?"

"I understand, my treasures." Francesca struggled to show some expression of empathy on her immobilized face. "Of course, it's out of discussion." She took a sharp little breath as if something very clever and practical had just occurred to her, "But certainly, there is another possibility."

"What's that?" Both boys looked at her earnestly.

Francesca almost breathed the words. "I could loan you some money from my personal account—just enough to get you started—and you could use the house as collateral."

The train back to Laveno was almost empty in the early afternoon, and the boys sat on the second level of the carriage where they could get a better view.

"Hey, did you notice Francesca's forehead and lips?" Fabrizio said.

"Yeah, I think she must have a fever or something. They looked all swollen."

"That's probably why she's going to the thermal spa for a couple of weeks. She needs to rest," Fabrizio said as the train rolled past the now abandoned 2016 Expo site, the gardens all gone, the shells of pavilions standing like empty warehouses, and the emblematic Tree of Life sculpture still sticking up in the air like a giant toilet brush. "So, what do you think about my idea for the B&B now?" Fabrizio said.

"I guess the only thing we can do is try." Enrico nudged his brother's shoulder. "You know, sometimes you're quite clever." Enrico smiled. "Even if you are a *cretino*."

FOR MORE than an hour after the boys had left, Francesca remained lounging on the sofa with a wineglass in her hand and smoking a cigarette.

"What did you tell them?" Pietro said as he walked in from his tennis lesson.

"The truth." Francesca took a long drag. "There's hardly any money left in the bank account." She blew out the smoke in her husband's face.

"Phew." Pietro fanned the air. "You didn't tell them about the Swiss account, did you?"

"Give me some credit! Of course I didn't." Francesca almost spit the words.

"So, you didn't give them the money for their stupid B&B?"

Francesca softened her tone. "I told them it was a wonderful idea, and at great personal sacrifice I offered them a loan."

"A loan?"

"Yes, a loan, with a two-year term and the house as collateral." Francesca held two fingers up. "And when their B&B flops and they default on the loan...."

Pietro broke into a grin. "The house becomes yours." Her husband bowed his head. "Then we convert the place into condos!"

"Exactly." Francesca ran her finger down her husband's nose. Then her tone became hard. "And they'll have to move to someplace they can afford and stuff their father in a home somewhere, if he's still alive."

Pietro picked up a glass and poured himself some wine. "That should give us enough time to quietly bleed off the rest of the money from the old lady's account and hide it beyond their reach in Switzerland."

"That's my money, not theirs! Those little bastards and their *frocio* father killed my mother," she growled.

CHAPTER SIX

FOLLOWING MONTHS of darkness and bitter cold, just when it felt like spring would never come, the days grew longer, spikes of tulips and crocus poked up from the ground that had been frozen rock-solid only weeks before, and the tiniest branches of the oak became swollen with reddish buds.

"Hey, guys," Jessy said as he walked into the kitchen and threw down his books. "You know my new FB, Peter?" He opened the fridge and took out a piece of cheese.

"That's not Facebook." Owen shot a look at Maggie, who nodded.

"Well, he's more of a suck pig than a fuck buddy, but anyway, he's the supervisor for the LGBT hotline." Jessy chewed the cheese.

"And they want us to give advice over the telephone?" A moping expression hung on Owen's face.

"Let me finish." Jessy sounded slightly irritated. "Their annual fundraiser is coming up fast and so far, they have no one to organize it. Of course, I told Peter all about you and your business," Jessy said.

"What business? We put together a few parties for some friends," Owen said in a flat sarcastic tone.

Jessy ignored him and continued. "And he agreed to having you two organize the fundraiser."

Owen scratched his head. "I don't think we're ready for something like that."

"Are you serious?" Maggie said.

"I'm dead serious," Jessy said. "Did you go to their fundraiser last year at the community center?"

"No. Why?"

"Because neither did anyone else!" Jessy waved his hands. "Not even half the volunteers showed up, and they ran out of soft drinks and sandwiches by nine." Jessy clasped Owen's face. "No matter what you put together, it couldn't be worse than that."

Owen cast his eyes up at Jessy. "So what's the catch?"

"No catch. I told him because it was such a special cause, you'd do it pro bono. Besides they have almost no budget anyway."

"Pro bono?" Maggie said.

"For nothing." Owen scowled.

"C'mon, it'll be great publicity. Oh, look at the time. Someone here with a life has swim practice, an evening class, and a hookup later on at Trexx. Ciao for now." He kissed the tip of his fingers and threw his hand toward them just before he darted out the room. "Don't wait up for me. I'll talk to you at breakfast and you can tell me about all the fabulous ideas you've come up with," he called as he went out the front door.

"For nothing?" Maggie mouthed the words and frowned. She sat back in her chair and brushed her hair back from her face with her fingers. "You know, this could be our big break," she said with a guarded tone of optimism.

Owen frowned back at her.

"There's just one thing I don't understand. How does Jessy carry on a conversation with these guys, if he has his dick in their mouths?"

Owen held up his hand. "I warn you. Don't ask or he will explain."

CHAPTER SEVEN

FABRIZIO SNUGGLED into one of the booths at the Old Milano Pub and chatted up Grazia and her best friend, Maria, while Enrico stayed out on the patio with Angelo and some friends and flirted with Luigi, Maria's boyfriend, as he served drinks.

A few years ago, Timmy Chan and his wife, Lilly, had taken over the management of the dingy old pub on the northern edge of Laveno. They remodeled the interior in pastels and glitter, hung a big TV on the far wall, and played music videos in between soccer games. It was too small to have a dance floor, but now that it was spring and the warmer evenings had returned, every weekend after nine on the cement patio in front, a DJ pumped out house beats. Timmy hired local boys and girls as bartenders and waiters, who were, not by accident, all good-looking, and all their friends from all the surrounding villages came, along with all those not wanting to go as far as Luino near the Swiss border. In no time the Old Milano had become the hottest nightspot on this side of Lago Maggiore.

By two in the morning the DJ shut down and pockets of boys and girls raised their hands in the air, blew kisses, and called out a last ciao as they wandered off toward their cars parked haphazardly along the street. Fabrizio came out with his arm wrapped around Grazia's waist. Her sequined sweater barely contained her jiggling breasts. Perched on her stilettos she was as tall as him. Fabrizio looked over at Enrico, smiled, and winked as Luigi walked past them with a tray of empty glasses and glared at Grazia. She scowled back at him. He scoffed and continued on into the bar. Unaware, Fabrizio steered Grazia across the street and along the dark shoreline promenade. A few minutes later, Maria came out, propped her butt against one of the high chairs, and folded her arms as if she were bored or angry. Luigi came out, rushed past her with a tray, and went back inside.

Enrico sat at the far end of the patio on a cement planter playing with his cell phone. He scrolled down the profiles of guys, some with face shots and as many without. Some had changed their photos. Some had changed their names. But he pretty much knew who most of them were. There were the usuals: the local hotties on the circuit, the escorts, the old guys who kept sending him photos of their dicks, and the ones too frightened to show their faces. There was also a variety of younger guys wanting to get off on dirty talk but who lacked the courage to actually follow through and meet up. Enrico clicked on a photo of new guy with nice eyes and a great chest. He scrolled down his profile: *twenty-eight, 172 cm., 62kg, athletic, single, straight, looking for hook-ups with guys, Verbania.*

He was right across the lake, only twenty minutes away by ferry, but the ferry had stopped running hours ago.

Maria remained propped against the windowsill fiddling with her cell phone. Luigi came over and put his hands on her rump and pulled her pelvis up against his. She held out her cell phone and continued to gaze sideways at the screen. Casually, she turned and looked at Luigi. He leaned forward and kissed her, then went back inside. Maria plopped her cell phone in her bag and slung it over her shoulder. As she clicked her heels across the patio toward the street, she threw a tiny wave at Enrico, who was still sitting on the cement planter engrossed in his phone.

Luigi came back out and pulled the tables across the patio and formed them into a corral. The chain made a clinking sound as he wove it through the legs and secured it with a padlock. Then he disappeared back inside the bar.

Ten minutes later Luigi reappeared, called out, *"buona notte,"* and walked past Enrico, who didn't look up from his screen. At the edge of the passageway leading to the back street, Luigi paused and stared back at Enrico. When Enrico eventually looked up at him, he slipped into the shadows. Enrico swiped his screen closed, stood up, and casually followed him.

As Enrico rounded the corner, a hand shot out from the darkness, grabbed hold of him, and pulled him in, pushing him back against the wall. Luigi pressed his loins against Enrico and slid his hands under Enrico's T-shirt, caressing his stomach and pecs. Enrico held Luigi by his hair with one hand, shoving his other hand down the back of Luigi's underwear, grasping his left buttock and kneading it like pizza dough. After tugging the front of Enrico's T-shirt up, Luigi sucked and teased Enrico's nipples while he worked his hand down Enrico's stomach and past the band of his underwear. With a rattle of belt buckles and the zip of flies, both men opened their pants, slid the front of their underwear down, and set their constrained passions free. Like a sommelier gripping a wine bottle by the neck, Luigi grabbed a hold of Enrico's hard cock while stroking his own. Enrico pressed his hand on the top of Luigi's head and Luigi dropped to his knees. Without hesitation he engulfed the head of Enrico's cock as if he were sucking on a Chupa Chups lollipop. Enrico clasped the sides of Luigi's head with both hands and slid his hard dick down Luigi's throat like a snake slipping down its hole. Luigi flinched, his stomach heaved, and he began to gag. Enrico withdrew. Luigi gasped and gripped Enrico's slippery saliva-covered cock, kissing and licking his balls. Enrico moaned. Then Enrico's balls tightened and Luigi once again engulfed the head of his cock. Snatching short rapid breaths, Luigi stroked himself more vigorously while he sucked and pumped Enrico. Enrico clasped Luigi's head, slid his cock down Luigi's throat again and, with a low grunt, released himself. Luigi pulled back and gasped for air like a free-diver coming to the surface. He licked the remaining cum off the head of Enrico's cock while pumping himself like a piston until he shot across the toe of Enrico's tennis shoe and out onto the pavement.

Enrico pulled Luigi to his feet and they clung to each other, breathing in and out like two prizefighters at the end of the final round. Then they separated, bent over, and pulled up their underwear and pants, refastened their buckles, and straightened their T-shirts. Luigi shifted his weight to move away, but Enrico caught him and pulled him in for a kiss. Luigi turned his head sideways and Enrico kissed him on the neck. Without a word, Luigi darted down the passageway and out onto the empty street. Enrico smoothed his hair and went in the opposite direction, back toward the bar where Angelina was parked.

Two minutes later, Enrico rolled up to the steps at the edge of the lakeside promenade. He rotated Angelina's handlebar back and forth until the headlight caught two figures down below in a dark spot at the water's edge, stretched out on the cement landing near the break wall. Enrico could just make out Fabrizio, lying on top of Grazia with his face buried in her bare breasts and his ass bouncing up and down.

Enrico turned off the engine and the light and waited. With one last thrust and a groan, Fabrizio flopped down and splayed himself out on top of Grazia like a beached seal.

"Come on! Let's go," Enrico called out.

Fabrizio looked up and squinted at Enrico on the walkway above them. He pushed himself upright, peeled off the condom, and tucked himself into his shorts. Grazia sat up and straightened her skirt and hair.

"Ciao, Enrico." She waved as she pulled her sequined sweater over her head and tucked her breasts back in.

"Ciao, Grazia." Enrico waved back.

Extending his hand, Fabrizio pulled Grazia to her feet, and the two climbed up the steps to where Enrico sat astride the motorbike. Grazia leaned over and kissed Enrico on the cheek, then turned and pressed herself up against Fabrizio and made an expression like a puppy begging for a biscuit.

With both hands cradling her rump, Fabrizio kissed her. "Got to go!" He pulled on his helmet and hopped onto the back of Angelina, gripping hold of his brother's waist. Enrico gunned the throttle and Fabrizio jerked backward. "Later," he called, leaving Grazia behind in a cloud of exhaust.

As they raced up the hill, around the curve, and along the lakeside road toward home, Fabrizio pressed up against his brother's back and with his mouth at the side of Enrico's helmet, he yelled above the roar of the bike and the rushing air. "I've never been able to get past first base with her before, but tonight she was all over me!" Fabrizio stretched his arm out in front of Enrico's face and dangled the used condom for him to see.

"Why the change in attitude?" Enrico called out, not taking his eyes off the road.

"Who knows? Must be a full moon. You know how horny women get during a full moon."

Enrico laughed and yelled back, "Guys too!"

CHAPTER EIGHT

"You won't believe this!" Maggie said as she burst through the door.

"Already heard. Eminem is not really a homophobe."

"Yeah right." Maggie swatted the air. "No, I want to tell you something much more interesting."

"Breathe, woman. You're turning blue."

Maggie took a big breath of air. "Do you remember Skate-O-Rama, the old roller rink just north of the city on Mattydale Street? It was huge during the '70s and '80s, but it's been closed for years."

"How old do you think I am anyways? Of course I don't remember it," Owen said.

"Well, that's not the point." Maggie threw out her hands. "The point is, it's been marked for destruction. They're going put up a condo or a shopping mall or something. Part of that urban redevelopment program."

"Fascinating! But what has this got to do with us?" Owen crossed his arms.

"My dad's the agent handling the property transfer?"

"Same question," he sang out.

"My dad spoke to the owners, and they were thrilled at the idea of one last bang-up party before the place goes on the block and, well…."

"No!" Owen gasped.

"Yes! It's ours for the night. Free of charge!"

Owen grabbed Maggie and bounced her up and down as they burst into squeals.

"Oh, oh, put me down or I'm going to pee my pants," Maggie said.

"And guess what?" Owen flexed his eyebrows. "I convinced my boss the fundraiser would be great advertising for the party store, and he agreed to let us have all the miscellaneous bags of glitter and mismatched balloons in the storeroom. And there's a shitload in there."

"Yeah, but what kind of a theme can we do in an old roller rink, with a whole lot of different colored balloons and bags of glitter?"

"Are you kidding me!" Owen gave Maggie a mock shove and brought his hands together in a praying position. "After all these years of homo indoctrination, have you learned nothing my child?"

Maggie squinted at him.

Owen cocked one eye at her. "All we need is a DJ and a honking big mirror ball and we'll have a night of disco inferno Syracuse will never forget!"

They started jumping and squealing again just as Jessy walked in the door.

He dropped his books on the floor, ran over, and joined in.

"Hey, what are you squealing about?" Maggie said.

"Or are you just channeling your inner thirteen-year-old girl?" Owen jested.

Jessy came to a stop and so did Owen and Maggie. "Do you remember that apprenticeship in screenplay writing I applied for?"

"Yeah," Maggie said.

"Well, I got it! I'm going!"

"Wait a minute." Owen stood still. "What apprenticeship in screenplay writing?"

"You know, the one in California."

"You're going to California!" Owen's head began to spin.

"C'mon, it's just for six months." Jessy bumped Owen on the shoulder.

Owen remained frozen with his mouth hanging open. California might as well be on another planet. Owen felt nauseous. Once Jessy left, that would be it. He would never come back to Syracuse or to him.

CHAPTER NINE

As THEY came up the path from the lake and through the garden gate, Enrico and Fabrizio called, "Ciao, Papà," to the skinny old man who was hunched over pruning a rose bush with surgical care. The old man continued to examine and clip the delicate branches without pausing to look up.

"I'm going to get changed," Fabrizio said to his brother. "My balls get itchy if I sit around in a damp swimsuit." He bounded up the steps and went directly into the house. Enrico followed him but went onto the terrace.

The sun was sinking behind the mountains on the other side of the lake, staining the sky the color of a ripe melon. Even though the hot weather had arrived early, there was still a tiny tip of white snow on Monte Rossa in the distance. The afternoon wind had subsided, and the surface of the water was as smooth as a fresh bedsheet, except for intermittent rolling waves from the hydrofoil out in the middle of the lake making its last run back to Laveno and the wake from a speedboat cruising along the shoreline heading to the marina in time for cocktail hour.

Tata stood there looking out at the lake. "I love this time of day," she said as Enrico walked up to her. "It always makes me melancholy for Sicily."

"But this is your home." Enrico kissed her on the cheek.

"Born Sicilian, die Sicilian." Tata shrugged. "Even though I've been here for almost fifty years, no matter how lovely the lake is, this will always be a foreign land for me."

"Why didn't you ever go back to Sicily?"

Tata brushed her hand through Enrico's hair. "You know, your mother was like a little sister to me, and she was alone with your sister, Francesca." She kissed his forehead. "And then, of course you two boys arrived and I was up to my eyes in dirty diapers and baby formula." Tata laughed.

"Tell me about Mamma again, Tata."

Tata had told them the story many times before, but each time she told it in a slightly different way or added a small detail. She knew that her memories were their only connection to their mother. "Your grandmother was a stern woman, with little understanding for what grows inside a young girl's heart." Tata shook her head. "Ha, it was me who had to explain to your mother about her monthly visitor and what to do."

Enrico frowned. "How could she not know about menstruation?"

"It was like that for good Catholic girls back then." Tata rolled her eyes and shrugged. "Then, when she had just turned fifteen, she met an older boy from across the lake.

"Every day that summer, as the sun was hanging low over the mountains, just like it is now, he would paddle across the lake and whistle for your mother to come to the shore and meet him. And like so many innocent young girls who are drunk on the wine of their first love, she gave her heart to that boy." Tata shook her head vigorously.

"As these things so often do, it ended in tragedy." She took Enrico's hands and held them. "By the time your grandmother discovered their romance, it was too late. Your mother was already pregnant with your sister."

Enrico bit his lip and swallowed.

"Your grandmother accused the young man of raping her daughter and sent the police across the lake to look for him, but he had already disappeared. They say he went to Bologna to join the Marxists." Tata shook her head. "I don't know why your grandmother didn't send your mother to Switzerland and have the problem taken care of like most girls do. Maybe it was because her family was so Catholic and word had already spread throughout the village anyway."

Tata let go of Enrico's hands and brushed back a strand of hair from her face. "After that, your mother's life was almost destroyed. She had your sister and raised her, facing the scorn of the other women and vulgar innuendos of the men in the village. But she always held her head high.

"When your sister Francesca was six, your grandmother insisted on sending her to boarding school in Milan, and from then on your mother and I looked after the old lady.

"Many lonely years passed. And by the time your sister was seventeen, your mother was only thirty-one. Then one day she met your father, who had just left university in Milan and returned to the lake. Even though he was almost ten years her junior, the two of them fell in together like left and right feet. Oh, you can imagine how those viperous tongues in the village wagged, but all the same, it wasn't long before your father proposed to your mother and they were married." Tata patted Enrico's cheek. "And eventually your mother became pregnant with you two." Tata stopped.

"Go on," Enrico encouraged.

Tata put her hand to her face and spoke in a low tone. "After your mother died in childbirth your father became ill." Tata's eyes were glassy like she was fighting back tears. "By then your grandmother was too far on in years, so I stayed to look after her, your father, and the two of you. That's why I never returned to Sicily." Tata smiled, but her lips were trembling as if there was more to the story.

"When I die, you'll send my body home to Siracusa." She leaned over and kissed Enrico's cheek. "But right now, I can smell my broccoli, asparagus, and cheese torte in the oven." She brushed her hands and went back into the kitchen.

"ALL TUCKED in?" Enrico said as they walked into their father's room after dinner.

Fabrizio picked up the blue plastic pillbox from his nightstand and examined it. "I see you've remembered to take your pill?"

"Look Papà, we brought you a rose," Enrico said.

"*Ah, com'e bella.*" Papà lifted his head off the pillow.

"Just lay back. I'll put it here where you can see it," Fabrizio said.

Papà's eyes followed him as he placed the vase on the table. "I think I will call her Isa, after my wife."

"But you call all your roses Isa," Enrico said as he and Fabrizio sat on the edge of the bed.

Papà studied their faces "You look so much like her. Are you her brothers?"

"No, Papà." Enrico swallowed. "I'm Enrico, your son, and this is Fabrizio, your other son."

Papà relaxed his face, reached out and took Fabrizio's hand, and patted it. "*Che bei raggazzi,*" he said, speaking to the rose. He closed his eyes and drifted off.

The boys remained sitting on the edge of his bed until they were sure he was asleep.

"C'mon, the pill has kicked in. He'll rest quietly until morning."

CHAPTER TEN

"WE'VE GOT a problem," Maggie said as she came into the house and found Owen staring into his computer screen. His eyes were red, and his hair was greasy. "What time did you go to bed last night?"

"I didn't."

She sniffed. "You didn't shower either."

"What's the latest problem?" Jessy said as he came out of the kitchen with a cup of coffee in his hand.

"Fire inspection. The certificate is way out of date. I talked to the fire marshal, and they said they couldn't do it before the end of June. We're sunk."

Jessy placed the cup of coffee on the edge of Owen's desk, took out his phone, and dialed.

"Hey," Jessy said into the phone.

Pause.

"I was thinking about you too." Jessy voice was as sweet and slippery as lube.

Pause.

Maggie rolled her eyes. "Was he born with a permanent hard-on?" she whispered.

"Yes," Owen whispered back.

"Listen, I need a little favor." Jessy proceeded to outline the problem of the fire safety inspection over the phone while Maggie and Owen stared at him with an expression of bewilderment. "Of course it's for a good cause. The LGBT hotline."

Pause.

"Was there ever any doubt." Jessy practically licked the phone. "Oh, and give my love to the boys at the station. Especially that new guy with the hairy chest. What's his name? Marco. Yeah, tell him he's welcome to join us after the party if he wants."

Pause.

"You're the best, big boy." And he hung up.

"Problem solved. The inspection will be next Thursday at three, as long as no buildings catch on fire or no cats get stuck in trees." Jessy picked up his coffee and went back into the kitchen. "Oh, and don't forget to get the publicity balloons printed up with your name and number."

Maggie mouthed the words and grabbed her hair. "What planet does he come from?"

"I'm not really sure, but I wouldn't touch his cell phone without rubber gloves if I were you."

That Monday morning Maggie came with the keys to Skate-O-Rama and wrestled the rusty lock free. The graffiti-covered metal doors made a loud groan as she pushed them open. It was the first time in many years the light of day had penetrated the lobby.

Owen and Maggie walked in, stepping over something decomposing on the floor. They cautiously navigated around other mounds of nondescript garbage, past the front ticket bank, and into the cavernous roller rink.

"It's like a time capsule," Owen said as they stood and waited for their eyes to adjust.

"Yeah, a very dusty time capsule," Maggie said.

"And it smells like mold and pee," Owen moaned.

"Well, at least the wooden floor is still intact."

By the end of the day Maggie had got the water and power temporarily reconnected and, with the precision of a military drill sergeant, organized the LGBT hotline volunteers into cleaning squads. They hosed down and scrubbed everything they could, and what they couldn't, they covered with tarps. Owen arranged for portable latrines to be set up in the parking lot, procured a liquor license, and hung the decorations and mirror balls. Jessy, wanting to do his part, solicited everyone he knew to publicize the event. He convinced his ex, Eddy Lataro—a DJ who specialized in old-school disco, ecstasy, and light chems—to do the music.

By Friday afternoon, after he had inflated, tied, and hung the last balloon, Owen stood next to Maggie in the middle of the large empty roller rink. "I'm so exhausted I can't even tell what it looks like."

"I'd ask you to shoot me, but I think that would just be a waste of a good bullet." Maggie leaned on a broom handle.

"I'm afraid to ask, but have we missed anything?" Owen said through a deep yawn.

"Thankfully, the hotline volunteers are handling the staffing. They'll all be here at seven. Just enough time to go home, take a shower, and lay down for an hour. Oh, by the way, who's covering security on the door?" Maggie could barely speak.

"Security?" Owen wheezed.

"Yes, sir!" A voice from behind startled them.

They spun around to face a mountain of a man in rumpled fatigues who looked like he had spent more than one night sleeping on the street. Both Maggie and Owen stared up at the figure with their mouths hanging agape.

"What do you want?" Owen was too tired to be frightened.

"My name's Big Eddy. I'm looking for a job, sir, and this good-looking guy by the name of Jessy told me to talk to you."

"Can you do door security tonight, Big Eddy?"

"Yes, sir. Military police, two tours in Iraq." He saluted them.

"Good. I can pay you a hundred bucks, cash. You're on the door, all night. Be here at 1900."

"Yes, sir." Big Eddy saluted again and marched away.

"Oh, and just don't kill or maim anybody," Owen called after him. "That's an order!"

"Where did you learn to speak military?" Maggie sneered.

"Where else?" Owen shrugged. "Porn videos."

CHAPTER ELEVEN

THE HOT, humid Italian summer settled in—like being trapped in an enormous steam room—and the rich families from Milan took up residence in their grand summer villas, along with the colonies of German and Dutch vacationers on their seventies-style summertime estates. Of course, most Italians were passionate beach babies, and by August, many would shun the dark green fresh water and its unpredictable weather in favor of the marine breezes and endless days of cloudless sky along the salty blue Mediterranean, leaving the lake pretty much to the Germans, Dutch, and the locals.

Enrico stood back and examined their work. Fabrizio came up behind and wrapped his arms around his brother, just as he had done during the nine months they'd shared their mother's womb.

"What do you think?" Enrico said.

"Not bad. Not bad at all. It won't be long before we're ready for our first guests."

"I have to admit, the two rooms in the tower look pretty good." Enrico smiled.

"It's amazing what a deep cleaning and a coat of paint can do." Fabrizio let go of his brother.

"Not to mention new bed linen and curtains." Enrico smoothed the bedcover. "We were lucky the mattresses were in good shape."

Fabrizio yawned. "At least the tower is presentable."

"Presentable!" Enrico put his hands on his brother's shoulders and turned him toward the window. The gloaming sky streaked orange, and the bluing mountains on the other side of the lake cast a silhouette onto the pinkish mirror surface of the water.

"Okay, it's got a view that could make Naples weep, but what about the rest of the house?" Fabrizio stretched his arms over his head.

"As long as our guests are looking out the window, they won't see the cracks in the plaster."

"Tomorrow we'll start on the dining room," Fabrizio said.

"And we'll keep the doors to the rest of the house shut." Enrico shrugged.

"Never underestimate the power of fresh cut flowers and candles." Fabrizio spread his hand out in front of him like he was spreading light across the room. He had read in his online business course that special touches like fresh cut flowers, candles, and local color would create the magic that guests will remember.

Enrico shot him a curious look.

"What?" Fabrizio said.

"Sometimes you really sound gay, you know?"

Fabrizio sneered. "You don't have to suck dick in order to have a sense of design."

"No, of course not." Enrico made a taunting expressing. "But it helps." Enrico bobbed his eyebrows.

"It's not the dick itself that I object to. It's the sweaty balls." Fabrizio flicked his tongue in and out.

"Speaking of sweaty balls, you really stink." Enrico made two sharp sniffs at his brother's chest.

"That's the smell of a real man, little brother." Fabrizio punched Enrico's shoulder.

"Could have fooled me. I thought it was the smell of a dead pig."

"Come on, let's have a swim before dinner." Fabrizio bent over and grabbed hold of one of the handles on the trunk that contained their mother's memorabilia and their father's secrets.

Enrico grabbed hold of the other handle. "First thing tomorrow we need to go to the community office and see why they haven't sent us our B&B permit yet."

The next morning Enrico and Fabrizio hopped on Angelina and zoomed off to Castelveccana.

"Aldo, why haven't you approved our permit for our B&B?" Enrico said as they walked into the community office. "It's already June and we want to start booking guests."

A slightly rounded man in his midthirties sat behind the large wooden desk. A brass nameplate that read *vice-sindaco*, was carefully positioned on the front edge of his desk. "We need the certificate from the electrician and plumber," Aldo said with a bored tone.

"They did the inspection two months ago. We sent it to you," Fabrizio said.

"And then there's the community health inspection." Aldo lazily swirled his hand in the air. "These things take time."

"That was also sent a month ago," Enrico said, barely able to keep the irritation from his voice.

"Look, Aldo, stop busting our balls!" Fabrizio barked.

"Hey, it's not up to me. It's the hotel association that blocked your request. You'll need to take it up with them," Aldo barked back.

"What hotel association? There's only one hotel in Castelveccana," Enrico said.

"Who's the chairman?" Fabrizio said.

"Ottavio." Aldo hunched and shrugged.

Enrico's hands flopped to his side and he growled.

"They're meeting next month. I can put it on the agenda and you can present your request then."

"Come on, little brother. We're getting nowhere here." Fabrizio put his hands on his brother's back and pressed him out of the community office door.

Outside Enrico put on his helmet and straddled Angelina. "This is why nobody can ever get ahead in Italy."

"Oh wait, I forgot something." Fabrizio darted in through the doors again and walked back into the office wearing an expression on his face that said *let's play hardball.*

Aldo looked up. "Listen, Fabrizio, you know we're friends and everything, but my hands are tied here. I can't risk making Ottavio angry. You understand."

Fabrizio held up his phone with the screen facing Aldo. *Butt Pig 97.*

Aldo went white and gripped the sides of his desk.

"The face is a little hard to make out, but it's a nice shot of your ass."

"What! That's not me! You can't prove it," Aldo snarled.

"Then you won't mind if I push this key and send a link to everyone I know." Fabrizio's tone was casual, almost lyrical.

"Wait! Wait!" Aldo shuffled through the pile of papers and documents on his desk. "See, here it is. I've got your certificate right here. All I have to do is sign it."

"Good. Sign it and I'm out of here, and the identity of Butt Pig 97 remains a secret."

Aldo scribbled his signature across the bottom of the page, stamped it with the community seal, and handed it to Fabrizio.

"Hey, Aldo, since we are friends, take my advice. It's time to change your Grindr name. Maybe the photos too."

Two minutes later Fabrizio emerged from the community office grinning with the certificate in his hand.

"Nooo! But how?" Enrico said.

"Your Grindr account. Tell you all about it back at the house." Fabrizio threw his leg over the seat and grabbed onto his brother's waist.

Enrico hit the gas and they zipped up the street toward the lakeside road and home.

CHAPTER TWELVE

IT WAS ten o'clock. Maggie and Owen stood nervously by the door as people began to line up.

"Don't let them in until we have at least a hundred people waiting in line." Owen looked up at Big Eddy, who was guarding the doorway with his legs spread apart and his arms crossed in front of his massive chest.

"Why not let them in now?" Maggie said.

"Studio 54 tactics. I want them to beg for it," Owen said.

From inside the DJ was pumping out the disco beats, and by ten thirty, the parking lot was full and people were getting impatient. At ten forty-five, Owen looked out at a group of drag queens, all glitter, high heels, and wigs, standing in the middle of the parking lot, posing and smoking. He stood on his toes and said to Big Eddy, "See them?"

Big Eddy nodded.

"They're in."

"You're the boss." Big Eddy made an ear-piercing whistle. "Ladies!" He pointed directly at them. "You're in!" He jabbed his thumb toward the door.

People jeered and cheered as the gaggle of drag queens, waving and blowing kisses, sashayed through the crowd and strutted up to the doorway.

Owen handed them tickets for complimentary drinks and pointed to the DJ stage. "VIP section straight ahead, ladies."

"Now, that boy has class, girls," said one drag queen in an enormous blond wig. She fluttered her hand and gave Owen a series of Hollywood air kisses.

"Mm, mm, and ass too!" her friend in a pink wig sang out as she reached back and squeezed Owen's butt.

"Why did you do that?" Maggie said.

"Because I want a vision of glamour to be the first thing that everybody sees, and besides, ten forty-five is international drag queen time. Everybody knows that."

Just then Jessy and four beefcakes appeared in the parking lot all wearing firefighter T-shirts that looked as if they had been sprayed on. Maggie and Owen and half the parking lot turned and gawked.

"His timing is impeccable, as always," Maggie said, shaking her head.

"What must it be like to be him?" Owen gazed at Jessy with equal measures of envy and adoration as he and his entourage paraded up to the door.

Jessy reached out and swept both Maggie and Owen into his arms, first kissing Maggie on the neck and then Owen on the lips. "You're stars."

"Go in and get the boys a drink. We'll be in in a minute." Owen beamed back with pride.

You could almost hear a collective sigh from the crowd as Jessy and his American wet dreams marched in through the doors.

Owen patted Big Eddy on the back. "Okay, Big Eddy. Let 'em in."

The crowd pushed forward.

"One at a time!" Big Eddy growled and the crowd shied backward.

"C'mon, girl," Owen said to Maggie as he took her by the elbow and steered her inside. "It's showtime!"

By eleven, the roller rink was filled with drag queens poised on stilettos, aging queens stuffed into spandex, muscle Marys waiting for the opportunity to bare their pecs, posers and label queens with gelled hair and too much cologne, closet queens, and gentrified weekend fags. Biker gals in leather and denim in the company of their high-heeled, lipstick-toting girlfriends, clustered round the bar. While those who defied gender designation squeezed into whatever space they could. Even twinks and twinkies, brats clad in neon vinyl and street rats covered with homemade tattoos, all who were much too young to remember Gloria Gaynor and The Trammps, came to revel in the camp and glitter. It seemed as if just about everyone in Syracuse and the Finger Lakes area who thirsted for fun was here tonight to relive those magical days of disco.

Across the floor, a sea of bare torsos undulated to the throbbing beats like surfers waiting for the perfect wave. Owen's eyes were fixed on Jessy, his body swaying to the rhythm and his head following, as if it were only surreptitiously attached. Like a layer of flawless latex, Jessy's skin stretched over the plates of his pecs, rippling down past his turtle-shell-like abdomen. The band of his underwear clung just under the cut of his lats, kept in place only by the bulge of his butt, with the crotch of his jeans hanging forward like a package waiting to be ripped open and engulfed.

Jessy reached over and pulled Owen's T-shirt up over his head, then pressed his warm torso, glistening with moisture, against him and the two gyrated and writhed to the rhythm, flesh upon flesh. Beside them, Maggie, in baggy shorts and a black athletic top, stretched her arms outward and swayed back and forth as if she were swimming through a tropical sea of exotic fish, their beauty and sensuality intoxicating her and filling her with grace and confidence. A bare torso swam past, strobe lights licking his flesh and accentuating the tide marks of sweat and glitter. Maneuvering in between, he pressed himself up against Jessy with a pill held in his teeth. A smile spread across Jessy's face and he opened his mouth as if he were about to receive Holy Communion. The guy grabbed the back of Jessy's neck and engulfed him in a kiss. Without missing a beat, Owen turned toward Maggie. They both knew the drill. Jessy would disappear into the dark room while they danced on. Maggie let her arms float like an Indian deity. She spun around and, as water fills a void, bodies flowed between her and Owen and they melted into the crowd and into the night.

The next day Owen and Maggie spotted their publicity balloons everywhere, on dashboards and in coffee shops. Maggie saw a group of schoolkids volleying a red one back and forth as they skipped down the street. The LGBT hotline made more money that night than they had made all year in donations, and word on the street was the party had been legendary. Owen's phone began to ring incessantly. While Jessy finished his first year at college, Owen and Maggie quit their jobs and became full-time event organizers.

Chapter Thirteen

"Come over here and look at what I've found." Fabrizio was sitting cross-legged in front of the old trunk holding an open letter in his hand. There was another on the floor next to where he sat.

"Stop going through everything. We'll never get the place cleaned up at this rate." Enrico came over and sat down next to his brother. "Those are Papà's old letters. You shouldn't be reading them." He had a sour look on his face.

Fabrizio turned to his brother. "Our whole lives we've heard stories about Papà and Mamma. I want to know the truth…"

"…and Papà's not able to tell us." Enrico finished Fabrizio's sentence, as they so often did.

Fabrizio read:

> *Dearest Achille,*
> *My hand is shaking as I write to you. I pray you*
> *not think of me only as a silly schoolboy of seventeen*
> *infatuated by an older university man. But I must tell you*
> *I am almost a man and, I say to you with the heart of a*
> *man that to me you are invincible in body and spirit, like*
> *the god whom you are named after.*
> *Your adoring servant*
> *Antonio*

Like a mirror image the two boys stared at each other with expressions of bewilderment on their faces.

"What the hell…," Enrico said.

"Sounds like this Antonio guy had the hots for Papà," Fabrizio said.

"Well, remember those old photos. Papà was really *fico* when he was young. Here, give me the other one." Enrico fluttered his hand at Fabrizio.

"I thought you didn't want to read these letters." Fabrizio handed the other letter to his brother.

Enrico unfolded it and read.

> *My Sweetest Antonio,*
> *I am unworthy of your adoration. But please know this, my heart is true and if it were not such an abomination in the eyes of the church and God, I would profess my love for you from the top of the Duomo in Milan.*
> *Forever yours in spirit and flesh,*
> *Achille*

Enrico locked eyes with his brother, and then Enrico shivered and looked away. He picked up the envelope, turned it over, and studied the front. "It looks like Papà's handwriting. The stamp hasn't been cancelled, so I guess he never sent it."

Fabrizio grabbed the letter from his brother's hand and examined it, then held it up and waved it in the air as if it bore a perfume or an odor. "Wow, did they ever use at lot of drippy language back then, just to say they were horny."

"You *cretino*, that's not the point." Enrico snatched the letter back from Fabrizio.

"Well, what's the point, then? It looks like Papà and this guy, Antonio, had a bone for each other," Fabrizio said. "So what?"

"So what?" Enrico sputtered out the words. "It means that old gossip was true. Papà really was a *finocchio*."

"And so are you." Fabrizio shrugged.

"It also means he didn't love Mamma, like Tata told us." Enrico had a tone of panic in his voice. "Their marriage was a lie!"

"There's one way to find out." Fabrizio sprang to his feet.

"Where are you going?"

"Well, we can't ask Papà, so I'm going to ask Tata." Fabrizio darted toward the door with the letters in his hand. "Come on, you said you wanted to know the truth."

Chapter Fourteen

Normally Owen avoided Asian fusion restaurants the same way he might avoid a European fusion or African fusion restaurant, if there really were such things, but he hadn't picked the place, Becky had. She was a great promoter and an important business contact, but her tastes only ran as deep as shopping mall chic.

Owen was nervous. But maybe it wasn't the restaurant and meeting the client for the first time that was making him nervous. Maybe it was something much bigger bothering him—something he couldn't quite put his finger on or name. He had created a new job and identity for himself as an event organizer. So why did it all feel as uncomfortable as he used to feel in that horrible Sunday suit his mother made him wear to church when he was a kid? Suddenly the image of Jessy popped into his mind, always self-assured, always in control.

Jessy and Owen had been the Jessy-Owen duo since that day back in fifth grade when Owen sat alone during recess in the corner of the schoolyard, sulking because his father had left them, and Jessy came up and shared his pack of cookies with him. After that, you rarely met one without the other. Even though many had tried over the years, no boy or girl could come between them. Like the time when Norman Elgin told Jessy not to be friends with Owen because he was a sissy boy. During recess, to illustrate his point, Norman grabbed Owen, put him in a headlock, and told him he wouldn't let go until Owen admitted he was a fairy. Jessy came up behind Norman, grabbed the back band of his tighty-whities and reefed them up as hard as he could. There was a loud ripping sound and Norman, hollering like he was mortally wounded, released Owen. When the principal heard the commotion and came running, Norman accused Jessy of attacking him.

"No! That's not true!" Owen yelled. "I started it. I called Norman a douchebag!"

The principal looked shocked as Owen spit out the words, and while she sent Norman home to get new underwear, she told Jessy and Owen to write lines on the board, *I will not call people names*, and

I will not get into fights. Of course, this only served to cement their friendship further.

"Hey, Owen," Jessy said as they stood at the front of the classroom wiping the chalkboard clean after all the other students had gone home. "What's a douchebag?"

"I don't know," Owen said. "It's something my mother called my father when he left us, so it's got to be really bad."

Of course the story of Norman, with the back of his underwear wrapped over his head, was greatly exaggerated over the years and followed him through grade school.

There was also that time in their freshman year when Sharron, spelled with two Rs, had her thirteenth birthday party and invited all the cool kids, and especially Jessy. When Jessy and Owen showed up at her door, she said to Owen that he wasn't invited because she didn't want losers at her party.

"Now, that's a douchebag," Jessy said as the two of them turned away and walked down the street. "C'mon, let's get a pizza and go to the movies."

But then there was that night during their sophomore year, when Jessy bought a bottle of vodka with his fake ID and the two of them got really drunk down by the waterfront. Owen suddenly kissed Jessy on the lips and professed his love. Jessy kissed him back and affirmed his undying love and commitment to Owen but qualified it in the same breath with the phrase, "like a brother."

Owen, terrified of losing the person most precious to him, repeated, "like a brother."

It tortured Owen, keeping him awake at night and keeping him just out of reach of anyone else who might make a serious bid for his heart. Jessy, after every adventure and conquest, always returned to the comfort and security of Owen's arms.

Now Jessy was finally leaving him, going to California for that writer's apprenticeship, and this time Owen feared he would never come back to him. He still had Maggie, but that wasn't the same. He also knew she'd never find a guy of her own as long as he was around. Owen needed to set her free and break free himself.

Owen reached into his pocket and touched the tiny plastic bag. He still had a tiny bit of coke left over from the disco night. He stepped through the doors of the restaurant and went directly into the washroom.

He'd do a line. Just enough to take away the jitters, that's all. He held one nostril closed and took a sharp sniff, then the other nostril—just enough for confidence. A wave of relief shot through him, and he blew out a breath of air. Time to meet the client. He glanced at his watch, then stepped out of the bathroom. There at the far end of the restaurant was Becky sitting with a young man.

"Actually, I'm a special events planner, but I do weddings," Owen explained after Becky had introduced him and they ordered.

"Well, what do you think?" said the young man, who looked like a poster boy for health tonics. "Will you do it?"

Owen looked at Becky, who was sitting across from him. Her harsh makeup accentuated her age.

"If I understand you correctly, you want an early-afternoon wedding," Owen said.

"Yes," Becky said. "With a lunchtime reception because they're leaving for their honeymoon in Australia that same evening."

Owen held up his hands and made a frame in the air. "Tim, a twenty-year-old bronze-medalist diver with Neil, his forty-year-old businessman boyfriend, diving hand in hand into a swimming pool after saying their vows." He nodded. "Becky, I have to say you're right. The press will gobble it up."

"I know what the press wants." Becky smirked.

"This should make quite a splash," Tim said to Becky, and they laughed.

Owen smiled but didn't join in. "Was Neil going to wear Speedos or boxers?" Owen's tone was serious.

"What do you mean?" Tim furrowed his brow.

"Because you also know how unforgiving the press is," Owen said as he dipped his sushi into the wasabi and popped it into his mouth.

"Ohhh. I didn't quite picture it that way." Tim bit his lip.

"Yes, but that's what makes headlines," Becky said with a slight shrill to her voice.

Owen swallowed and looked directly at Tim. "It could be at Neil's expense."

"Oh no, we can't do anything that might embarrass Neil." Tim had a tone of panic in his voice. "I just want our wedding to be special!"

Becky's overenthusiastic expression soured. She stiffened her body, and her face became hard. "What do you suggest we do, then?"

"Well, your idea is certainly in the right direction, but we might need to consider some slight modifications," Owen said.

Becky opened her mouth to say something, but Owen continued, "Listen, rather than trying to find an indoor pool large enough for your wedding, what about considering an alternative theme?"

"Like what?" Tim sounded concerned.

"Didn't you say that you and Neil met at the theater?"

"Yes, the Broadway production of *Mamma Mia!*"

"What do you think about a musical theme with a backup chorus line and dance routine? It would certainly look less like self-promotion than a swimming pool theme."

"And where will you create this off-Broadway musical wedding?" Becky's tone was sharp.

"Right here at the Syracuse Landmark Theater. It's been restored—faux orientalism, dripping in crystal, gold, and opulent murals, straight from the 1920s golden era of movie palaces—and it's fabulous."

"Yes, yes, it's spectacular," Becky interrupted, waving her chopsticks.

Owen continued, "We'll do the service in the theater and the reception in the lobby." He paused and looked at Tim. "Now, I can't promise anything at this late notice, but…."

"But what?" Tim leaned forward in his chair with his eyes trained on Owen.

Owen smiled. "Since it's an early-afternoon wedding, we just might be able to get it."

"Yes, yes," Tim said.

"And what about the song-and-dance routine?" Becky said with a note of sarcasm as she popped a piece of tuna sushi into her mouth.

"My best friend is tight with the director of the Visual and Performing Arts program at Syracuse U. And there are two things actors thrive on, an audience and a paid gig."

Tim squealed with delight and clapped his hands. "Neil will love this. What do you think?" He turned to Becky. "Can we do it all by the second-to-last weekend of June?"

Becky looked at Owen, who gave her a single nod.

"Of course we can!" Becky forced a smile and rolled out the words "That's why I called in Owen. He's a genius!" She sneered at Owen and mouthed the words, *I hate you.*

Owen smiled and shrugged.

Chapter Fifteen

SLAP.

"Ow, what did you do that for?" Enrico said as he rubbed the side of his face.

"Young man, don't you come into my kitchen and say things like your papà never loved your mamma."

"But what do these letters mean, Tata?" Fabrizio said.

"Pour me a grappa," Tata barked as she flopped onto the chair.

Enrico placed a small glass in front of Tata and filled it with the fruity brandy.

She took a sharp swig. "Now sit down and listen," Tata said. "Your papà was in his nineteenth year, his second year studying pharmacy at Cattolica University. Every morning and every evening he took the train between here and Milan. It was a three-hour trip back then because it stopped in all the villages along the way, but he used that time on the train to study." She took a large swig of grappa. "And yes, he and the Castagna boy, Antonio, had a story together. But of course he hadn't met your mother yet. Is that what you wanted to know?"

"What happened?" Fabrizio pleaded.

"Come on, Tata. Tell us more." Enrico refilled her glass.

"I can't tell you more. I didn't know him back then. But I can tell you that the Castagna family was an important family, and when they found out what was going on, they reported your father to the university and had him expelled. They also threatened to report him to the police for corruption of a minor should he try to contact the boy further."

"What happened to the Castagna boy?" Enrico said.

"They sent him to the US." Tata shrugged as if it were usual for rich families to send their sons to the US when a scandal emerged. "Or at least that's what everyone said."

"And?" Enrico coaxed.

"And your father returned home to the lake in disgrace and got a job at the pharmacy. Even though he lived a quiet life, didn't drink or gamble, was a good son and went to church every Sunday...." Tata paused, then slowly took another drink. "Scandal like that has a way of clinging to a man like a bad smell.

"Then one day your mother went to the pharmacy to get your grandmother's medicine and that's when they met. The two of them fell in together like two best friends, and it seemed as if the gloom that had hung over this house for so long had been swept away with a summer's breeze. Francesca had been sent to boarding school by then, and of course, tongues continued to wag, but no one could deny that there had never been a couple more beautiful and two souls more alike than your father and your mother." Tata twirled her hand like she was stirring the air.

"It wasn't long before your papà asked your mamma to marry him, which as you can imagine was the answer to your grandmother's prayers. And so they got married, and that was that." Tata emptied her glass.

"And?" Enrico urged.

"Get her another glass of grappa," Fabrizio said. "She's holding out on us."

Tata scowled at Fabrizio but held up her glass and Enrico refilled it. "Okay, you're grown men now. I guess you're old enough to know the rest." She took a sharp swig. "That was not the end to it. When your father confessed to the priest that after a year of marriage they had not consummated the sacrament, the priest informed him that in the eyes of the church and God the marriage was not sanctified until they did so."

"And so…," Enrico started.

"What happened?" Fabrizio finished.

Tata looked sternly at the boys. "Don't ask me for details, but as far as I know, they consummated the marriage that one time, and that's when your mother became pregnant with you." Tata shook her head. "I don't know whether to thank that old blabbermouth priest, because without his meddling there would never have been the two of you, or to curse him for what came to pass."

Tata's face drooped, and she got a faraway look in her eyes. "I remember sitting there in church with the two of you bundled in my arms, not more than two days old, at your mother's funeral service. When the priest gave his final benediction, I bent my head down and kissed each of you on your foreheads and asked myself what kind of God could give such joy and take it away so cruelly. That was the last time I ever stepped inside a church."

"But Tata, what happened to Papà?" Fabrizio said.

"What made him, you know, so sad?" Enrico said.

"I'm no doctor, but over the years I watched your papà—burdened with shame for who he was and guilt over the death of your mother. It ate away at him until he eventually retreated into his own world."

"But he didn't cause Mamma's death!" Fabrizio cried out.

"So, it's true what they say about Papà," Enrico said.

"I was there. I saw with these two eyes of mine. Your papà loved your mamma in every possible way he could, and your mother loved him with all her heart." Tata threw back the last of her grappa. "Now go. Get out of here. I have dinner to make." She pointed to the door.

Enrico and Fabrizio got up, kissed her on the cheek, and left the kitchen.

"And make no mistake, he loves you two boys more than life itself," Tata called after them as she reached over, took the bottle, and poured herself another drink.

Chapter Sixteen

IT WAS Wednesday evening, the evening when just the three of them went out together, no boyfriends, no lovers, no fuck buddies, and no hangers-on were allowed. Those were the rules.

"Package from Amazon," Jessy said as he came through the door.

"Hey, how was school?" Maggie called from the kitchen, where she was sitting with her laptop.

"Fine. Got an A on my story." He walked in, bent over, and kissed her on the cheek from behind.

"Wow! Congratulations." She turned her head and looked up.

"And I didn't have to blow the professor or anything." When it came to sex, you could never really tell if Jessy was joking or not. "So, what's in the package?"

"Owen's latest scheme toward efficiency," Maggie said as she swiveled around in her chair.

"What?"

"He decided to no longer do any laundry." Maggie shrugged. "He sends all his clothes out, and, get this, he's started ordering seven sets of socks, boxers, and T-shirts from Amazon every week." Maggie took the package and put it on the far end of the table.

"What does he do with the dirty stuff?" Jessy scrunched up his nose.

"Throws it out. He says it's easier than washing it."

"Man, that boy's getting weirder every day."

Maggie nodded. "He keeps working harder and harder, like he's trying to prove something to somebody."

"Yeah, but how do I tell my best friend no matter what he does or how successful he becomes, he's never going to win his mother's love and approval?"

"He really needs to get away for a while," Maggie said. "He promised me if I could secure the Landmark Theater for the Dally-Burman wedding, he'd take me to Italy."

"A last-minute booking for Italy in July, are you crazy? Rome, Venice, Tuscany. Even if you can find something decent, they'll be crawling with tourists," Jessy said.

Maggie let out a puff of air. "Well, I was also thinking about the northern Lake District. Italian charm without the tourist swarm—just peace and quiet." She looked back at the screen and scrolled down. "Oh, look, this one is pet and gay friendly." Maggie tapped the screen.

"Oh goodie, I wonder if both the pets and gays have to wear muzzles and pee in the backyard?" Jessy quipped.

"Stop being so negative." Maggie looked up at Jessy.

Jessy reached over and scrolled down the sites. "*Lago B&B*. Hmm. I have to admit this one looks grand."

"Oh, and look, it's got a view of the lake and the mountains. I'd be able to see Switzerland from my bedroom."

Jessy studied the screen. "Yes, and there's Julie Andrews singing 'The Sound of Music.'" He pointed at the corner of screen. "Oh no, maybe it's just one of the Von Trapp brothers in drag."

"Would you be serious?" Maggie said. "And then we'll do the usual tourist tour through Venice, Rome, and Florence after we've chilled out.

"What do you think?" Maggie grit her teeth. "He did promise me, and I just confirmed the theater this morning. I've got his business credit card." She held up the card between her fingers and waved it back and forth.

"Just book it." Jessy nodded.

"Come with us." Maggie clasped Jessy's hand.

"Oh, what a cliché. Two gay men traveling with their...."

"You say that name and I'm not going to dinner with you!" Maggie shook her finger at Jessy. She knew the name people had for girls like her. But what kind of a life did she have before them? It was not likely that some Prince Charming was going to knock on her door and sweep her off her feet. Without Jessy and Owen, she was destined to be just another Pathetic Patty.

"What name?" Jessy had a look of false innocence pasted on his face. "I was going to say, two stunningly handsome gay men traveling to Italy with their gorgeous best girl."

"So you'll come?"

"No, no, this is your thing." Jessy leaned away. "If I wanted to see ladies with big hair, push-up bras, perched on stilettos, and old guys with Tuscan cigars, white belts, and big bellies, I could go to a family reunion."

"Ah! That's so racist." Maggie scowled.

"Honey, I'm allowed to say these things. I'm half Italian, you know." Jessy propped a bent wrist on his hip. "Besides, you were at my last family reunion."

"Okay, so you have a point." Maggie flicked her hand backward like she was shooing a fly. "But what about all the famous designers, the wine, and the great food?"

"I can get all the shoes, booze, and spaghetti I want when I go to California, without the bad plumbing and musty churches." Jessy made a mock genuflection.

"Yeah, but it's not the same. Italy is the real thing. Just look at this villa." Maggie pointed at the photo on the screen. "It must be, I don't know, really old."

"I wish I could, but my writing apprenticeship starts in two weeks." Jessy stood up straight. "Go and have your little Merchant Ivory fantasy and take Owen with you before he completely loses it."

"I guess this is it." Maggie looked at him with sorrowful eyes. "The end of the Terrible Trio."

"My dear woman." Jessy extended his arms full length like he had just sung the theme song in a musical. "We will always be the Terrible Trio." Jessy put the back of his hand to his head, leaned against the desk, and swooned the way Greta Garbo did in the silent movies. "But sometimes the best way to say I love you"—he thrust his hand outward and looked away—"is it to let go."

"Okay, clown, enough with the movie camp. I'm trying to be serious." Maggie swatted Jessy. "Hey, do you remember that time when you guys first invited me to skip class with you?" She had begun using the phrase, *do you remember that time*, more and more often, and when she did, she felt old. Maybe it was because she longed for that magical time back in high school when they were adventurers out to discover the world. For some time now, it seemed like all they did was work. They no longer went out to have fun and tear up the night; now they went out to schmooze, make appointments, and talk about proposals for the next event, gig, or happening. When had the sparkle disappeared?

"What time are you talking about? We always skipped class."

"No, I know. I mean that time you guys chose me to be your bestie."

"Our beasty?" Jessy cocked one eye at Maggie.

"No, you idiot!" Maggie nudged him and took him by the arm. "Not your beasty, your bestie."

"I beg to differ," Jessy said. "We were two lost puppies in a pet shop. It was you who chose us."

Jessy always had a way of giving something you said a whole new perspective, and she had no doubt he would make a brilliant writer.

Back in high school, while the other girls in her class were wearing makeup and push-up bras, Maggie's apparel and hair accentuated her androgynous appearance that boys and girls of her age sometimes have. In her shapeless black sweatshirts and skirts, with her black hair pulled down in front of her morbidly mascaraed eyes, she kept to herself and nobody really took the time or interest to get to know her.

One day, Sharron-spelled-with-two-Rs tagged her with the nickname Morticia and it stuck like poo on Maggie's shoes.

"Hey, Morticia," Sharron-with-two-Rs said as she passed Maggie in the halls. "How are things down at the morgue?"

The name drove Maggie even deeper into that dark place.

Then one morning in her senior year, while Maggie was sitting at her desk counting the months ahead and praying for it to be over, for no apparent reason Owen leaned across the desk and whispered in her ear, "We're busting out of here. Meet you at your locker at two."

She had sat next to Owen and Jessy in homeroom for two years, but they had hardly ever spoken to her. Well, there was that time she loaned Owen a pen and that other time she let Jessy copy her math homework. Then there was that time in art class when they asked her if she could draw a skull and she made this elaborate design of a skeleton dancing on a disco stage. They did say hello to her when they passed her in the halls, and they always remembered that her name was Maggie, not Morticia. Even if their invitation was a joke, or some kind of cruel setup, what did she really have to lose, anyway?

The afternoon bell rang and a horde of kids flowed into the corridor and gathered in front of their lockers. Maggie dug through the pile of notebooks and textbooks in the bottom of hers. Suddenly, out of nowhere, Jessy and Owen appeared on either side of her locker. "C'mon, let's go."

Maggie glanced back and forth at them nervously as she pulled her physics book out of the pile.

"Where?"

"Anna's Café." Jessy suspended his large frame from her open locker door.

"Or would you prefer physics class?" Owen rested his back against the locker next to hers. He was so close she could feel his body heat and smell the spicy scent of his deodorant or cologne, or whatever it was.

"With Mr. Molecule?" Jessy crossed his eyes and wobbled his head back and forth.

"Hell no!" She tossed her physics book back in the pile and grabbed her ragged vintage black velvet jacket from the hook. Jessy let go of the door, and Maggie slammed it shut.

"We need to sign out first," Jessy said as they maneuvered through the flow of kids coming down the corridor.

"We've got fake notes, but you'll need a good excuse," Owen said.

"I can say I'm going to my dad's real estate office for my career day project?" Maggie whipped out her cell phone and made a call. Two minutes later she hung up and smiled. "I'm covered. Let's go."

Sharron-with-two-Rs pressed herself back against her locker and stared with her mouth agape as Maggie, sandwiched between Owen and Jessy with their arms wrapped over her shoulders, swept past her. She continued to stare as the three of them skipped down the stairs and out of sight. Of course, by the time Sharron-with-two-Rs recounted the episode to only her most trusted friends, the word in the corridors was that Maggie did threesomes.

"Oh, it's just gross!" Sharron-with-two-Rs said loudly to her entourage of friends the next day as Maggie passed them in the hall. "If Jessy and Owen wanted a threesome, why did they ask Morticia and not me?" She propped her hands on her hips and scowled.

After that, it seemed as if everyone, except Sharron-with-two-Rs, remembered Maggie's real name.

With the inclusion of Maggie in their tight little bubble, Jessy and Owen had expanded the strict boundaries of the Jessy-Owen duo. Sure, there was a label for a girl who dedicates herself completely to a couple of boys like Jessy and Owen, but she didn't care. They were her boys and she was their bestie.

But they were no longer kids in high school, and now the friendship, which had served to protect and nurture the three of them through their final years of adolescence, was beginning to stunt and strangle them as adults. Each, in their own way, was too comfortable to acknowledge their truth and too frightened to let go, but the day was fast approaching when their paths would part. Maggie knew that Jessy's apprenticeship in California would be his big chance and that he would leave them. Even more than that, she knew that someday she would have to break free from Owen. No matter how she tried to prepare herself, she couldn't quite imagine what her life would be like without her boys.

Just then her cell phone rang. "Where are you? Jessy and I are starving," she said into the phone while Jessy mouthed the words, *Where the fuck is he?*

"Yeah, I know," she said. "Work comes first. Later." She made a halfhearted kiss and hung up. "Owen's ditching us again. He said he's got a dinner meeting with a potential client."

Jessy scowled. "Another lame excuse. What was it last week? Alien invasion? Natural disaster? Oh, he forgot." Jessy rolled his eyes and shook his head. "Well, I guess we should cut him some slack. He's seeing some new guy named Lane or Lance or something like that."

"And he's the source of the problem." Maggie wore an uncharacteristic look of deep disapproval.

"What? Is there's something else going on?" Jessy's voice suddenly became serious.

"His new boyfriend...." She paused. "Is a cokehead." She almost spit out the words. "I found this under the sofa pillows." She held up a miniature ziplock bag dusted on the inside with powder.

Jessy slapped his forehead. "Shit!"

"He thinks I don't know." Maggie's face drooped and she shook her head.

"How long do you think he's been snorting?"

"I don't know, but he's not sleeping at night, and as you said he's getting weirder every day."

"We've got to do something before it's too late." Jessy shot his hands outward as if he were grasping for an answer in the air. It was the first time Maggie had ever seen Jessy looking lost and desperate.

"If I can get him away for a few weeks, I'm sure I can reason with him," Maggie said.

CHAPTER SEVENTEEN

"OKAY, ARE you ready?" Fabrizio said.

"Ready for what?" Enrico eyed his brother suspiciously.

"I posted our website last night." Fabrizio held his hands up.

"But the pictures and description of the house don't exactly match reality!"

"Did you just fall off the vegetable wagon?" Fabrizio jabbed his elbow into Enrico's ribs. "That's why they call it virtual reality! Everybody knows the internet is a bullshit. Nobody expects a B&B to actually look like the pictures on the site. Besides, we've already got a booking." Fabrizio gestured toward the screen.

"A booking!"

"Yeah, some American guy and his wife."

"Oh, Mother of God, let me see." Enrico plunked down next to his brother and swiveled the laptop toward him. "How do you know they are husband and wife?"

"Because they booked separate bedrooms." Fabrizio curled his lip. "Who travels with their girlfriend and books a separate bedroom?"

"Got a point." Enrico nodded.

"And if they give us a good review, we're all set!" Fabrizio said.

Enrico stood up and grabbed hold of his hair. "We are so fucked."

Fabrizio jumped up, wrapped his arms around his brother's waist, and lifted him off his feet. "Fucked? We're going to be rich!"

Chapter Eighteen

"OKAY, PACK your bags!" Maggie said as she burst into Owen's bedroom.

"What?" Owen didn't look up from the Excel chart on his screen.

"Our trip to Italy!" Maggie was beaming. "I hope you haven't changed your mind and want to go Germany instead? Those leather shorts look like they chafe, and sausages give me gas."

"What are you talking about?" Owen turned his head sideways toward Maggie.

"Owen. You promised me if...."

Owen's phone rang and he held his finger up to Maggie and looked at the screen. "It's the bakery." He spoke into the phone. "Yes, of course there are two grooms. It's a gay wedding!" He tilted the phone away and mouthed the words, *they're idiots*. "Well then buy two bride and groom statue sets and keep the two brides for your next lesbian wedding!" He rolled his eyes and shook his head. "Good, send me a photo when the cake's ready." He hung up. "Surely this can't be their first gay wedding. It's two grooms! How hard can the concept be! Sorry, honey. What were you saying?"

"As I was saying, you promised me if I could secure the Landmark Theater, we'd go to Italy." Maggie had her hands propped on her hips.

"Maggie, I can't possibly leave right now." Owen looked back at his flow chart.

"Look, I had to use every connection my dad had, and I even had to flirt with that greasy booking agent."

"The theater may be booked, but we still have to pull the wedding off, and I'm swamped." Owen stood up and breathed in deeply.

"The Dally-Burman wedding is the second-to-last weekend in June, just before Pride. Everything is on schedule." Maggie used that same flat, stern tone she used when a subcontractor phoned with an excuse. "Owen, we had a deal!"

"Maggie, I can't." Owen walked toward the door. "I'll make it up to you. I promise."

"You can't imagine how much you sound exactly like a straight guy when you say that," she growled.

Owen's phone rang again. "Ask Jessy," he said as he pressed it against his face to answer.

"Jessy's going to LA. Or did you forget that too!" Maggie said.

I'll call you later. He mouthed the words and blew her a kiss.

"Don't worry, everything is going as planned," Owen said into the phone "Oh, listen. I found a white 1960 Mustang convertible we can rent for the big day. I thought you might prefer that to a hardtop." He stepped out of his bedroom and into the living room, leaving Maggie standing in front of his computer desk.

Maggie threw her hands in the air and stomped out of his bedroom, past him, and into the kitchen.

"Oh, just a moment! I'll call you back later." Owen hung up, ran back into his bedroom, and riffled through his drawers. Next, he dug into his jacket pockets. Nothing. "Shit," he muttered. It was only five and he already wanted a little snort. He really had to stop before it got out of hand, but first there was the Dally-Burman wedding. He'd stop after that. Seriously.

CHAPTER NINETEEN

THE BOYS came up into the back garden from the lake carrying the paddles.

"We can offer our guests a tour of the lake," Fabrizio said.

"Tomorrow I'll take the boat over to the boatyard and get Dario to look at the engine. It sounds a little rough. Probably just needs a good grease job," Enrico said.

"Yeah, and maybe he can give you a good grease job too." Fabrizio bobbed his eyebrows.

"Pig!" Enrico bunted his brother with his shoulder. "Besides, I think that's best left for my fantasies."

They laid the paddles down under the eaves of the garden house.

"I'm starved." Fabrizio trotted off toward the house with Enrico in close pursuit.

"Hey, Tata," they called as they burst in through the kitchen doorway. "What's for lunch?"

Standing in front of the stove staring into a large cauldron of boiling water, Tata remained motionless.

"Tata, are you all right?" the boys said in unison.

"Oh, yes, yes, fine." Tata turned and kissed them on their cheeks. "Your sister and her husband are here in the living room." Tata turned back toward the stove.

"Oh great! We really need to talk with them," Enrico said enthusiastically, and they bounded out of the kitchen.

"You're staying for lunch, right?" Fabrizio called out as they came into the living room. Francesca was standing in the center of the room pointing at one of the large impressionist paintings while Pietro photographed it.

"No, we can't possibly." Francesca waved her hand behind her ear. "But Pietro did want to make a record of all of the paintings we have. Our dear great-uncle Donato Frisia has become quite notable in the past few years, and I wanted to be sure we have a complete record of the collection."

"Did you get the ones in the dining room too?" Fabrizio said.

"Yes, yes, I got them all." Pietro clicked the shot and put his phone in his pocket. "And the antique furniture, as well. A lot of these are pretty valuable, you know?"

Francesca shot Pietro a disapproving look.

"Actually," Pietro continued, "we had some important business in Switzerland to do so we just dropped by to get your signatures on some documents." He went over to the Versace briefcase that was open on the dining room table, took out a collection of official-looking papers and a Montblanc pen. He put the papers on the table and handed Fabrizio the pen. "Sign here." He pressed his finger on a line at the bottom of the page.

"What is it?" Fabrizio said.

Enrico reached past his brother, took the document, and scanned the first page. "It's all in legal language. I'd have to read it carefully."

"There's no need to read it." Pietro took hold of the top corner of the document and tugged it from Enrico's hand. He placed it flat on the table in front of Fabrizio again and smoothed it. "It's strictly for bureaucratic reasons. Of course you're free to hire a lawyer first, but that will be costly and tie up things further."

Francesca cleared her throat. "It's just a formality to close our grandmother's estate." Francesca glanced in the mirror and fixed a strand of hair behind her ear.

"As soon as you sign, we can deposit it with the notary in Milan," Pietro said, waving the pen.

Francesca flashed her big yellow teeth. "After that I can access my personal account and loan you the money you asked me for."

"We trust you." Fabrizio took the pen from Pietro. "Where do I sign?"

"Here, here, and here at the bottom." Pietro pointed.

Suddenly, Tata appeared behind Fabrizio and took hold of his wrist. "If you are going to be a responsible businessman you need to know what you're signing first, don't you?"

Francesca shot an acidic glare at Tata.

"Tata's right," Enrico said. "It's time we take responsibility for our own finances. We can't expect Francesca to always look after us."

"Of course, my dears." Her voice was dripping with sweetness. "I will leave you a copy so you can study it at your leisure." She held her wrist up and glanced at her gold Rolex. "It's just we're late, and if we are to make it to Switzerland before the bank closes, we'll need your signatures right now."

"Like Pietro said, it's just for bureaucratic reasons." Fabrizio's hand flinched, but Tata held it firmly.

Enrico bit his lip. "I don't want you to think that we don't trust you." He took the pen and the document from his brother's hand. "But we need to study this first."

"Oh, my darlings. I would never think that." Francesca took Enrico by the chin and kissed his cheek, then leaned over and kissed Fabrizio's cheek.

"I don't have a second copy here with me," Pietro snapped.

"No worry," Enrico said. "We can photograph this one."

"We really have to go," Francesca blurted out.

"It'll just take a second." Enrico held the paper flat on the table while Fabrizio dug for his phone.

"Better I email you a copy when we get back to Milan." Pietro snapped the document back, folded it, put it into the briefcase, and closed it shut. With a firm grip on the case, he took the Mont Blanc pen from Enrico. "We'll be in touch." His voice was as stern as his face.

He leaned to kiss Tata's cheek, but she turned and walked away. "I smell something burning in the kitchen."

Francesca glared at her through squinted eyes. "Come, Pietro." She clicked her tongue. "We'll just have to deal with the signatures another day. This will certainly slow down the process for everyone, but we must be on our way." She threw a kissing sound toward the boys and walked out of the room with Pietro following closely.

CHAPTER TWENTY

DURING THE weeks leading up to the Dally-Burman wedding, Owen had barely slept, attending to every detail, from making sure the chorus had practiced "Singing in the Rain" with umbrellas, just in case it rained, to color coordinating the toilet paper in the washroom. Maggie organized the crews of caterers and musicians with the precision and efficiency of a military operation.

The big day, with all the sparkle and magic of a Broadway musical set in the spectacular Landmark Theater, was beyond what anyone could have imagined. After the reception in the lobby, the teary-eyed newlyweds, about to make their grand exit, paused to give Owen and Maggie their gratitude and a substantial check.

"Holy shit," Becky said loudly as she staggered away from the bar and out of the theater smelling of wine and packed into a dress that reminded Owen of an old expression about a silk purse and a sow's ear. "That was sure the classiest fuck'n wedding I've ever been to."

As Tim and Neil emerged out the front doors of the theater and bounced down the outer steps, the chorus group burst into their song-and-dance routine with twirling umbrellas even though it was a glorious sunny afternoon. Just before they climbed into the Mustang convertible, Tim launched his bouquet of flowers at the expectant crowd, who leaped into the air like a squad of seasoned volleyball players. As soon as the newlyweds had driven off, the guests showered Owen and Maggie with accolades and asked for their business card.

In the week that followed, Owen and Maggie barely had time to wrap up the accounts and pay the bills for the wedding before Pride was upon them.

"Now comes the fun part, where we see if we have anything left over," said Owen as he made a last entry on his Excel chart.

"I just did our final balance and well...," Maggie said as she completed a bank transfer to the florist and looked up from her screen.

"Well what?" Owen leaned across the kitchen table.

"We just made a killing on the Dally-Burman wedding! Look." She swiveled her laptop around so Owen could see the screen.

"Wow!" he said as he stared at the final balance. "Maggie, my dear woman, it's time to celebrate!"

"Let's hope Pride is better this year than it was last year." Maggie let her head flop backward with exhaustion. "I still can't say the word *T-shirt* without cringing."

The previous year, Jessy had decided that they should make and sell T-shirts at Pride. When Jessy got an idea in his head, it was pretty hard to convince him otherwise.

"This is our first Pride. Can't we just dance behind one of the floats?" Owen whined.

"C'mon, we need the money," Jessy said.

He produced a gothic black image of a man and woman and the words *faggot and dyke* printed in graffiti scroll across them.

As Owen and Maggie stared at the design doing their best not to make sour faces, Jessy explained, "Everybody is sick and tired of those banal rainbow flag designs. What people really want is something edgy with a message."

"Are you sure people really want to wear a T-shirt that says that?" Owen pointed at the words.

"Absolutely! Pride Day is all about asserting our identity and reappropriating words that hurt," Jessy said.

Owen and Maggie suspected Jessy of taking Queer rhetoric a little too literally but said nothing. They pooled their resources and came up with enough money for T-shirts, silk screening, and the kiosk fee at Pride.

"I don't think I have the courage to wear one of these, and I'm not even a lesbian," Maggie confessed to Owen as they examined the T-shirts when they came back from the printers.

On the day of Pride, the three of them, each sporting a T-shirt, set up their table in the park at the end of the march, along with the scores of other tables selling rainbow-colored products of every imaginable kind, from key chains and necklaces to underwear and sex toys. Maggie and Owen stood and watched as the throng of people shuffled by. A few people stopped and asked if they had any other designs. Jessy didn't seem to notice. He was busy explaining the concept over and over again to numerous guys who seem much more interested in the vendor than the product. By the end of the day Jessy had sold twenty-five T-shirts to guys who only agreed to buy one if he gave them his telephone number. Maggie got propositioned by a biker woman, and Owen was lectured numerous times for the *inappropriateness and insensitivity* of his T-shirt.

"That was the longest Pride Day of my life," Owen said to Maggie as they packed up the boxes of unsold T-shirts and their table.

"Honey, that was the first Pride Day of our lives," Maggie said. "It can only get better after this!"

"What are we going to do with all these horrible T-shirts?" Owen groaned.

"I don't care as long as I never see one again." Maggie moaned.

The boxes of T-shirts, which were piled up in Jessy's mom's basement for weeks, miraculously disappeared one day.

With the grand success of the Dally-Burman wedding behind them, this year's Pride would certainly be different. They started out on the gay swim team float and wound up dancing with the leather daddies. At the end of the parade they did their rounds past the promoters and vendors and watched the drag queens on stage. After a few hours of banal conversation and predictable gossip barely audible above the thump of the music, they wound up at the beach party. There, the afternoon melted away with the house beats, and evening washed in like the tide. By nightfall they were swept along with the crowd to the dance floor at the Rain Lounge. Maggie and Jessy kept a close eye on Owen for most of the evening, steering him away from anyone who might offer him nose candy. At some point Owen met up with his new boyfriend, Lane or Lance or something like that, and they disappeared.

It was well after four in the morning when Maggie went back to the VIP corner near the DJ, to find Owen sprawled out on the sofa by himself. He looked exhausted.

"This was a lot better than our last Pride!" Owen said into her ear over the throbbing bass as Maggie plunked down on the sofa beside him.

"Don't even mention that disaster with the T-shirts." Maggie laughed.

"I thought we agreed never to use that word again," Owen said.

"Where's Lance?" Maggie couldn't help but notice a little white dust along the edge of Owen's nostril.

"Lane. He went off with his friends." Owen sounded as if he didn't really care where he had gone.

Good, Maggie thought as she pictured him surrounded by his club kid friends, bent over the bathroom sink with a straw up his nose, but she bit her lip and changed the subject.

"Hey, do you remember our high school prom, and the principal told you that you couldn't bring Jessy as a date?"

Owen smiled and nodded. Maggie always got nostalgic in the early hours.

She pressed in close against him. "Sharron-with-two-Rs and her anorexic band of evil cheerleaders just about pooed themselves when I walked into that rented ballroom in a full-length Versace gown with the captain of the swim team on my one arm and the top of the class on my other, both dressed in tuxedos—the two best-looking boys in school."

"Oh, they sound very sexy. Anybody I know?" Owen smiled and scrunched up his nose in that way that always made Maggie's heart go ping.

She stretched over and kissed him on the cheek.

"Before you two came along, the only boy who had ever asked me out was Norman Elgin. Remember him? Bad teeth and breath to match."

"Norman Tighty-Whitie Elgin." Owen let his head fall backward against the sofa.

"He came over to my house in his pickup truck and we went to the drive-through at the Burger King. We made out in the parking lot. I figured, what the hell, it's not like I'm ever gonna get a better offer. Afterwards, he dropped me off in front of my house. All I wanted to do was get away, so I dashed, leaving my panties lost somewhere under his seat."

"I hate it when I leave my panties behind." Owen slurred out the words.

Maggie batted him on the arm. "The next day he had my panties dangling from his rearview mirror, bragging loudly how he'd popped my cherry."

Owen's eyes were now closed, and he was almost asleep. "I hate it when I pop my cherry," he mumbled.

Maggie continued. "That morning, during homeroom, everyone was staring at me and laughing. I wanted to die. You and Jessy had skipped homeroom. Of course, Mrs. Tomar didn't report you; you had her wrapped around your little fingers."

"Mrs. Tomar. She had this mole on the side of her lip with a giant hair growing out of it," Owen said without opening his eyes.

Maggie stared off into the distance as she spoke. "I'll never forget the look on Norman's face when he went out to his pickup during lunch and found his side window smashed and my panties gone."

She stared directly at Owen. "They never figured out who did it."

Owen said nothing. He leaned over and kissed Maggie on the lips, then reclined back and closed his eyes again. His breathing slowed and he drifted off.

Maggie's eyes became moist. "You know, I get the Pride stuff, but I don't know if it gets me. When do I get a letter in the LGBT lineup?"

Owen didn't stir.

"What I'm trying to say is, where's my Pride? I mean, someday you and Jessy are gonna find guys of your own and settle down. And what will happen to me? I'll just be this pathetic old fag hag still hanging around in the shadows."

Owen breathed in and out deeply.

Maggie smoothed back his hair, and he stirred and opened his eyes. "C'mon, honey," she said. "It's time to find out where Jessy and your boyfriend are."

They knew where Jessy would be: dance floor, dark room, or hanging over a toilet throwing up. As for Owen's new boyfriend, Lane or whatever his name was, Maggie really didn't care.

THEY WEAVED and wormed their way through the dance-trance-induced crowd to the far back corner where the dark room was. Owen could barely keep his eyes open. After all the nights without sleep preparing for the wedding, he was completely burned out. Maybe Lane had some coke left. Just a little pick-me-up snort, that's all he needed.

"Wait here. I'll see if Jessy's in there." Owen swept back the heavy black curtain and ducked into the darkness. The pungent odor of men filled his nostrils. A hand slid across his pelvis and down onto his crotch, and he felt himself getting chubby. He swiveled away. By now his eyes had adjusted enough that he could make out figures pressed against the walls. In the corner, there was a cluster of silhouettes. Owen squinted to see their faces.

Leaning back against the wall, he spotted Jessy with his pelvis thrust forward, humping some guy's bent-over ass. Someone else was holding onto the guy's head with both hands and pumping his face. Owen's boner strained against the zipper of his jeans as he watched Jessy thrust harder and then come with a grunt.

"Psst, Jessy," he called out in a church whisper.

Jessy pulled out, peeled off the condom, tossed it on the ground, and tucked himself back into his pants.

Owen leaned over and whispered into Jessy's ear, "C'mon, lover boy, time to go."

It was a ritual almost half as old as their friendship.

Jessy stepped away from the cluster and someone else moved into position.

But before Owen turned to leave, he paused. He couldn't help but notice that, even in the darkness, there was something familiar about the bent-over figure's form. Out of curiosity, or maybe jealousy, Owen briefly glanced down at the guy's face. "Shit!" Owen turned and darted out of the darkroom.

By the time Jessy emerged from behind the heavy black curtain, Owen was now standing next to Maggie.

"How was I to know he was Lane?" Jessy said as he hurried up to them.

Owen refused to look at him.

"They call it a darkroom because it's dark! Next time I'll be sure and inquire first if anyone has a boyfriend," Jessy huffed.

"Thanks a lot!" Owen spit out.

"Oh, don't act so indignant." Jessy held up his hands in surrender. "So I just fucked your party boy. So did three other guys." Jessy made a stupid face and shrugged.

Owen tensed his jaw and glared at Jessy. "He was my boyfriend!"

"Oh yeah right." Jessy crossed his arms. "He wasn't a boyfriend. You don't even know anything about him. He was just a fashion accessory. You had him penciled in between appointments and working dinners, just like you've been doing to Maggie and me." Jessy's permanent carefree expression had disappeared, and his face was now hard.

"That's not true," Owen said with a conviction that sounded forced. But it was true. Owen didn't know anything about Lane, and he didn't really want to. In fact, it wasn't Lane he was jealous of. He stood speechless for a moment. Suddenly, all his feelings for Jessy that he had buried for so long came boiling to the surface. "And what about you? You expect me to stand by and watch while you fuck whoever you want!"

"I may be a slut, but I don't lead people on like there's anything more to it than sex," Jessy continued. "Oh, and don't think we don't know about your new best friend—the nose candy."

Owen felt the blood drain from his face. "What do you care! You're the one who's abandoning me!" He gasped as his unspoken truth escaped from his mouth.

"So that's it! You're pissed because I'm going to California and you're looking for an excuse to dump on me and hurt yourself."

Owen spun around toward Maggie. Her eyes filled with tears as she nodded agreement.

"And what about your promise to go to Italy with Maggie?" Jessy continued. "Or are you just going to brush her off too?"

Maggie stood frozen.

"Fine!" Owen spit out. "If you haven't cancelled the plane tickets and hotel bookings, we'll go to fuck'n Italy!" He looked back at Jessy. "Have a nice life in California!" Owen was trembling and his eyes were moist. Suddenly, he reached up and clasped his nose as a trickle of blood ran onto his lip. "Oh shit!" He turned and raced off.

PART TWO

CHAPTER TWENTY-ONE

"IS IT nine in the evening or nine in the morning?" Maggie said as they stepped through the exit doors of Malpensa International Airport.

"Nine in the evening." Owen pointed across the parking lot toward the taxi stand.

Maggie looked back at the large red letters over the entrance. "*Malpensa*. Even the name sounds European."

"Oh right, like LaGuardia sounds so American."

"Yes, but everything feels so European." Maggie held up her hands. "It even smells European."

"Maggie, so far we've seen the airport. And, by the way, that's diesel fuel you're smelling."

"I don't care. This is my first time to a foreign country." Her face was beaming. "No, wait a minute, remember that school trip to Niagara Falls back in final year? We crossed the bridge into Canada. That was my first foreign country."

"Oh yeah." Owen furrowed his brow. "I'd forgotten about that."

"Well, I remember the Horseshoe Falls and the people were really polite, but the money looked like Monopoly money."

"Well, I remember Jessy made out with the guard at the Ripley's museum," Owen said with a sneer.

"It's always sex with you two boys, isn't it?" Maggie said, doing her best imitation of Miss Morality, their old Social Studies teacher.

"It was Jessy, not me!" Owen said, pointing at his chest.

"Hey, do you remember Jessy bought a bottle of vodka with his fake ID and the three of us got drunk in the back of the bus on the way home?" Maggie said.

"Yeah. You spent half the trip barfing in the toilet," Owen said.

"You two were always getting me into trouble." Maggie pouted. "Well not this time. This time I'm going to immerse myself in the culture and savor the local flavors."

"That's just what Jessy said before he blew that guard." Owen curled his lip and feigned disgust. "But I don't want to talk about him." Owen pasted a stern look on his face. "I came here to forget Mister California."

"You miss him, don't you?" Maggie took Owen's hand and stroked it.

"It feels like a stake through my heart."

"I miss him too," Maggie said.

Owen started to say something, but a jet taking off drowned him out. Instead, he took out his cell phone. "Oh no! My cell phone won't work here!" he yelled as the roar of the jet faded into the distance, while he repeatedly jabbed the screen.

"We'll have to buy SIM cards when we get to the B&B," Maggie said calmly.

"Well what am I going to do until then?" Owen had a slight tone of panic in his voice.

"We could go back inside and look for one in the airport, but I'm sure that the Facebook and Twitter networks won't collapse without you."

He stopped and breathed in deeply. "Sorry. I'm just a little jittery, that's all. Let's find our taxi." Owen hadn't snorted anything since that fateful night during Pride. The Prozac his doctor prescribed took the edge off, but he still had a dull headache even after the Tylenol Extra he took just before landing.

"They say it's like quitting smoking," Maggie said.

"I wish it were only cigarettes."

"Hang in there, big boy." Maggie patted his arm. "Oh, that must be our taxi." She pointed at a strange-looking minivan.

"Mr. Muller and Miss Tun?" the taxi driver said as he slid open the door to his white Fiat Multipla.

"That's us," Maggie said in a perky tone.

"Your luggage?"

"Just this." Maggie held out her carry-on. "The airline lost our bags."

The driver shrugged. "Welcome to Italy."

Maggie climbed in and Owen crawled in beside her.

"Ahh, my butt is killing me. I must be suffering from economy ass," Owen said, squirming from side to side. "I'll probably never be able to dance again."

"As long as you can have sex, what are you worried about?" Maggie poked Owen with her elbow.

Owen patted the left side of his chest. "I've taken a vow of celibacy. No sex without love."

"Yeah right, like my vow to diet. No potato chips without beer." Maggie snorted. "Save it for your memoirs, Madame X."

"No, seriously. I read this article about sex and porn addiction. Did you know the newest trend is celibacy?"

"It's not new. It's called the priesthood."

"Oh yeah, like they're celibate." Owen rolled his eyes.

"Shhh." Maggie jerked her head toward the diver. "Be careful!" she whispered. "We're in Big C country now."

The driver adjusted his rearview mirror and looked at them. He fiddled with his navigator, then pulled away from the curb, barely missing a couple who had stepped onto the striped crosswalk. He sped up the exit ramp, navigating the spaghetti pattern of overpasses and merges. They cruised along a double-lane highway for about ten minutes, then passed through a toll and out onto a multilane highway.

The car ahead was driving the speed limit in the center lane. The driver flashed his headlights. "*Testa di cazzo*," he muttered as he swerved right into the slow lane and raced past.

"I'll bet that means dickhead," Maggie whispered to Owen.

"We're gonna die," Owen whispered.

"Oh, relax. You said the same thing during takeoff and landing." Maggie pressed her nose against the window and looked out. "Too bad it's getting too dark out to see the scenery."

Owen grit his teeth and gripped the spongy corners of his seat. "Perhaps it's best we can't see too much."

Thirty minutes later, they took the off-ramp and passed through another toll. Twenty minutes after that they exited the multilane highway and continued along a rolling two-lane highway.

"I hope he knows where this place is," Owen whispered to Maggie.

"Of course he does," Maggie said. "Besides, he has the navigator, so how could we get lost?"

"Maybe we're being kidnapped and he's going to sell us as sex slaves," Owen whispered.

"They'll probably turn you into a eunuch."

"Ahh!" Owen held his hand over his groin and pressed his legs together.

The taxi raced on into the night, only slowing to maneuver around the traffic circles that were placed about every ten miles along the road.

"If we go around another traffic circle, I'm definitely going to barf," Owen said.

"Well, roll down the window a crack and get some fresh air."

Owen hit the button, lowered his side window, and let the warm night air blow on his face.

Suddenly the window rose up, hitting him in the chin.

"Air-conditioning!" the taxi driver said sternly.

"Hang on, I'm sure we're almost there." Maggie patted Owen's knee as they rounded another traffic circle. Looming up ahead was a dark silhouette of mountains sprinkled with lights.

"Laveno." The taxi driver pointed.

They slowed to cross a railway track and glided into the town.

"Oh, that must be the lake." Maggie pointed at the deep blue expanse beyond the town.

The taxi driver swerved around a curve at the Old Milano Pub, barely missing a group of young people standing partway in the street with cigarettes and cocktail glasses in their hands.

"At least we know there's a nightlife here," Owen said.

As the taxi continued, the road became progressively narrower. Owen inched away from his door and pressed closer to Maggie. "There's no way two cars can pass each other on this road."

Just as he spoke the headlights of a car appeared from around a blind corner heading straight toward them. Without slowing down the driver guided the taxi closer to the rock embankment. The weeds growing from the crevices made a slapping sound along the body of the car and against Owen's window. Just as it appeared that the oncoming car was going to hit them, the driver made a sharp little flick of the steering wheel. Only inches from clipping their mirrors, the two cars zoomed past each other.

"If we meet a bus or a truck, we're dead!" Owen said loud enough for the driver to hear.

The driver raised his hand and sliced it back and forth through the air just as they entered a gallery. As they came out the other side, the taxi driver jabbed his thumb toward the lake. "Gay beach."

"Gay beach?" Owen said.

"Yes, many gays, nudists, and *scambisti* come here."

"*Scambisti?*"

"Yes, to trade wives," the driver said.

Owen and Maggie looked at each other, furrowed their brows, and shook their heads as the taxi wound around a curve and up over a hill.

"Oh look!" Maggie pointed ahead to a small, lit chapel resting on the side of a cliff overlooking a cluster of lights nestled in a bay below.

Owen leaned over closer and peered out the window. "That doesn't look real. It looks like a postcard."

"Castelveccana." The taxi driver pointed. Five minutes later the taxi slowed and veered off the roadway onto a street bordered by stone walls, and up a hill toward a church. He turned left at the church and continued down a maze of poorly lit descending and ascending roads. Finally he came to a halt in front of an ancient-looking wrought-iron gate and flicked his headlights.

"I think we've arrived at Dracula's summer home." Owen stared out at the dark building looming in front.

"It really is a classic Italian villa!" Maggie said as she peered out her window.

A figure stepped out of the shadows into the headlight beams and opened the gate.

Owen pressed his face against his side window. "That's probably Igor," he said as the taxi drove in through the gate past the figure. "And from what I can see in this light, Igor sure looks hot."

Maggie swatted Owen. "That'll be one of the servants. I'm sure they have a huge staff here."

They drove down the gravel driveway and stopped in front of the house. Owen and Maggie got out of the car and stretched while the taxi driver placed their carry-on bags on the front step. The young guy from the gate trotted down the driveway and directly up to them. Owen watched with curiosity as Maggie held out her hand limply toward him.

He looked at her hand, then took it and kissed it. "Signora."

Maggie shivered.

Owen shot her a look and rolled his eyes. "Oh please," he muttered through tightly stretched lips.

He turned toward Owen, took his hand, and shook it vigorously. "Hey, guy, how's it go'n? I'm Fabrizio," he said with a contrived American accent.

Just then another young man appeared in front of Owen.

"And my name is Enrico." He smiled.

Owen quickly glanced at Fabrizio, then back at Enrico and beamed. "Very pleased to make your acquaintances." Owen's eyes remained locked on Enrico.

Maggie shot Owen a look and rolled her eyes. "Oh please," she muttered back at Owen.

"Welcome to our home." Enrico gestured in the direction of the steps lined with tea candles in clay pots. "We'll take your bags."

"Oh, we only have our carry-ons. The airlines lost our bags."

"Luckily I have all my personal stuff in here," Maggie said.

"I'm afraid I packed all my electronic stuff in my carry-on, and I don't have a change of clothes." Owen blew out a breath of air. "But Air Italia said they would deliver our bags first thing tomorrow," he quickly added.

Enrico shot a nervous glance at Fabrizio. "I better call them in the morning just to make sure they have the address."

"Oh, the other thing is, we need SIM cards," Owen said. "Our phones don't work here."

"Don't worry, we can get them in the village tomorrow." Enrico gestured again. "Go in and make yourselves comfortable. You are welcome."

"I'll take your bags, Miss Maggie." Fabrizio flashed a smile at Maggie.

As Maggie and Owen walked along the pathway and up the steps, Maggie whispered to Owen. "So, do you think they're gay or straight?"

"I'm definitely getting a reading, but I forgot to set my gaydar for Italian guys."

"I'm getting a reading too," Maggie said.

"You can't get a reading." Owen sneered. "There's no such a thing as straightdar!"

"Well, I'm certainly seeing double. And I'm liking the view!" Maggie bobbed her eyebrows.

"It's like my favorite porn video." Owen held the door open. "Of course, you're not in it."

"I'm thankful for that," Maggie said, and they went inside.

FABRIZIO AND Enrico waited in the driveway until the taxi drove off. "See, I told you they were husband and wife," Fabrizio said to his brother in Italian.

Enrico inhaled deeply. "You were right. Only a married woman would be brave enough to wear sweatpants and sports shoes outside the gym."

"I'm always right," Fabrizio said. "I've got a sixth sense for these things. Especially about married women."

"When have you ever been with a married woman?" Enrico cocked his head sideways.

"Signora Bianchi." Fabrizio shrugged. "What about her?"

"You haven't been with Signora Bianchi. You only fantasize about her when you wank." Enrico scowled.

"Well, that's almost the same." Fabrizio shot him a grin.

"C'mon, *cretino*. Let's get them settled. By the way, why did you kiss her hand?" Enrico said as they strolled up the path with the carry-on bags.

"She stuck it in my face, and I didn't know what else to do with it."

"And since when did you become a cowboy? Cut out the Texas accent. They're from New York."

"Just making them feel at home." Fabrizio held up his thumb and winked like he'd seen Fonzie do on the reruns of *Happy Days*.

Chapter Twenty-Two

"OWEN, COME quick!" Maggie appeared in Owen's doorway. She was making jittery little bounces as she disappeared back into her room and into her bathroom. "Hurry, I'm about to pee my pants."

"What's wrong?" Owen followed her and stood in the doorway.

Maggie stood pointing at the porcelain bowl next to the toilet. "What's that thing?"

Owen broke into a smile. "It's a bidet."

"I don't care what it's called. I just want to know if I'm supposed to pee in it or wash my feet in it."

"No! You're supposed to wash your girlie bits in it after you've done your business." Owen snorted a laugh. "Just don't ask me to demonstrate."

"No! Get out of here and let me pee in peace."

"You're the one who called me in here." Owen swatted the air and turned to leave.

"No! Don't go!"

"What now?"

"How do I flush?"

"With the big silver handle. You have to twist it on and off. It's manual."

"Okay, get out of here."

Owen walked out of Maggie's room. "Just be careful. *C* stands for *caldo*—hot!" he called back to her.

Owen had just returned to his room when there was a knock on his door. He opened it to find Enrico standing there holding a toothbrush in one hand and a small pile of clothes in the other.

"Is everything all right?" Enrico's voice had a slight nervous twinge.

"No, fine. Everything is fine." Owen looked directly into Enrico's eyes. "More than fine," he said and quickly broke his stare.

Enrico stood there for a moment, not saying anything. Then he glanced down at the pile of clothes in his hand. "I thought that maybe you would like to change into something fresh after your flight, so I brought you some clean socks, underwear, and a T-shirt you can borrow until your bags arrive." Enrico looked up and down at Owen. "You're a bit bigger than me, but these should fit. Oh, the toothbrush is new."

"Thanks." Owen took the pile from Enrico. "Especially for the toothbrush. I'm sure I have airline breath." He chuckled.

Enrico smiled nervously and turned to go but stopped. "Have you eaten?"

"We ate on the plane," Owen said. "Right now, I think I need a shower."

"If you'd like to come down in an hour, Tata has prepared something light for you before bed." Enrico turned and went down the stairs.

Two minutes later, Maggie appeared at the door.

"Did you figure out the plumbing?" Owen said.

"Fresh as a daisy. You know I could learn to love this bidet thing. It's like a little swimming pool for my vagina." She leaned against the doorsill. "So what did Enrico want?"

"He loaned me some clothes until my bags come."

"Oh, how sweet." Maggie chirped.

"Yeah, but I don't know if I'm comfortable wearing some guy's underwear." Owen frowned.

"Are you kidding me?" Maggie cocked one eyebrow. "You'd go into a dark room and stick some stranger's dick in your mouth who you can't even see, but you're squeamish about borrowing a pair of underwear?" Maggie shook her head. "There are things about gay men I'll never understand." She turned and went back into her room. "For the record if some hot guy like that were to loan me his underwear," she called back, "I wouldn't know whether to wear them or eat them!" She slammed her door shut, leaving Owen standing there with the pile of clothes in his hand.

Owen posed in front of the mirror and admired himself in Enrico's underwear. He was a boxer shorts guy and hadn't worn jockeys since he was in grade school. They weren't some fancy Italian designer that he recognized, like Armani or D&G, but he had to admit they were nice. He turned sideways and examined himself. He liked the way they hugged his butt and held his package. They seemed to complement his form better than his usual five-to-a-pack boxers. Then he imagined the underwear hugging Enrico's lean Mediterranean form, the little line of hair leading down from his navel under the wide band, and of course his cock, resting in the pouch like a snake asleep in a hammock, not that

Owen had ever seen a snake sleeping in a hammock, but he began to get hard all the same.

Just as he was about to slide his hand down the front of his underwear, the door banged open and Maggie walked in. Owen jumped and turned sideways in an attempt to hide his chubby. "Hey! Don't you ever knock?"

"Why? After living with you and Jessy for a year, these poor eyes of mine have witnessed more than any sane woman ever should. Here's my toothpaste. Don't squeeze it from the top of the tube." She tossed it on the end of the bed. "Oh, nice underwear. Really shows off your package." And she walked out again.

Chapter Twenty-Three

WHETHER IT was withdrawal, the medication, or just jet lag, Owen was up and wide-awake at sunrise. He had figured out how to use the Moka coffeepot and was standing on the terrace with a tiny cup of coffee as dark as old motor oil in his hand, watching the morning light tickle the tops of the mountains on the other side of the lake, when one of the boys came out of the kitchen.

"Enrico, right?"

"Yes." Enrico beamed.

"Hey, I'm getting good at this." Owen smiled back "Thanks again for the change of clothes. Listen, I need to get an Italian SIM card. Do you know where I could do that?"

"Right here in Castelveccana at the newsstand. It's about a fifteen-minute walk, but I'll give you a lift on the bike." Enrico pointed to Angelina sitting in the drive below them.

He hadn't intended it as an excuse to get to know Enrico, but it seemed like the perfect opportunity, except it would mean riding on the back of a scooter, not something Owen was quite comfortable doing. "No, I don't want to trouble you." He waved his hand.

"No trouble." Enrico placed his tiny coffee cup on the cement banister. "I'm going to pick up something for Tata. Come on."

Owen followed him as he trotted down the steps and over to Angelina. Enrico slipped on his helmet, straddled the bike, and pumped the foot pedal until the engine sprang to life. He braced his legs wide on either side of the bike, twisted around toward Owen, and handed him the other helmet. "Hop on."

"I've never ridden on a motorbike before. What do I do?" Owen had that same clumsy and awkward feeling he had felt so often growing up, like when he was afraid to skateboard or when he stood frozen on the end of the diving board at the pool unable to jump off.

"First come here and let me fix your helmet." Enrico reached up and took hold of the strap dangling under Owen's chin. Owen stood there like a child whose mother was tying on his hat before he went out to play.

"There you are." Enrico pulled the strap tight. "Now, brace yourself on my shoulders and climb on behind me."

Owen threw his leg over the seat. "Like this?"

Enrico bent over and took hold of Owen's ankle. "Put your feet here on the foot pegs." Then Enrico took Owen's hands and wrapped them around his waist just inches above his crotch. "Hang on." He revved the throttle and the bike jolted forward and Owen jerked backward. The scooter growled down the gravel drive and out onto the pavement. Enrico torqued the accelerator and they climbed up the hill and past the church.

As they came down the other side and flew around the corner, Owen clung harder onto Enrico's waist and squeezed his thighs against his hips. Pressed up against Enrico's warm backside, with the vibration of the engine and the exhilaration of the speeding bike, Owen began to get hard. He thought about sliding back in the seat a little so that Enrico wouldn't feel his boner, but he was too nervous to relax his grip.

Even if this wasn't really sex, not since he and Jessy had first fooled around when they were still in junior high had Owen surrendered his body to the moment like this. For some strange reason, the lines to an old song by Marianne Faithfull that Jessy's mom always used to sing off-key popped into his head. It was about a woman who had turned thirty-seven only to realize she'd never ridden through Paris in a sports car with the warm wind in her hair. Owen was a long way from thirty, this wasn't Paris, and they weren't in a sports car, but all the same, with his arms wrapped around Enrico and the warm wind in his face as they swerved and swayed down the roadway, he felt like he understood what the woman in the song had longed for.

"Everything okay?" Enrico turned his head and called back to Owen over the sound of the roaring engine.

"No problem," Owen yelled back.

Chapter Twenty-Four

"Good morning, *tesoro*," Tata said as Maggie came in through the kitchen door.

"Oh, good morning." Maggie blinked and inhaled the rich coffee aroma. "What time is it?"

"It's eight o'clock, dear. I heard you coming, so I put the coffee on. It will just be a moment. Sit down here at the table."

"I must have jet lag." Maggie fought back a yawn as she sat down. "Have you seen Owen?"

"Yes, he got up earlier. Enrico took him to Castelveccana to get something for his phone." The Moka pot steamed and gurgled. Tata took it off the fire and poured the brown liquid into a tiny cup. "Sugar?"

"Yes, one please."

Tata added a spoonful of sugar and placed the cup of coffee in front of Maggie.

Maggie picked up the tiny cup daintily in her fingers and took a sip. "Oh my, that's good! It's like super-coffee."

"We Italians love our coffee." Tata laughed.

"But Tata, where did you learn to speak English so well?"

"My father worked at the Gerbini American aeronautic base after the war, and he insisted that all his children learn English. I was sixteen when he died, and since I was the oldest, I came north to work and help support my mother and eight younger brothers and sisters back in Sicily."

"Wow, that must have been really heavy," Maggie said.

Tata shrugged. "It was. But I'm strong." She spooned three tablespoons of sugar into a large glass bowl. With a sharp strike on the edge of the bowl, she cracked an egg in half, skillfully separating the yolk from the white by pouring it back and forth between the two halves of the shell. Then she put the egg yolk in the large bowl and the egg white in a smaller bowl and did it again.

"What are you making?"

"Tiramisu."

"Ahh, I love tiramisu! It's my favorite dessert," Maggie said. "Oh, I'm sorry. I'm bothering you, aren't I?" Maggie caught herself.

"No, not at all. I live in a house full of men. Do you know how long it's been since I've had another woman in my kitchen to talk to?"

Maggie laughed. "I know exactly what you mean. I live with two men. They're great roommates, but sometimes I crave the company of another woman."

"What about your mother, dear?"

Maggie breathed in deeply. "Don't get me wrong, I love my mother, but we've never really connected in that way." She paused. "It was like we had left too many things unsaid and no longer knew how to restart the conversation."

Tata nodded in that wise and understanding way of older women have who have known the joy and sorrow of raising children.

Maggie continued to watch Tata as she picked up the bowl of egg yolks, cradled it in her arm, and beat the mixture until it was light and creamy. Then she placed the bowl back on the table and added a large white fluffy blob.

"Is that whipped cream?"

"No, it's mascarpone cheese," Tata said as she picked up a wine bottle and poured a couple of sloshes over the mascarpone. "And this is marsala." She handed the bottle to Maggie. "It's a sweet Sicilian wine." Tata picked up the bowl again and stirred. "My mother passed away years ago, so I like to get up in the morning and prepare something special the way she always used to. It makes me feel like she is still with me." Tata put down the large bowl, picked up the small bowl with the egg whites, and beat them until they were stiff. Then she added them to the large bowl and gently folded them into the mascarpone cream.

Maggie smiled. "My mom always used to make us waffles on Sunday morning."

"Now comes the fun part." Tata took the Moka pot off the stovetop and poured the remains of the coffee into a shallow glass pan. She reached out and Maggie handed her the bottle of marsala. She poured a few sloshes in the pan with the coffee and stirred. One at a time, she dipped some biscuits that were sitting next to the pan, into the coffee and marsala, putting half of the soggy biscuits aside in the small bowl and using the other half to line the bottom of the glass pan. She spread half the mascarpone cream over the biscuits and sprinkled them with a heavy dusting of cocoa. On top of this she added a second layer of biscuits, covering them with the remaining mascarpone and dusting them with cocoa.

Maggie watched, mesmerized by the process. "It's like magic! I had no idea that's how tiramisu is made. Is this your mother's recipe?"

Tata chuckled. "Yes, with a few modifications. Everybody's recipe is slightly different. Now I'll leave it in the fridge until tomorrow evening, because it's better the next day." Tata smiled. "Would you like another cup of coffee?"

"No thanks. If I drink too much coffee I'll start to sweat, and I don't have a change of clothes."

"Ahh, Fabrizio told me the airlines lost your luggage."

"Yeah, but they said they would deliver it today."

"Mmm, I don't want to cast disparaging remarks, but I wouldn't put too much faith in Air Italia," Tata said, making Maggie worry.

"As soon as I'm finished here, I'm going to the Luino market." Tata brushed a strand of gray hair back behind her ear. "I know you've just arrived, but perhaps you would like to come along with me and pick up a few girl things just in case."

"Oh, but what about Owen?"

"Don't worry about your husband, dear. He's in good hands with Enrico."

"Oh no, he's not my husband." Maggie waved her hands back and forth. "We're just friends." Maggie paused, considering her words. He was not her husband and he would never be. She needed to stop mothering him and let him look after himself. "Actually, yes. I'd love to come along."

"Well then, let's go, *tesoro*," Tata said as she opened the fridge door and slid the pan of tiramisu onto the top shelf. "The Luino market is one of the oldest markets in Italy. People come all the way from Germany and Switzerland. So we want to get there early and avoid the crowd." Tata took off her apron and folded it. "While you go up and get your things, I'll change and meet you out front."

As they walked down the lane to the gate, Tata said, "Don't worry. We'll be back before lunch."

Up ahead, waiting at the side of the road was a strange three-wheeled vehicle that looked like it was the offspring of a motor scooter that had mated with a pickup truck.

"It's a little tight, but we're small and I'm sure we can squeeze in." Tata held the door for Maggie.

Inside the tiny cab, with his right hand gripping a steering bar and his left shoulder and arm hanging out the window and down along the door, was a thin weathered man about Tata's age who smelled of tobacco.

"This is Giovanni," Tata said as she gave Maggie a gentle push from behind. Maggie wedged herself in next to Giovanni, and Tata climbed in next to her and slammed the door shut. Giovanni revved the engine, popped the clutch, and the strange contraption lurched forward. They roared down the highway at what Maggie estimated to be twenty-five miles an hour. In the rearview mirror she could see cars collecting behind them in a cloud of blue smoke. They rounded the curve and as soon as they were on a straight section of the road along the lakeshore, the cars zipped out from behind and raced past.

Twenty minutes later, Giovanni pulled up to the curb and Tata threw open her door and jumped out. Maggie unfolded herself from the vehicle and stretched her back and legs. She looked around. It seemed as if all the streets were filled with market stalls.

"We'll do the food shopping first," said Tata.

Maggie followed her into the labyrinth overhung with giant canvas umbrellas, almost unable to walk without tripping over something. Everything around her was colors and textures, and the air was pungent with intoxicating smells. They passed stacks of fruit and vegetables that Maggie didn't recognize. Tata stopped at what seemed to be specific stalls where she pointed and gave instructions to the vendors as to what she wanted and how much. She handed two cloth bags filled with fresh eggplants, zucchini, and tomatoes to Giovanni, who stood patiently behind her. Next they went over to a stall piled with loaves of bread. Tata pointed at a large loaf. The woman behind the counter handed it to her and she passed it to Maggie.

"It's still warm," Maggie said.

Tata looked at her with a curious expression. "Of course it is, my dear."

Next, they went to a stall with vats of olives. "Do you prefer green or black?" Tata said to Maggie as the woman reached forward and offered Maggie a large green olive.

"It's almost the size of a plum," Maggie said as she took a bite.

"*Mezzo chilo*," Tata said to the woman.

They maneuvered through the crowd over to a stall displaying cheese. Before Tata could speak, the man behind the counter held out a wooden board to Maggie. Tata pointed. "This is gorgonzola. This one is sweet and this one is sharp. Which do you prefer?"

Maggie took a piece of sweet and then a piece of sharp from the board. "I think I like the sharp."

Tata held up her forefinger and thumb to the man, who nodded and cut off a large wedge, weighed it, wrapped it in paper, and handed it to Tata.

"Okay, that should do us." Tata passed the final cloth bag to Giovanni, and he disappeared into the labyrinth.

"Where's Giovanni going?" Maggie said.

"Back to the truck with the food. He'll hang out at the coffee bar playing cards with his friends until we're finished." Tata took Maggie by the arm. "Come now, let's find some fresh clothes for you to wear until your bags arrive. I'm sure women in the United States must wear something other than boy's sporting clothes." She led Maggie into a new section of the labyrinth, hanging with leather bags and clothes, shoes and housewares.

An hour later they reemerged with their parcels. "If you know how to shop, you can always find Italian quality in the market without designer prices," Tata said. "Now, come with me." She led Maggie into a small shop filled with underwear and brassieres that read *Segreti Intimi,* over the door.

Maggie went to a rack and examined some plain white bras that looked to be her size.

"Oh, look dear." Tata came up to her holding a hanger with a delicately laced burnt-rose bra and matching panties with a lace front panel. "What do you think?"

"Ah, they're almost too beautiful to wear," Maggie said.

Tata smiled. "Well, no matter what you're wearing on the outside, these will make you feel elegant on the inside, where it counts, even if you're the only one who sees them." She winked and handed her the hanger. "Now go in and try them on."

As Maggie sauntered off to the changing room with the underwear in hand, she felt as if she were exploring something new about herself. Owen would never believe she had gone clothes shopping, much less bought such girlie things. Of course, she'd show him what she'd bought, but she certainly wouldn't model the bra and panties for him. She wondered why she should be shy with Owen. After all, she'd seen him in his underwear many times, but that was more like a brother and sister thing. It was true, they were like brother and sister, and they would never be anything more.

"I've only been in Italy for less than a day and I've already bought more clothes than I have all year," Maggie said as they stood on the street outside the shop. Then she reached up and tugged at the split ends of her hair. "I really should have got my hair cut before we left," she said, giving voice to her thoughts.

"What would you like to do with your hair?" Tata said.

"I don't know, but after buying all these beautiful clothes, I think I need to change my look."

"Well, we've got time. Come with me." Tata took Maggie by the arm and led her down the street to a hair salon. As Maggie sat in the salon chair, Tata combed her fingers through her hair. "You have such thick, lovely black hair. Why do you wear it in front of your face like a burka, child?" Tata then said something in Italian to the woman poised in front of her with a pair of scissors in her hand. The woman gave Maggie a sympathetic look and nodded. Without further instructions, she spun Maggie around in the chair, lowered her head back into the sink, and washed her hair. As she snipped, teased, blow-dried, fluffed, and sprayed, another woman filed, polished, and painted her nails. After almost an hour, the hairstylist stood back allowing Maggie to see herself in the mirror. Instead of covering it, her glistening black hair now followed the contours of her face, accenting her eyes, cheekbones, and jawline.

Maggie gasped. "I no longer look like I'm from the *Muppet Show*! I look like, like a woman!"

"Of course you do, my dear," Tata said as the stylist removed the white poncho from around Maggie's neck. "Now go into the back room, put on your new *intima*, and slip into that new tan skirt and cream silk blouse you bought. Oh, and don't forget your new shoes." Tata handed Maggie a lovely pair of beige suede midheel pumps, open at the toes.

It was a good thing Owen had reminded her to shave her pits and legs before they had left home. Then she remembered the night of her prom.

She had just put on her fuzzy pajamas when the doorbell rang. At first, she thought it must be the pizza delivery, but when she opened the door with a twenty in her hand, there was Jessy and Owen wearing tuxedos and holding a wardrobe bag and women's shoes.

"What are you two doing here?" she said.

"Where are your parents?" Jessy said in a serious tone.

"They've gone out to dinner."

"Good," Owen said.

"Why?"

"Because we're kidnapping you," Jessy said as they marched in through the door.

"And the fewer the witnesses the better," Owen added.

"You can't kidnap me. I'm in my pajamas."

"We've decided that the principal has no right to tell us who we can and cannot bring to the prom," Jessy said.

"And so we're going as a threesome," Owen said.

"But look at me!" Maggie cried. "How can I go to the prom like this!"

Jessy snorted and looked at Owen. "Haven't I heard that line before?"

"Yes, my dear, as you can see your pumpkin awaits." Owen pointed out the open door to Jessy's beat-up old Chevy Comet parked by the curb.

"And your gown? Versace, of course, my dear. Direct from my mother's closet." Jessy held up the wardrobe bag. "Oh, they didn't have any crystal slippers in your size at the magic kingdom, so you'll have to settle for my mom's red Jimmy Choos." Jessy dangled his mother's best high heels in front of Maggie.

"Now get into a shower and for heaven's sake shave your legs and pits while we prepare your gown," Jessy commanded.

Fresh from the shower, Maggie sat wrapped in a bath towel in front of the mirror. Jessy held up the damp mound of Maggie's hair in his hands. "What do you think, hair up like this or down like this?"

Owen stood back and examined it. "What about coming up here on top?" Owen framed his hand around Maggie's head.

"And flowing down here in the back." Jessy gestured with his fingers.

"Hey, who's the little cutie?" Owen reached out and took the photo that was clipped to the corner of Maggie's mirror.

"That's me when I was ten." Maggie's lip trembled.

"Wow, you sure looked like a boy when you were young," Owen said.

Maybe if she had been a boy, Owen would have looked at her with different eyes. Maybe not. Owen only had eyes for Jessy.

Owen clipped the photo back onto the mirror and picked up the blush pallette.

Jessy leaned over and took a quick glance at the photo. "Hmm. Well, when we're finished here, you'll be so glamorous you'll make Helen of Troy and Cleopatra weep."

"Hey, easy with the rouge. I'm not a hooker," Maggie said as Owen brushed her cheeks with color.

"Hold on, I still have to blend it," Owen said as he lightly fluttered the powder brush on Maggie's cheeks. "Okay, now for the dress and the shoes."

"Oh my gawd woman!" Jessy shrieked. "Don't you have anything but military surplus undergarments and sports socks?" He held up a sturdy-looking bra.

"Oh the horror!" Owen said as Maggie grabbed her underwear out of Jessy's hand.

"Give me the dress and the shoes," she barked.

"Where are you going?"

"To raid my sister's underwear drawer and get dressed." Maggie hobbled into her sister's bedroom holding the wardrobe bag and the shoes.

After ten minutes Jessy called through the closed bedroom door. "C'mon, how long does it take to slip on a dress and put on a pair of shoes?"

"Naked or not, we're coming in." Owen opened the door a crack.

"Okay. I'm ready."

Maggie was standing in front of the full-length mirror perched on the pair of ruby heels. The silky black gown cradled her breasts, hugged her abdomen and hips, and flowed down around her legs to her ankles. Her jet-black hair was piled up on top and cascaded down her shoulders.

"Apart from the fact I can't breathe in this dress and can't walk in these shoes, what do you think?" Her voice was jittery.

Both Owen and Jessy stood gazing at her.

"What do you think?" Jessy said to Maggie with a tone of adoration.

"I think I'm beautiful," Maggie said with tears in her eyes.

"Believe it, you're beautiful," Owen said. "But whatever you do don't cry and mess up my makeup job."

"IS EVERYTHING okay in there, dear?" Tata called.

"Yes, fine," Maggie said as she stepped out of the change room. "How do I look?"

"Oh my, you are beautiful!" Tata and the hairstylist nodded their approvals.

"I look so different. I haven't felt... I don't know, it's stupid, but I haven't felt this much like a woman since my high school prom," Maggie said. "I feel like I'm in a fairy tale."

"Ha!" Tata waved her hand as if she had a magic wand. "Cinderella is a child's story, but you, my dear, are real."

Maggie almost floated out the door of the salon behind Tata. Tata gently took Maggie by the arm and the two women sauntered down the sidewalk together passing directly in front of two teenage boys. One boy turned his head and stared. "*Che fica!*"

Tata leaned in close. "I'm sure he was referring to you and not me, my dear."

They strolled over to a café and sat at a table by a potted northern palm. The waiter brought them two glasses of sparkling wine and set down a plate of olives and salami.

"Champagne?" Maggie asked.

"No, only a light prosecco. *Cin*," Tata said as she held up her wineglass to Maggie. "Welcome to Italy."

"*Cin*," Maggie said and clinked Tata's glass. "I've only just arrived, and I think I've already figured out what the expression *la dolce vita* means."

Tata laughed.

"But, Tata, I want to confess something to you." Maggie's expression was serious.

Tata patted Maggie's arm. "Later *tesoro*. Right now, *carpe diem*. Seize the day!" Tata winked.

CHAPTER TWENTY-FIVE

IT WAS a little awkward maneuvering Angelina with this big American guy on the back. Instead of leaning into the curves, he leaned away, making it difficult for Enrico to balance the bike, and every time he touched the brakes, Owen slid up a little closer, forcing Enrico to inch ahead until he was sitting too far forward to be comfortable. Of course, he could feel Owen's boner pressed against his ass. Owen was squeezing him so tightly that now he had a chubby and had to go pee. But Enrico was used to married guys getting all touchy-feely with him when nobody was looking. Besides, everyone got horny on vacation. According to Fabrizio, American men talk about sex like they're talking about the weather, but when it comes to intimacy with another guy, they're too terrified to follow through. Enrico liked this guy from the moment he first saw him, but he was their first guest and he couldn't afford to screw it up by letting his cock take control of his brain. Besides, from Luino to Varese, there were dozens of guys on Grindr—gay, straight, curious, and bi—tracking Enrico and all he had to do was respond.

"Hey, your luggage finally arrived," Fabrizio announced loudly as Enrico and Owen pulled up to the house. "I put it in your room."

"Oh, thank heavens," Owen said as he climbed off the back of the bike. "And I got a SIM card for Italy, so I'm back in action." Owen took off his helmet. "Did they also bring Maggie's?"

"Yes, but she had already left with Tata for Luino," Fabrizio said.

"Luino?"

"They went shopping."

"Maggie? Shopping?" Owen furrowed his brow.

"Yes, it's market day," Fabrizio said as if everyone knew Wednesday was market day in Luino.

Owen shook his head. "But Maggie is allergic to two things, peanuts and shopping."

Fabrizio shrugged.

"Woo! It's hot as Hades." Owen tilted his nose over and sniffed at his armpit. "And I'm beginning to smell a little ripe."

"What about a swim?" Enrico suggested as he took off his helmet and hung it on the handlebars. He was sweating, too, but it wasn't just because of the heat and sun.

"Grand idea," Owen said. "Give me a minute to get changed into my swim shorts now that I've got them."

"Okay, we'll meet down at the water," Enrico called as Owen dashed up the steps and into the house.

"You go without me," Fabrizio said to Enrico.

Enrico frowned and cupped his hands to gesture, *Why, what's the problem?*

"I'll stay here and wait for Tata and Miss Maggie to come back." Fabrizio grinned and shot a wink at his brother.

Enrico rolled his eyes and went inside, shaking his head.

Down at the water, Enrico stood on the end of the dock and waited. Finally Owen appeared. He watched him walk down the concrete steps and out onto the dock with his eyes trained on his cell phone.

"What took you so long?" Enrico said.

"Oh, I had to check my Instagram and emails." Owen didn't look up from his cell phone. Enrico continued to watch as Owen pushed off his canvas loafers with his foot and pulled his T-shirt over his head, keeping his eyes trained on the tiny screen. His skin was pasty like a plant that hungered for the sun. Enrico wondered if he wore those ridiculously large boxers because he was modest, or maybe he was ashamed of his body. Owen continued to stare at his cell phone, giving Enrico the impression that what was inside that tiny box of electronics was much more interesting and important to him than what was right in front of his eyes. "Ready?" Enrico said with a note of exasperation.

Enrico dove off the end of the dock, flying through the air and slicing into the water as Owen suddenly looked up from his screen. He surfaced, stole a breath of air, and slipped under again. Then he surfaced again, rolled over, and floated on his back. Owen carefully placed his cell phone on his shirt, stepped to the end of the dock, then leaped, hurling through the air in a sitting position and coming down with a splash. He instantly surfaced in a cauldron of bubbles, the back of his baggy shorts filled with air and his behind floating upward, giving him the look of an ungainly water mammal. Even though he could swim well enough, it seemed as if his aquatic genes were closer to wallowing hippopotamus than gliding dolphin.

"Let's swim out to the buoy," Enrico said and set off with Owen slapping and splashing behind him. By the time they reached the buoy, Owen was winded and grabbed on to its algae-covered metal surface.

Enrico flipped around, swam underwater, and up behind Owen, almost touching his feet. "You okay?" he said.

"Fine," Owen said as he puffed in and out. "I need a moment."

"Take your time." Enrico smiled as he treaded water next to Owen. "We have all the time in the world." He rolled over lazily and floated on his back.

On the way back from the buoy, Enrico swam closely behind Owen, just to be sure. He certainly wouldn't want their first guest to drown, but more than that, he felt strangely protective of this American guy.

As they reached the dock, Owen's cell phone began to play a tune.

"Oh. It's my phone!" Owen said as if it were something to be excited about. He scrambled up the ladder onto the dock and rushed over and picked it up. But as he did so, the cell phone slipped out of his hands and went flying through the air and fell into the water with a plop.

"Ahhh! Nooo!" Owen cried.

"I'll get it." Enrico dove under and disappeared into the murky green. Ten seconds later he broke the surface with the cell phone held high.

Owen dropped to his knees and took the phone from Enrico's hand, holding it up like a poor drowned kitten. Water ran out from the behind the screen, dribbled along the seams, and down Owen's arm. "It's dead!" Owen cried. "I can't believe I killed my cell phone!" Owen looked as if he were hyperventilating.

Enrico climbed up the ladder, bent down, and put his hand on Owen's shoulder. "Are you all right?"

"No, no. I'm fine." He was still breathing heavily. "It's just a cell phone, right? And we still have Maggie's," he said as if he were trying to convince himself. "It's just, I haven't been without a cell phone in my hand for years."

Enrico said nothing and stood up.

Owen followed, shaking his head like a prize fighter who had just taken a left hook. "You know, it's almost like a cosmic joke."

"What do you mean?"

"I mean, I came here to Italy to try and forget someone and move on, and it seems like fate is helping me do that."

By the way Owen talked, it sounded to Enrico as if he had just broken up with someone and that he and Maggie weren't a couple after all. Enrico didn't know what to say, so he paraphrased something Fabrizio had read to him from one of his internet seminars. "You mean that you need to let go of the past and open yourself up to new possibilities?"

"Exactly. I just wish the cosmos would have texted me instead of destroying my six-hundred-dollar cell phone." Owen laughed nervously. He placed the dripping device on the dock, put his straw hat on, and sat down with his feet dangling in the water.

Enrico sat down beside Owen. Out of the corner of his eye, Enrico could see Owen watching him as he leaned back letting the water trickle down his chest and the sun lick his skin. Enrico smiled and Owen quickly looked away.

"Do you and your brother have girlfriends?" Owen said, looking at his feet as he swirled them in the water.

Enrico had heard that Americans were very direct, but not in quite the same way Germans were. "No," he said and swirled his feet too.

"Me neither," Owen said.

Enrico smiled. As long as Owen was asking personal questions, Enrico thought it okay to reciprocate. "Miss Maggie?" he said.

"Oh no." Owen waved his hand. "She's not my girlfriend. We're just friends." Owen's eye twitched slightly. "Actually, I'm gay."

Enrico said nothing.

"Did you think Maggie and I were a couple?" Owen said, breaking the silence.

"At first my brother did, but I knew right away you weren't," Enrico said.

"How did you know?" Owen sounded more curious than defensive.

Enrico shrugged, and a slow grin spread across his face. "Because I'm gay too." He liked this frank manner of speaking. It was more like the way he and Fabrizio spoke to each other. Before Owen could respond, Enrico said, "So, do you have a boyfriend or a lover?"

"No," Owen said. "I mean, I did, but he kind of cheated on me."

"Oh." Enrico realized their conversation had just ventured into territory that was either too painful to talk about or would open a floodgate of emotions. "I'm sorry" was all he said.

"Ah, don't be. I wasn't in love with him." Owen swished his feet back and forth. "What about you?"

Enrico thought about that married architect. "I've been seeing someone, but I'm not in love with him, either."

Owen nodded. "The truth is, I've been in love with my best friend, Jessy, since we were kids." Owen breathed in deeply and slowly exhaled. "It's one of those friend-zone things, and I know it's never going to happen between us." Owen stretched his legs out straight.

There was something both bold and shy about this guy that made Enrico want to take him in his arms. He wondered if after sex would Owen just look away, like so many of his lovers did, or would he allow Enrico to stare deeply into his blue eyes and see who was inside?

Owen plopped his feet back into the water. "Hey, what's that old man doing?" Owen pointed to a figure walking along the stony beach with his head bent down. "Is he looking for clams?"

"No, that's my papà. He's looking for glass."

"Glass?"

"Yes. See all those old stone buildings? There used to be a glass kiln right over there where the marina is, and when the lake is low like this, you can still find chunks of melted glass."

"What does he want with glass?"

Enrico smirked and covered his face with his hand. "Do I really have to tell you?"

"Yes, absolutely!" Owen laughed. "I want to know!"

"Okay then. I'll tell you the story." Enrico threw Owen a coy grin. "There once was an old witch who took this beautiful young princess and locked her in a tower."

"Wait a minute, you're making this up." Owen nudged Enrico with his shoulder.

"No." Enrico chuckled. "Tata used to tell Fabrizio and me this when we were little. Anyway, the old witch was very jealous, and she cast a spell on the beautiful young princess so that if she ever left the tower, she would turn to glass." Enrico pointed up to the tower where Owen and Maggie were staying.

"Okay, since Maggie is out shopping, I will assume the role of the beautiful princess," Owen jested.

"Oh, but wait, there's more," Enrico said eagerly. "One day a poor boy was walking past the tower. He heard the princess crying, and he called to her and asked her why she was so sad. She told him she was crying because she was lonely. The boy said that he would visit her every day when he came in from fishing. Which he did. One day he picked a rose at the foot of the tower and threw it up to her. She kissed it and threw it back to him. And from then on they were in love."

"You know, sometimes I think love is easier in fairy tales," Owen said.

Enrico cocked his head and looked at Owen. "Why?"

"I guess because it comes instantly with a kiss." Owen smiled.

Enrico paused and looked at Owen's lips. They were thin and pale, not rich and full like his own or his brother's—probably because of the cool water—but all the same, he wanted to lean over and engulf his mouth with a kiss.

"Sorry, go on," Owen said.

"Okay." Enrico looked away. "The old witch soon discovered that the boy and the princess were in love and she cast another spell and sent a storm to drown the boy when he was out fishing. When, from her tower, the princess saw the boy's overturned boat floating ashore, she was so brokenhearted that she threw herself out of the window." Enrico paused and took a deep breath.

"But the boy had not drowned. He was a good swimmer and eventually he swam to shore where he found his true love shattered into a million pieces of colored glass. After that, every evening when he came home from fishing, he went to the foot of the tower and collected the pieces of colored glass—the green glass for her eyes, the black glass for her hair, the white glass for her skin, but he could never find any red glass for her heart."

"And what happened to him?" Owen looked directly into Enrico's eyes.

Enrico forced a mournful smile and shrugged. "He got stuck in the past and could never find his way out." He swallowed and looked back toward his father. "Papà, come on, it's time to go up to the house for lunch." Enrico turned back toward Owen. "Why don't you go up and get changed. We'll be along shortly."

Owen stood up, leaving the wet imprint of his bum on the dock. He bent over, slipped on his shoes, and picked up his towel, shirt, and drowned cell phone. "I knew I should have got the waterproof one," he said and climbed the garden steps up to the house.

CHAPTER TWENTY-SIX

"MY BAGS are in my room, but I still haven't seen Owen," Maggie said as she came back down from the tower after putting away her new clothes and having changed into a fresh pair of shorts and a T-shirt.

Tata poured flour into the mixing bowl and looked up. "Fabrizio said he's down at the lake having a swim with Enrico."

"Ah." Maggie glanced nervously out the open kitchen door toward the garden. "Do you know when they'll be back?"

Tata smiled. "Don't worry. They'll be back at two for lunch."

"You sure have your boys trained well." Maggie laughed.

"Do you cook, child?" Tata said.

"Not really."

Tata paused and looked up at Maggie. "Tell me, in America do the children go home to their mamma's house or to their papà's?"

Maggie furrowed her brow as she contemplated Tata's question. "Wow, I never thought about it that way."

"But make no mistake, being a good cook is not enough." Tata smiled and went back to kneading the dough. "It's hard work being a woman, so we have to be *furba,*" Tata took out a wooden roller.

"*Furba?*"

"Yes, smart, clever," she said as she worked the roller back and forth over the dough.

"*Furba,*" Maggie repeated. "I like that word."

"Now, there are two basic things you need to know about Italy." Tata rolled the dough paper-thin. "Food is the way Italians communicate." She then cut it into wide strips.

"And the second thing?" Maggie fixed her eyes on Tata as she fed the strips of pasta into a strange device that looked like a hand-cranked paper shredder.

"Italian men puff and blow in the street...." She turned the handle and long thin noodles emerged from the other side into her waiting hand. "But they're all the same when they sit down at their mamma's table— just little boys."

Maggie chuckled as she thought about Jessy and Owen. It was true. She often thought of them as little boys.

Tata looked up at Maggie and smiled. "And that's exactly why we love them, isn't it?"

Maggie smiled back and nodded.

"But make no mistake, even if Italy is a matriarchal society, there's not much choice for a woman without a husband and child. She can be a nun, a slut, or a nursemaid for the elderly." Tata breathed in deeply and let out a slow breath. "That's why it's so important a woman has her own money."

As Tata spoke, the image of her mother's credit card popped into Maggie's head. She knew her mother and father had a joint bank account and her father had his business account, but she didn't know if her mother had her own account. Then she remembered when her older sister got married her dad put twenty-five thousand dollars in her sister's account and instructed her that the money was her personal emergency fund and that she was never to tell her husband about it. Less than three months later, her sister and her sister's husband arrived at the house for Sunday dinner driving a new BMW.

"They have a great financing package," her sister's husband explained to her stone-faced father. It was less than a year after that when her sister's husband drove away in the BMW with another woman sitting in the passenger seat and her sister moved back in with her parents and took the bus to work.

"As for me, I came north from Sicily to work as a servant for the boys' grandmother. And when their mother died in childbirth, I took over their care." Tata hung the strings of pasta on a wooden device that looked like the bare struts of an umbrella. "I poured my heart into each plate of pasta and every bowl of risotto, and as the old lady slowed down and the boys grew, things changed."

"What do you mean?" Maggie said as if Tata was about to impart a wicked conspiracy to her.

"The old lady may have been the queen of the castle, but we both knew who ruled the kitchen and the dinner table. She couldn't cook a risotto to feed to pigs." Tata broke out into laughter, and Maggie, not knowing how to react, laughed along with her.

Tata brushed her floured hands back and forth and picked up another strip of pasta and fed it into the cutting device. "You can say a lot about Italian men, but almost all of them know what to do in the kitchen and the bedroom." Tata washed her hands. "But, as I'm sure you know, we women are not without our little secrets in the kitchen and the bedroom too." Tata winked.

Maggie felt her face harden.

"What's wrong, child?" Tata said.

"The truth is I don't know how to cook, and I've never really had a man."

Tata furrowed her brow and stared at her. "I don't understand."

"What I mean to say is…." Maggie waved her hand. "I'm not Owen's wife or girlfriend, or even his lover. I'm just his friend." Maggie paused and swallowed the lump in her throat. "And I've been in love with him for years." Strange. She had only just met Tata, but she felt as if she could tell her anything and she would understand.

Tata smiled at Maggie like an old lady to an infant. "I see." She patted Maggie's cheek. "When I was just seventeen, I met a boy here at the lake and we fell in love."

"What happened?"

"Let's just say I was a poor peasant girl from Sicily, he was from an important northern family, and they had other designs for him." Tata shrugged. "Love doesn't always follow according to plan. Life moves forward and we accept and adapt." Tata pursed her lips. "But when I look at my life and my two boys, even if they're not really mine, I wouldn't change a thing."

"But what man would ever want me?" Maggie said.

"I see a wonderful young woman here in front of me. I can assure you any man would be lucky to have you." Tata put her arm over Maggie's shoulder and kissed the top of her head. "I think you're stuck in liminality, my child."

"What's liminality?" Maggie said.

"It's where you've left the old you behind, but you haven't yet fully embraced the new you."

"What do you mean?"

"I mean, you know Owen will never be yours, but you haven't opened your heart to the possibility of someone else yet."

Maggie forced a smile back at Tata. That's exactly how she felt most of the time, stuck somewhere in betwixt and between. Maggie loved Owen, and Jessy, too, but whenever she was with the two of them, she'd always felt like she was number three. It was as if they spoke a secret language that she couldn't quite follow. Even if they were the Terrible Trio, she knew that Owen and Jessy must take their own paths and they would leave her behind.

"But how do I get out of this liminality?" Maggie said with desperation.

"I thought that was what we were doing this morning in Luino—*carpe diem*—seizing the moment and celebrating the new you." Tata smiled. "Now, enough morose thoughts. Roll up your sleeves and wash your hands. Tata is about to teach you how to make *pasta al prato*. I believe it translates as lawn spaghetti."

"Lawn spaghetti?"

"Oh yes." Tata chuckled. "You know, for most of its history Italy has been under some kind of oppressive rule: the French, the Spanish, the Austrians, the fascists, and the church, and through it all we've always had to make do with what we had at hand. That's the true art of Italian cooking—simple elegance."

Tata pulled out a large aluminum pasta pot, filled it with three liters of water, and set it to boil. "Come outside with me." She grabbed a pair of scissors from the drawer and they went outside into the garden.

A few minutes later they returned with a handful of rosemary, thyme, mint, basil, and a few stalks of lavender.

"I had no idea you could eat all of these things just growing in the yard."

Tata held the herbs up to Maggie's nose. "Can you smell it? We are going to translate these perfumes and your emotions into flavors, so only think about beautiful things, like making love." Tata flexed her eyebrows.

"But what about the lavender?"

"Ah, that's my little secret. While you wash the herbs, I'll prepare the pasta."

Tata added a fistful of course sea salt to the pot of boiling water. Then she put an ample palmful of pasta into the boiling water and set the timer for ten minutes. "Okay, now we chop the herbs until they are fine enough for pesto."

"I don't know how to chop pesto," Maggie said. "I've only ever used the stuff from a jar."

"Ahh!" Tata bit her knuckle. "Do like this." She took the large chopping knife and with machinelike precision reduced the basil to microscopic flecks. "Here." She handed Maggie the knife. "Now you do the same to the other herbs. Careful with the lavender, just a strand to give our sauce a very subtle high note, but no more or it will dominate the other notes like an old lady wearing too much perfume."

"Like this?"

"Yes, just like that. Okay, now for the hard work." Tata put the fine flakes of herbs in a brass mortar, held it firm, and ground it with a brass pestle until it became a green paste. "You can also use a food processor, but I like the old-fashioned way. It's my little workout so I don't get flabby underarms."

The timer rang.

"Can you check the pasta, *tesoro*?"

"How do I know if it's ready?

"Pick up a piece with a fork and taste it. It should be not too firm and not too soft—like a kiss."

"I'm hardly an expert on kissing." Maggie laughed.

"Close your eyes and think of some handsome boy kissing you."

Maggie fished out a piece of pasta from the pot and bit into it. She closed her eyes and tried to imagine Owen kissing her, but instead, for some odd reason the image of Fabrizio flashed into her mind, his soft lips firm against her waiting mouth. "I think it's right."

"Good. Stand back." Tata lifted the boiling pot over to the sink and poured it into a colander. Then she bounced it up and down a few times, draining off the water, and returned the pasta to the pot and covered it.

A beam of light sparkled in the stream of green liquid as Tata poured half a cup of olive oil into a small frying pan on the fire.

"Okay, now we heat the olive oil to a point just before it starts to smell burnt."

The oil began to sizzle, and Tata fanned the air over the pan with her hand. "You can smell when it's ready."

Maggie sniffed and nodded.

"Okay, put the herbs on top of the pasta." Tata lifted the lid off the pasta pot and Maggie spooned in the herb sauce. "Add three ripe cherry tomatoes and one tablespoon of tomato sauce for each serving."

"How many are we for lunch?" Maggie said.

"Six."

Maggie counted as she put six tablespoons of tomato sauce and eighteen cherry tomatoes into the pot.

Now, for the final step," Tata said. "Pour the hot oil into the pasta pot over the herbs, tomato sauce, and pasta."

Maggie held the handle of the hot pan with both hands as if she were afraid it might burst into flames at any moment. The oil sizzled as it ran down the side of the frying pan and into the pot of pasta.

"Quick, mix the pasta and sauce well with these wooden spoons."

"Like this?" Maggie said.

"Yes, fluff it." Tata swirled her hands as if she were about to dance the flamenco. "There, now you can hold any man captive at your table. I'll get the door."

With the hot gloves on both hands, Maggie picked up her large pot of *pasta il pratto* and carried it into the dining room where Owen, Papà, Enrico, and Fabrizio were waiting patiently at the table.

"Now tell me, dear, who do you think is in control here?" Tata whispered into Maggie's ear.

CHAPTER TWENTY-SEVEN

THAT EVENING, after the heavy pasta lunch, dinner was a light menu of fresh cantaloupe with smoked prosciutto ham, a simple spaghetti dressed with butter, black pepper, anchovy paste, and parmigiana cheese, fresh bread and gorgonzola cheese, and fresh figs for dessert, accompanied by spring water and a carafe of homemade red wine that Giovanni had given Tata.

After dinner Maggie and Owen went outside onto the terrace and reclined in the wicker chairs, gazing up at the canopy of stars. It probably wasn't any more spectacular than the night sky over the Finger Lakes district back home, but maybe here they felt like they could really take it in and bask in the *carpe diem* effect.

Maggie was right. She was always right. He really did need to get away. And, thankfully, the Prozac and Tylenol were helping.

"So, what happened to you this morning?" Owen turned his head toward Maggie.

"What do you mean?" Maggie looked nervous.

"When we arrived you were still under the manga curse of Pathetic Patty." Owen grinned. "And now, look at you." He made a circle with his finger.

"Do you like it?" Maggie's face went flushed.

"Like it?" Owen hung his mouth open. "Mothers of Syracuse, lock up your sons. Here comes the new Maggie—international sex-bomb!" Owen laughed and Maggie, giggling along, reached over, and swatted him on the shoulder. "By the way, whatever magical potion Tata brewed up, ask her if there some left for me. I could sure use a shot."

Owen cast his eyes back toward the purple sky and thought about riding on the back of the motorbike that morning, clinging onto Enrico's warm, hard body. Breathing in deeply, he could still smell the woody scent of the back of Enrico's neck. Then he pictured him on the edge of the dock, his long lean form packed into a black Speedo accented with a red strip, that clung to his buttcheeks and came around the front, cupping his package. He had heard Italian men liked to wear tiny bathing suits, but he supposed that was only a stereotype. It wasn't so much the Speedo as the way in which Enrico appeared completely at ease with his body, even though he was standing there in the open, almost naked.

Back in high school Owen had spent endless hours at the side of the pool, admiring Jessy to the point where he felt almost like admiring anyone else was a betrayal. But now, as he thought about Enrico, for the first time, Owen realized how much his devotion to Jessy had closed him off from seriously considering another boy.

His mind wandered back to the summer when almost every evening after he'd finished at Party Harty's he would race over to the community pool just in time for a dip before Jessy closed up. Owen would dart into the changing room, throw on his big baggy boxers, and emerge onto the pool deck, all white and pink. Just seeing Jessy perched there on his elevated lifeguard chair, his bronze muscular form clad in those tight red trunks, made Owen feel virile too. But no matter how Jessy coaxed, Owen could never quite muster the courage to dive off the twenty-foot platform and at the final moment, he always jumped off feetfirst.

The final week in August, that summer they'd graduated from high school, Jessy had just finished his shift, cleared the pool, and was in the office signing out while Owen waited poolside. As he sat there with his legs dangling in the water, he convinced himself that this was his last chance to show Jessy he was not a chicken. With everyone in the changing room and no one around to make him nervous, Owen got up, padded over to the ladder, and scaled it. The cool evening breeze tussled his auburn hair and tickled his skin. From up here he could see the roof of his house in the distance. Well, it wasn't his house anymore, not since his mother had thrown him out in June. He stepped cautiously out to the edge of the platform and stood with his arms held over his head like Superman about to take flight. He took in a big breath, bent his knees slightly like Jessy had told him to do, and leaped out into space.

Down he came like a dead weight and went splat onto the surface of the water, knocking the wind out of his lungs. Luckily Jessy had heard the splash and came running in time to pull him out before he drowned.

That's why their argument at Pride had made him so mad. It was like Jessy was pulling him out of the deep end once again. Most of all, he knew Jessy was right. He didn't care about that little cokehead Lane, or whatever his name was. He just wanted to be a party boy like Jessy. But Jessy was like Teflon. He could party with the pros and nothing ever stuck to him. More than envy, Owen despaired at the thought of losing Jessy. What would he do without him? The coke had given him the confidence he felt when they were together, but he was smart enough to know that coke was a poor substitution to his addiction to Jessy. Well, he'd certainly gone cold turkey from it all. He was a long way from work, the party circuit, and Jessy.

Owen thought about what Enrico had said when they were in the water as he'd clung to the buoy trying to catch his breath. He really did have all the time in the world. He had no deadlines, no clients to meet. He was young and gay and single. Sure, Owen knew it would probably come to nothing more than flirtation with Enrico, but that wasn't the point. He was on vacation and he was here to enjoy.

Suddenly, Owen was jolted out of his little daydream by the sound of a popping cork behind him. Both he and Maggie looked around at Fabrizio, who was standing with a bottle in his hand next to Enrico, who was holding wineglasses.

"Champagne!" Owen said.

"No, not really. It's Italian Franciacorta," Fabrizio said.

"Which is considered to be on par with many French champagnes," Enrico added.

Enrico handed Owen and Maggie each a glass and Fabrizio filled them.

"I chose the rosé especially for you, Miss Maggie," Fabrizio said with a toothy grin.

"Ah, how sweet. My favorite color is pink." Maggie beamed.

Owen turned his head toward Maggie and said out the side of his mouth, "Since when?"

"Since right now." Maggie flashed him a quick sneer.

After Enrico and Fabrizio had filled their own glasses, Fabrizio held his high in the air and said, "A toast. To new friends."

"And new possibilities," Owen added, darting his eyes toward Enrico.

No sooner had they finished the bottle of Franciacorta, than Enrico appeared with another bottle and held it up. "This is a simple pinot grigio. It's the most popular northern Italian dry white."

"It's a little lighter," Fabrizio added. "Or would you prefer prosecco?"

"No, that looks fine to me." Owen drained his glass and held it out.

"So, what do you guys do for fun in the evening?" Maggie said as Enrico filled her glass.

"Dance," Enrico said.

"There's a club around here?" Owen took a sip.

"No, the nearest disco is in Varese about an hour away," Enrico said.

"Where do you dance, then?" Owen's eyes were trained on Enrico.

"Here on the terrace or in the living room in the winter," Fabrizio said.

"With each other?" Maggie said in a tone that divulged an unfiltered thought.

"Of course!" Fabrizio said without the slightest indication that that might be unusual. "We practice here. There's a network of Latin American dancers and schools throughout the villages."

"They have competitions," Enrico said.

"We've been disqualified three years in a row," Fabrizio said proudly.

"Disqualified? Why?" Owen said.

"Well, we dance tango. You know it was originally a dance between men," Fabrizio said.

"The *gauchos* in Argentina," Enrico added.

"There's nothing in the rule books that says two men can't compete," Fabrizio continued.

"But the couples are scored on both the gentleman's and lady's performance, so the judges always disqualify us because neither one of us is a lady," Enrico said.

"But that's ridiculous!" Maggie said, almost spilling her wine.

"That's why we have so many rules in Italy," Enrico said.

"Just to be sure the playing field always slopes uphill in the winner's favor," Fabrizio said.

"Or in this case, the dance floor," Owen said.

"But here, let us show you our tango." Enrico took out his cell phone and connected it to a set of Bluetooth speakers. "Do you know Gotan Project?"

Maggie and Owen shook their heads.

Enrico and Fabrizio set down their glasses, moved to the center of the terrace, and stood face-to-face. Enrico raised his right hand and clasped Fabrizio's left. He put his left hand around Fabrizio's waist and Fabrizio placed his right hand on Enrico's shoulder. Sultry electronic music flowed out of the speakers and the two masculine bodies pressed together. With a slight gyration of his hips, Enrico stepped forward, sinking his pelvis into Fabrizio's and guiding him backward. In syncopation with the rhythm, they floated as one around the terrace, their feet entwining in a spiraling performance of desire and passion, domination and submission.

Tata leaned against the doorframe. "I remember your mamma and papà dancing like this." She pressed her hands to her lips.

Then, with a theatrical gesture, Enrico twirled Fabrizio and they seamlessly switched roles, Fabrizio taking command and Enrico following.

Owen shivered and Maggie squirmed in her seat.

"Who needs porn when you have tango!" Owen whispered.

With a gesture of defiance, Enrico pushed against Fabrizio and spun outward, but Fabrizio caught his hand and with a flick, like a boy spinning an old-fashioned top, he spun Enrico back into his arms. Enrico slid down the length of Fabrizio's body onto the floor. Fabrizio stepped ahead and, as if he were weightless, pulled his brother back to his feet and into his arms again, dipping him over like a drooping stem. Then the music crescendoed. Still holding onto each other's hands, they spread their arms outward like an eagle's wings and stood frozen in a pose as precariously balanced as a Degas bronze statue.

Owen and Maggie clapped enthusiastically.

"I think I just moistened my panties," Maggie leaned over and whispered at Owen.

"So did I?" Owen said. "And they're not even mine."

"And now it's your turn." Enrico reached out his hand toward Owen.

"Miss Maggie." Fabrizio bowed slightly and took Maggie's hand.

"There's no way I can dance like that," Maggie said as she followed Fabrizio to the center of the terrace. "Even after a bottle of wine."

"We'll start with a simple merengue," Fabrizio said. "It's easy, just move your feet like this, one-two, one-two."

"Like climbing the stairs," Enrico added.

"And sway your body back and forth." Fabrizio placed his hands on Maggie's hips.

At first Maggie and Owen bounced like two kangaroos during mating season while Fabrizio and Enrico floated and swerved like snakes in water. But after they had finished the second bottle of wine, Owen's hips had discovered a rhythm different from his usual shuffle and writhe he'd perfected from years at the clubs. Meanwhile, Maggie had become as malleable as putty, completely surrendering herself to Fabrizio's guiding arms. Punctuated by bouts of laughter—like when

Owen stepped on Enrico's foot and when Fabrizio dipped Maggie and she moaned—and pauses for wine refills, the two pairs danced on, letting themselves float along with the music into the night. By the time the third bottle of wine was empty, Maggie became dizzy and the evening came to an end as naturally as it had started.

"What just happened here tonight?" Owen said to Maggie as they climbed the stairs to their bedrooms in the tower.

"I have no idea." Maggie twirled around, gliding in through her bedroom door. "But whatever it was, I want more." She blew him a kiss and shut her door.

Owen went into his room and flopped down on the bed. As he lay there, he thought about the time when he had confessed his love to Jessy and Jessy had said, "I love you too, like a brother."

"Sorry, Jessy, but I want more too," Owen said out loud.

CHAPTER TWENTY-EIGHT

MAGGIE REMAINED in bed, not sleeping, just staring out her window at the morning sun caressing the mountains on the far side of the lake. Eventually she rose. She slathered herself with sun cream and put on that black swimsuit with the square-cut legs that her mother had bought her years ago when she had to go to swimming lessons at the local pool. It might look like an old-fashioned wrestler's costume, but it still fit. She put her father's white cotton dress shirt on over top to protect her from the sun, grabbed her bag and straw hat, and skipped down the stairs. "Tata, have you seen Owen?" Maggie said as she leaned in through the kitchen door.

"I believe he's already down at the boathouse with the boys, getting the boat ready to go out," Tata said without turning around. "Do you want coffee?" She lifted the Moka pot off the burner and filled two cups, then turned with the cups in her hand and looked at Maggie. "Ahhh! What are you wearing, child?" she cried, almost spilling the coffee.

"It's one of my dad's old dress shirts. I'm very sensitive to the sun."

"Not that." Tata placed the cups on the table and went over to Maggie, pinched the corners of the shirt, and held it open. "Oh no, child, you're not going out in public like that, are you?" she said as she inspected Maggie's swimsuit. "I've seen nuns wearing sexier bathing costumes."

"No one will see it except when I go in the water," Maggie said.

"Remember that discussion we had about underwear?" Tata winked.

Maggie frowned. "You really think it's that bad?"

"It's a tragedy. Come with me." Tata led Maggie out of the kitchen and into one of the back bedrooms. She opened an enormous closet, removed a box, and lay it on the bed. She took off the lid and lifted out a carefully folded pink-and-white bikini and placed it on the bed as if it were something rare and precious.

Maggie held up the bikini. "I don't have the hips or the breasts for this."

Tata then held up a simple red woman's one-piece, cut low in the front and high in the hips. "It's old, but nylon lasts forever. This was the boys' mother's. She wore it when she swam across the lake in the annual competition. After she became pregnant, she gave it to me." Tata grabbed her hips. "Of course, I'm a little too old for this bathing suit. But you, my dear, have the perfect shape."

Maggie held up it up and examined it. She liked vintage clothes, because they always told a story, but she felt a little uncomfortable about wearing a borrowed bathing suit. Then she remembered how silly Owen was about wearing the pair of underpants Enrico had lent him. "Okay, I'll try it on and see if it fits."

Enrico and Fabrizio were bent over in the stern checking the fuel and Owen was squatting holding the boat steady by the time Maggie walked down the garden steps to the waterfront and out onto the dock. The old wooden boat was about fourteen feet long and looked as if it could comfortably hold five people. Unlike the sleek decorated gondolas Maggie had seen in photos, the boat was much deeper and fatter, and quite plain. It had a tiny raised deck in the bow with a tapered stern and resembled a large, fat semifolded leaf. Its outer hull was painted blue with a red strip, and the rest of the boat was varnished mahogany.

Fabrizio stood up. "Okay, we're ready to go."

Maggie slipped off her shoes, tossed them into the boat, and Fabrizio held out his hand for her as she stepped on board. Owen stood upright and handed Enrico his pack, then made a little leap from the dock onto the gunwale of the boat. Just as he started to lose his balance Enrico reached out and grabbed him.

"Thanks!" Owen said with Enrico still holding him around his waist.

"Why don't you and Maggie sit up here on the bow deck. The view is better and it's not so noisy," Fabrizio said.

"Just hang on to the railing," Enrico added.

"I'm sure that little balancing act you did getting into the boat was a complete accident," Maggie muttered to Owen as he sat down next to her and they dangled their legs over the gunwales.

"Strange, I normally I have the agility of a cat." Owen grinned.

Fabrizio untied the mooring, and Enrico sat on the captain's seat, started the engine, and slowly pulled away from the dock. He drew back on the accelerator, the engine roared, and the bow rose. The breeze tugged at Owen's shorts and T-shirt and made Maggie's father's shirt flap like a flag. The water slapping against the hull splashed Maggie's and Owen's dangling feet as they sped out over the undulating surface of the bay and passed little camps of families congregated along the stony shore at the ruins of *Le Fornaci*.

"They used to mine limestone from this cliff and burn it in those kilns to make lime for concrete." Fabrizio pointed and called out above the sound of the breeze and the motor.

They watched as a boy, standing on top of one of the ruined lime kilns, ran out, leaped into space, and plummeted down into the water with a splash while his friends cheered and hooted their approval.

As they neared the bay of Castelveccana, a classic wooden Riva launch, with its throaty inboard engine and all the grace and elegance of a 1950s Cadillac, cut across their path. Enrico veered to the right, their boat bouncing and splashing as they traversed its wake. Maggie gripped tighter onto the railing with one hand and held on to her hat with the other. They cruised farther along the shoreline past elegant seventeenth-century villas with their steep tiled roofs and towers and their lush Italian gardens sloping down to the water's edge. Wedged between the classic villas were modernist terraced bungalows, possibly inspired by Frank Lloyd Wright, with their manicured golf course lawns and hedges.

Twenty minutes later, Enrico slowed the boat and they cruised in closer to the shore where there was a tiny patch of stony beach with a scattering of men, some wearing bathing suits, some nude.

"That's the gay beach," Fabrizio said above the motor. Two men sat upright on their beach towels and Enrico and Fabrizio waved.

"That's Antonello and Giorgio. They're undertakers, so they don't really get any holidays," Enrico said. "But as long as nobody dies, they can spend the day at the beach."

"They're getting married this spring," Fabrizio added.

Enrico pushed the accelerator forward. The boat sped up and they motored below *La Galleria*, where the road and railway passed through a tunnel along the edge of a cliff strewn with avalanched rocks. Up ahead, a rock about thirty feet high stuck straight up in air out of the water, like someone's middle finger.

Forty minutes later they reached Laveno. The ferry boat, filled with cars on the lower deck and passengers on the upper deck, left a white churning trail as it came out from the dock, heading across the lake to

Verbania. Fabrizio pointed at the cable lift that ran up the side of the peak overlooking the town. Hang gliders, riding the air currents, circled the peak like giant colored falcons.

They continued on past Laveno for another fifteen minutes until they spotted an ancient monastery hanging from the rock cliff like some secret lair or mythical fortress. Enrico guided the boat closer to shore, cut the engine, and they drifted below it.

"This is Santa Caterina," Fabrizio said and held out his hand.

"It doesn't look real!" Maggie said with her mouth agape.

"It looks like something out of Lord of the Rings!" Owen scanned the face of the cliff.

"The story goes like this…," Enrico said. "In the twelfth century there was a rich merchant named Alberto Besozzi whose boat capsized while crossing the lake and barely escaped being drowned."

"Afterwards, he decided to retire here and become a hermit," Fabrizio said.

Enrico continued. "And he built this *cappella*."

"What's a cappella?" Maggie said

"It's a, um, hat," Fabrizio said.

"It's a chapel," Enrico cut in.

"Anyway," Fabrizio said. "He built this chapel and dedicated it to Santa Caterina of Egypt."

"Egypt?" Owen said.

"Yeah, the Copts in Egypt were once a powerful part of the Christian world."

"At least, that's what we read on the internet last night." Fabrizio shrugged.

Enrico lightly put his hand on Owen's shoulder, stretched his arm out, and pointed. "See, the chapel's right there."

"Then, in the seventeenth century, five enormous rocks fell on the church," Fabrizio jumped in. "But they didn't really cause much damage."

"So they said it was a miracle." Enrico slowly withdrew his hand from Owen's shoulder.

"You know how Catholics love miracles," Fabrizio said, and Enrico gave him a sharp jab with his elbow.

Fabrizio held up his palms. "It's true."

Enrico climbed back behind the wheel and started the engine. They motored across the lake, bouncing up and down on the waves like a ride at an amusement park. As they approached a small group of islands, Enrico slowed the boat to a gentle cruise. Owen and Maggie slid off the bow deck and stood, staring up at a splendid Baroque palace surrounded by terraced gardens. Enrico cut the engine and they drifted along the shoreline.

"The garden is full of flowers and exotic plants, which can grow here because the island is protected in the gulf," Enrico said.

"It's a microclimate," Fabrizio added.

"Oh look! There's a fountain and some statues." Maggie squealed. "Did they make this for the tourists?"

"Not exactly," Enrico said. "The Borromeo family made it in the seventeenth century for themselves."

"There is a large a statue of a unicorn, which is the emblem of the Borromeo family." Fabrizio, who was standing close behind Maggie, stretched out his arm and pointed.

"Wow! They must have been loaded," Owen said.

"Oh! Look." Maggie pointed. "Over there, there's a white peacock! Can you imagine living here?" Maggie's voice took on a kind of dreamy tone.

"Yeah, you'd have to wear one of those big hoop dresses," Owen scoffed. "I'd probably have to wear a white wig, long stockings, and itchy leggings."

Maggie blew out a puff of air. "You have no sense of romance."

Fabrizio took a half step backward, swept out his hand, and made a deep bow toward Maggie. "My lady."

Maggie beamed and held out her hand.

Enrico covered his face with his hands while Owen shook his head.

Fabrizo took her hand in his and gently kissed it.

"Well at least there's one romantic gentleman on this cruise," Maggie cooed.

"*Smetti di baciarle la mano*," Enrico said in a flat tone and reached over and swatted his brother's shoulder.

"What did he say?" Maggie asked.

Fabrizio stood upright. "He said we'd better go to see the castle before we run out of gas."

Maggie furrowed her brow and looked at Enrico suspiciously. At which point Owen rolled his eyes, bent over the other gunwale, and began to fake like he was barfing. Enrico laughed and followed suit.

Maggie looked at Fabrizio and jabbed her head toward them. Just as Owen and Enrico stood upright, Maggie and Fabrizio gave them a sharp shove, sending them sailing overboard. They came up flailing and gasping. But before they could exact their revenge, Maggie and Fabrizio quickly grabbed a towel and cowered under it at the far side of the boat just beyond their splashes.

After they had climbed out of the water and toweled off, Enrico resumed his position in the driver's seat, started the engine, and maneuvered the boat around. Fabrizio stood next to his brother and held on to the back of the seat while Maggie and Owen reclaimed their spots on the little deck in the bow. Enrico pushed the accelerator forward, the engine roared, and they cruised along the western shore, heading back in the direction of Switzerland. The boat lurched and bobbed as they bounced across the wake of an antique paddlewheel boat filled with tourists. In the distance, sailboats fluttered back and forth across the lake, like cabbage butterflies in a summer meadow. Enrico piloted the boat toward a tiny cluster of rock outcroppings in the water.

"No!" Owen said in disbelief. "There's a castle sitting right there in the water!"

Maggie gasped.

As they drew closer Enrico pulled back on the throttle, the engine went from a growl to a purr, the bow dropped, and the boat slowed.

"This is called Castelli di Cannero," Fabrizio said. "It's all that remains of a group of castles built in the 1500s to defend the upper part of Lake Maggiore from the Swiss."

"But underneath is an older pirate's fortress, built by the five Mazzarditi brothers," Enrico said as he pointed to the base of the towers.

Fabrizio piped in, "After robbing and terrorizing all the villages along the lake for about a hundred years, the Visconti family from Milan finally got mad and surrounded the islands, starving the Mazzarditi brothers into surrender, and their old pirate fortress was destroyed."

As they puttered around the islets looking up at the gray stone towers, Maggie spread her hands like a movie director explaining a panorama. "It looks like the set from *Beauty and the Beast*!"

"Can you imagine doing a wedding here?" Owen said.

"Yours or mine?" Maggie chuckled and nudged him with her shoulder.

Enrico shut off the engine and they glided to a gentle float. "You two can dive in if you want."

Owen pulled off his T-shirt. "Aren't you coming in with us?" he said as he made his way to the wooden ladder in the stern.

"You go ahead," Enrico said. "We'll stay here and set up the umbrella and prepare the picnic."

Maggie slipped from her sitting position in the bow to her feet. Leaning against the side gunwale, she unbuttoned her baggy shirt, pulled it off, and tossed it on the deck. She was just about to follow Owen into the stern when she realized the twins were standing frozen with their eyes fixed on her.

"What!" Maggie said. "What's wrong?"

"No, nothing's wrong." Enrico said. "It's just we have an old photograph of our mother…"

"…wearing a bathing suit exactly like that and standing in exactly the same place where you are right now," Fabrizio said.

"I'm sorry. I didn't mean to upset you. Tata lent it to me."

Maggie grabbed her shirt and was about to put it back on when Fabrizio cried, "No, no, don't!" He waved his hands back and forth. "You're a vision, like an angel." He had tears in his eyes.

Fabrizio's and Maggie's eyes locked together.

"Hey!" Owen looked back over his shoulder. "C'mon."

Maggie grinned nervously and jerked her head away, breaking their stare. "Yes, I'm coming." She moved into the stern to where Owen was perched on the bottom rung of the ladder. With a splash Owen leaped out into the water and Maggie followed.

"I know it sounds like a cliché, but I feel like we're inside a storybook," Owen said as they swam away from the boat.

"Oh, look who's the romantic now," Maggie said with a mocking tone and splashed him with water.

Treading water, Owen looked back toward the boat. "I wish they had read me fairy tales like this when I was little because right now, I can see a castle and an old wooden boat with a large red umbrella." He gulped some air and coughed. "And two gorgeous, half-naked Italian guys, holding a bottle of prosecco, a French loaf, salami, and cheese."

"First one back takes all!" Maggie laughed and started back toward the boat.

"Unfair advantage!" Owen called, slapping the water after her.

It was midafternoon by the time they returned home, and while the twins secured the boat, Owen and Maggie went back up to the house.

Maggie burst into the kitchen to find Tata putting a broccoli and artichoke pie into the oven.

"Remind me to give you this recipe," Tata said as she stood upright.

Maggie walked over to her and kissed her cheek.

"What was that for?" Tata said.

"You're very... what was that word, oh yeah, *furba*," Maggie said and waved her finger at Tata.

"Whatever do you mean, child?" Tata laughed. "Oh, by the way, you can keep the swimsuit," she called as Maggie skipped out of the kitchen and up the stairs to her room.

After she had changed, Maggie came downstairs onto the terrace and found Owen sitting in the wicker chair with his feet stretched out resting on the cement banister. "So how is your day going, my dear?" he said in a lyrical tone.

"Splendid!" Maggie only used the word splendid for the most splendid of things. She slid her chair closer to the railing, slumped low in it, and stretched her legs out as far as she could but couldn't quite reach. She sat back up, slid her chair even closer, and propped her feet up.

"There. I knew you could do it, Stumpy." Owen handed her a glass of prosecco.

"I'm not stumpy! My legs are petite." Maggie's voice always rose a little when Owen pushed the right buttons.

"Aren't you going to ask me how my day is going?" Owen said.

"How is your day going, my dear?"

"Splendid. I spent the day on a boat on a lake in Italy in the company of my bestie and two lovely young Italian gentlemen," Owen said in a mock Bostonian accent and held up his glass.

Following his cue, Maggie held up her glass. "What are we toasting?"

"To you, my petite treasure." Owen chuckled. "And your wisdom. This is exactly what I needed."

"To me," Maggie said, and they clinked their glasses and took a sip.

"You know, I can't believe I'm here in Italy." She slopped a little wine onto her leg as she waved her glass in the air.

"It really is like a fairy tale."

"Complete with two handsome princes," Maggie said as she gazed across the garden at one of the twins walking up the path from the lake carrying a pile of life vests and the other coming up behind him carrying the paddles.

Just then a car honked. And both of the brothers suddenly looked up. The first dumped the life vests on the lawn and trotted across the garden toward the gate. The second dropped the paddles and ran after him.

Maggie and Owen turned to look as a BMW sedan, the sunlight glimmering off its chrome and onyx surface, pulled up to the gate and honked again.

The boys held the gate open as the car glided through, down the hibiscus-flanked gravel lane, coming to a stop in front of the house.

The car doors opened and a short man with a plastic-looking mop of mousy-colored hair, wearing a pink polo shirt, red chinos, and driving moccasins with no socks, stepped out, stretched, and scratched his belly. From the passenger side, a bony woman with a stretched-back face got out and strutted to the front of the car. She was wearing a white blouse, black linen skirt, and white-and-black patent leather pumps that could only have come from one of the finest fashion houses in Milan. The woman glared at Maggie and Owen with an expression of deep disapproval, took out a cigarette, lit it, and blew out a long puff of smoke.

"I may not have gaydar, but I think my bitch alert is sounding." Maggie dropped her feet from the railing and sat upright.

"My little gay genes are screaming, 'Hang on to your wigs and your ruby slippers, the wicked witch and her flying monkey have just swooped in.'" Owen remained in his slouch.

From behind them on the terrace they heard Tata growl. Startled, they looked back over their shoulders at her.

"*Strega!*" She made a loud spitting sound toward the floor, then turned and walked back inside.

"Oh shit," Owen said. "I hope Tata didn't hear us."

Maggie snorted. "I wouldn't worry. Even if I don't speak a word of the language, I suspect that Tata doesn't like them too much, either."

CHAPTER TWENTY-NINE

"WHAT A surprise!" Enrico called out as he jogged up to the car and kissed his sister on her cheek.

"I'll tell Tata you're staying for dinner," Fabrizio trotted up behind him, leaned forward and kissed her.

"No, we can't possibly," Francesca said, elongating the vocal sounds and pushing them out through her nose. "We had some banking to do in Switzerland and we just stopped by to get a few photos of the house. For a keepsake, you know."

Pietro reached into the back seat of the car, pulled out a professional-looking camera, pointed it at the house, and snapped a few photos of the roof gables, walls, and foundation. Then he walked over to the terrace where Owen and Maggie were sitting. Eyeing Maggie like a lizard to a fly, he snapped off a few more photos of the façade.

"I see you have guests," Francesca said with a condescending tone. "How nice."

"Come up and meet them," Fabrizio said cheerfully.

"No. As I said, we can't stay." Francesca took a long drag on her cigarette.

Pietro returned to the car and placed his camera on the driver's seat. "It's a fine example of Liberty style, but the façade is in rough shape. The foundation looks sound. Very marketable," he said as if he were writing a sales description. "Are there any major cracks in the plaster?"

"Well, there's a large one in the kitchen," Fabrizio said.

Pietro waved his hand. "The kitchen was added onto the main structure later, so it doesn't surprise me."

"Maybe you could help us decide what to do first to fix up the old place," Enrico said.

"You wouldn't have any plans of survey and the original deed, would you?" Pietro said.

"It's all bureaucratic," Francesca quickly added. "Just to ensure the equitable separation of our dear grandmother's estate." Francesca genuflected and kissed her large diamond ring.

Fabrizio and Enrico both shrugged. "We could look. There might be something in the attic, somewhere."

"I bet Tata would know." Fabrizio turned his head toward the kitchen and didn't notice, but Enrico caught a glimpse of his sister curl her lip at the mention of Tata.

Fabrizio looked back. "I can ask."

"There's no need to right now. But if you find anything, anything at all, please let Pietro know as soon as you can." Francesca cleared her throat. "As Pietro said, it's just for the bureaucracy. As soon as we've done that…." She flashed her big yellow teeth. "I can access my personal account and loan you the money you asked me for." She held her wrist up and glanced at her gold Rolex. "We're late and if we are to make it back to Milan in time, we'll have to leave now."

Pietro shook the boys' hands. "Be in touch."

"Come, dear." Francesca clicked her tongue. "We must be on our way." She threw the boys a Hollywood kiss. "We'll visit when we have more time." She flicked her cigarette onto the drive, climbed into the passenger side and closed the door.

Pietro reached into the driver's side and put the camera on the seat behind, then climbed in.

Francesca rolled down her window partway. "Be sure and let us know if you find any old documents. Anything at all." Her big diamond ring sparkled in the light as she fluttered her fingers goodbye.

Fabrizio ran up and opened the gate while Pietro turned the sedan around, drove up the lane, and onto the street.

Enrico stood in the gravel drive in front of the house watching as they disappeared down the hill. Francesca was normally a nervous person, but ever since they'd told her about their plans to make the old house into a B&B she seemed especially agitated. And why were they making so many trips to Switzerland? Other than watches and chocolate, Switzerland was also famous for expensive medical clinics and questionable banking practices. Francesca and Pietro certainly didn't look like they were sick. On the other hand, Francesca did suggest that their money was tight, and Pietro was a bit *furbo* when it came to business deals. He hoped they weren't foolish enough to try and hide money in Switzerland from the Italian fiscal police.

CHAPTER THIRTY

THE SUN had sunk below the silhouette of mountains an hour ago, but the humid heat from the day still hung in the night air. The twins and Maggie and Owen stood on the shore looking out at the dark water. Just then a red meteor shot up over their heads and out across the lake. With a crack it exploded into a thousand little green stars that sparkled and twinkled as they floated back down and disappeared just before they touched the surface of the water.

"What are they celebrating?" Maggie said.

"Summer," Fabrizio said.

Maggie leaned comfortably against Owen's robust frame, as they so often did whenever they were in a crowd or at a concert. Out of the corner of her eye she watched as Owen's hand surreptitiously brushed against the back of Enrico's.

Enrico didn't flinch or move away.

Fabrizio continued, "My online business course said we were supposed to do something memorable, but we really can't take credit for this. Almost every weekend one of the villages along the lake makes a fireworks show." Fabrizio looked over at Maggie and grinned. "It's very romantic all the same, no?"

Instantly, like a boy who'd just been caught in the cookie jar, Owen pulled his rogue hand away and Enrico quickly stepped back and placed his hand on his brother's shoulder.

Maggie tilted her head back and gazed upward at the rockets bursting into cinders of light over the lake. "Ah, what more could a girl ask for?"

"It's a good thing Jessy's not here." Owen nudged Maggie. "He'd give us a detailed answer to that question."

Maggie snorted out a laugh that was partially masked by a second round of fireworks exploding in the night sky.

Later that night, up in her tower room, after she'd showered, she decided to slip on her new burnt-rose lace bra and panties. It was true what Tata had said, she thought as she admired herself in the mirror. They did make her feel special even if she was the only one who could see them. She sauntered over to the large open window and leaned against the sill. Gazing out at the moonlight casting a silvery patina on the dark silhouette of the trees and licking the surface of the water against the purple stain of mountains in the distance, she imagined Fabrizio's strong hairy arms wrapped around her, and she hugged herself.

Suddenly, jolting her from her little fantasy, there was an odd thumping on her door that sounded as if someone was butting his head against it.

"Coming, Owen," Maggie sang out. She turned away from the window and sauntered past the bed, then stopped abruptly. Sure, she'd seen Owen and Jessy in their underwear hundreds of times before and they'd seen her too. But these were not just everyday underwear; they were special—they were sexy. She was sexy. Perhaps this was the first time in her life she'd ever allowed herself to think that. Yes, she was sexy, and she didn't need to hide from Owen.

"Hey, have you seen where I put my passport?" she said and threw open the door.

But instead of Owen, standing there in her doorway wearing a shy grin and holding two bowls of tiramisu in his hands was Fabrizio. It was as if her fantasy had been hacked into.

"Ah!" she squealed and crossed her arms over her breasts. "It's you! I thought it was Owen."

Fabrizio looked to the floor. "I'm sorry to disturb you, but Tata thought you might like a little snack before bed." He held out the bowls.

Maggie cast her eyes longingly at them and then at Fabrizio. "Um, well, come in. Oh, wait. I'm half naked. Let me cover up first." Maggie scurried back across the room and threw on her father's white shirt. "There. All decent."

Fabrizio stepped in through the door. "Should I take this other bowl over to Owen?" he said with a smile that left little room for interpretation.

"Nah." Maggie swatted the air. "He's probably asleep already." She closed the door and let her shirt fall to the floor.

CHAPTER THIRTY-ONE

EVEN IF Fabrizio was the one with the head for numbers, Enrico didn't need a business degree to understand the column labeled expenses was bigger than the one labeled earnings. While he sat at the dining room table studying the spreadsheet on the screen, he heard someone in the kitchen and looked up. Maybe Fabrizio was making himself a midnight snack? He shut off the computer and went to see.

There in the kitchen, he spotted Owen's backside poking out from the fridge. Through his boxers, his buttocks looked like two grapefruits waiting to be peeled. He watched as Owen took out a pan of tiramisu, turned, and closed the fridge door with his hip.

"*Buona notte*," Enrico said.

Owen gasped and jumped, practically dropping the pan. "Oh, you scared me." Owen placed the pan on the wooden kitchen table. "I couldn't sleep, and I was looking for something to eat. Tata said we could help ourselves," he quickly added.

Enrico smirked. "Yes, but if you eat that you won't sleep for the rest of the night. Tiramisu is full of caffeine." Enrico sauntered over. "What about a glass of *Vin Santo*—it's a sweet wine from Tuscany—and some *biscotti cantucci*."

"You're the boss," Owen said with a playful lilt and returned the pan of tiramisu to the fridge.

Enrico took a bottle from the cabinet and poured two glasses of thick golden wine. Then, from the cookie tin, he took out some biscotti that looked like Scottish shortbreads with almonds and piled them on a plate.

"I've seen these at Starbucks, but I've never tried them."

"Come on. The kitchen's hot. Let's go out onto the terrace." Enrico handed Owen a glass and gestured for him to lead the way. Enrico followed with his eyes locked on Owen's behind.

They sat down and Owen raised his glass and took a sip. "Oh, that's really sweet." He bit into a biscotto and crunched it. "Wow. You could break a tooth on one of these."

Enrico chuckled. "Yes, but normally we do it like this." Enrico dipped his biscotto into the glass of wine, shook off the drops, and held it out for Owen.

Owen leaned over and took a bite of the wine-soaked cookie. "Mmm, that's better," he said.

"Can you do it on your own or do you want me to do it again for you?" Enrico shot Owen a coy look.

Owen made a bashful grin, causing a wave of goose bumps to flow down the back of Enrico's neck.

"For now, I think I can manage, but I'll keep your offer in mind." Owen dipped his biscotto in his wine and took a bite.

They sat in silence listening to the night, a cricket in the garden, a dog barking in the distance, and a lone car coming down the roadway.

"Enrico," Owen said, breaking the silence. "I don't know why, but I feel like I need to tell you something."

"What?" Enrico looked at Owen. He felt both intrigued and concerned about what Owen might confess.

Owen looked away. "I have a substance dependency problem." His voice was flat.

Enrico furrowed his brow. "I don't understand."

"I had some problems with coke before we left."

"Ah." Enrico nodded. "Some of the guys here have tried it. A few of them have tried heroin as well."

"At first it was just when I went out on the weekends." Owen frowned. "But then I started using it more and more often."

"Why?"

"I guess because it made me feel brave, in control, and desirable." Owen shrugged.

Enrico said nothing.

Owen looked to the ground. "Or maybe I just wanted to hurt myself because I'm none of those things."

"Do you still use it?"

"No, and it cost me my best friend to realize what an idiot I was."

"I'm sure he's still your best friend."

Owen slouched down in his seat. "Maybe, but he's gone now. He went to California." Owen breathed in deeply and slowly exhaled. "So I guess I'm looking for the guy who can make me forget about him."

"I'm not sure we're so very different." Enrico dipped a biscotto into his wine and took a bite, chewed, and swallowed. "I have to make room in my heart for someone else as well. But I can't imagine living without my brother." Enrico paused. "Do you think that sounds strange?"

"No, not at all. Jessy was like my brother, and more. He was always there for me."

"I know someday Fabrizio will find a woman and fall in love with her." Enrico stared into his glass at the tiny crumbs of biscotto floating in the wine. "And I'll be in the way."

"And I know that if Maggie is ever going to have a life of her own, she'll have to leave me too." Owen took a sip of wine. "Maybe it's for the better."

Enrico felt a pang of longing shoot through his chest. He could really fall for this American guy. He wanted to take him in his arms and kiss him, but if he did, what would it lead to? A one-night stand, just a vacation romance, nothing more. Owen was leaving tomorrow, and he would be left behind with a broken heart. Maybe that was for the better too. Enrico stood up. "I think I'll go back to bed. Are you okay?" He placed his hand tenderly on Owen's shoulder.

"Fine." Owen placed his hand on top of Enrico's and said, "I'm going to sit here awhile longer until I become sleepy." Owen's blue eyes seemed to radiate light. "Good night, Enrico. Oh, and thanks."

"*Buona notte,*" Enrico said as he slid his hand away and headed back toward the kitchen, not really sure what Owen had thanked him for.

CHAPTER THIRTY-TWO

MAYBE IT was all the fresh air yesterday out on the boat or the wine and biscotti he'd shared with Enrico on the terrace late last night, but this morning Owen woke up feeling more invigorated than he'd felt in a very long time. It was a spectacular day—hot and sunny—and their last morning at the lake before they continued on their tour of Italy after lunch. It would be hard to leave, but he was looking forward to seeing Venice. Maggie was so right. He did need to get away. Even though the B&B wasn't quite what he'd expected, it turned out to be a perfect refuge.

While Owen finished his cappuccino and fresh-baked brioche on the terrace, he gazed up toward Maggie's window in the tower. After what he had heard through the wall last night, he was sure that she would be snuggled in bed with Fabrizio for the rest of the morning. They'd probably do it again, once or twice before she had to get up and pack. With her new look—the new clothes and haircut—it was obvious Maggie was doing her best to move forward and set her heart free from him. The same way he was trying to set his heart free from Jessy. If only he and Enrico had shared something more.

His eyes wandered out across a cloud of brilliant blue hydrangea bushes at Enrico's long, lean Mediterranean physique as he came down the gravel walkway, and Owen couldn't help but smile. As he drew closer Owen could make out the crop of curly chest hair peeking out from his white low-cut undershirt, giving him the appearance of either a bricklayer from Calabria or a porn star. Why did Italians look so damn sexy in undershirts?

The image of Jessy wearing an undershirt at the swimming pool flashed through Owen's mind. Until last night his heart had refused to believe that any guy could ever measure up to Jessy. But there was something about Enrico—the way he seemed to glide when he moved, the little dimples in his cheeks when he smiled, and the dimples in his buttcheeks that poked out from his beneath his Speedo. Most of all it was the way Enrico listened and looked at him with those rich, deep understanding eyes.

Owen continued to stare as Enrico bent over and picked up a large fallen *tiglio* branch, his glutes straining against the back of his shorts. His biceps bulged and his lats pressed beneath his undershirt as he balanced the branch on one shoulder.

No matter how sweet the temptation, Owen thought, nothing could ever possibly come of it. It was just a simple vacation infatuation. Besides, the Atlantic Ocean lay between him and Italy. He had heard enough tragic stories over the years to know a long-distance love affair is a roller-coaster ride that empties your wallet and leaves you in tears. Enrico was an unobtainable fantasy best left unexplored. Who knew? Maybe there was a guy like Enrico on the American side of the pond? He blew out a puff of air. Unfortunately, he had yet to meet him.

Then, counter to his better judgment, as if he were thumbing his nose at Cupid, Owen leaned coyly with one buttcheek propped on the banister and his other leg extended. "Hey, when you're done in the garden, how about one last boat ride before we go?" He rolled out the words and winked.

"A boat ride?" Enrico looked up at Owen and then around the garden and toward the gravel drive where Angelina was usually parked. "Sure." He shrugged. "Why not? Let's go."

"Give me a minute. Got to get my stuff and I'll be right down." Owen darted across the terrace and through the door. He flew up the stairs, coming to a sudden halt in front of Maggie's door. He pressed his ear against it. Not a sound.

He grabbed his towel and day pack and jaunted down the stairs. "I'm good to go," Owen sang out as he skipped across the terrace and into the garden to where Enrico was waiting with the life jackets in his hands. Owen followed him down the steps to the dock. Enrico jumped in the boat, untied it, and Owen leaped in.

The engine roared and the bow rose as they motored away from the shore and sailed out across the smooth surface, cruising past the old lime furnaces of *Le Fornaci*. Up ahead, a couple of laser sailing boats chased each other across the bay of Castelveccana. As they headed out toward the middle of the lake, Owen slipped off his T-shirt, letting the sun lick his skin and the warm wind tease his hair and ruffle his nylon boxers.

"How about one last swim?" Enrico pulled the throttle back. The bow dropped and the boat glided to a drift in the middle of the lake.

"Here?" Owen said.

"Yes, this is where all the fish pee, so it'll be warmer." He shot Owen a grin. "C'mon, Americano, get your balls wet."

Out of the corner of his eye, Owen watched as Enrico pulled his undershirt up over his head and slipped off his shorts leaving nothing on but his small black Speedo—the sun glistening off his olive skin. Enrico then climbed up onto the gunwale and dove over the side, his sleek form slicing into the mirror-green surface of the water.

Owen climbed onto the gunwale and leaped in after him, coming up for air in a cauldron of bubbles. Owen dove under again, grabbed hold of Enrico's foot, and pulled him under too. They surfaced, splashing and frolicking like two kids. Then they swam back to the boat, climbed up the ladder, and flopped down beside each other onto the mattress-covered deck, the water glistening as it ran in little streams off their skin.

Owen rolled over on his side, his face only inches away. "Hey, I hadn't noticed that scar above your eyebrow before." Owen touched the scar with the tip of his finger.

"That's what I earned for making my brother angry at me. I have a talent for it, you know."

As Owen's eyes followed the line of Enrico's Romanesque nose down to the stubble on his chin, he felt his rising boner pushing up the front of his boxers.

"Are you going camping?" Enrico chuckled. "Because it looks like you're setting up a tent in those boxers."

Strange, Owen thought, *Fabrizio is the one who's always makes wise cracks. Enrico is usually more reserved.* He hadn't noticed it before but they seemed to share the same sense of goofy humor. Must be a twin thing. Owen grinned and looked up and around. They were out in the open, but there were no other boats nearby, and they were far enough out that nobody could really see much from shore. If Owen was ever going to make a move, it was now or never. With one smooth gesture he reached over and slid his hand under the band of Enrico's Speedo.

"Hey, Americano, what're doing?" Enrico flinched as his stomach muscles contracted and his cock began to swell, peeking out from its confines.

"Giving you something to remember me by." Owen grasped the shaft of Enrico's cock firmly and it blossomed full.

Enrico looked nervous and tried to shift away, but before he could Owen had tugged the black spandex down capturing his penis in his mouth as it sprang upward. Like a dog licking a wad of peanut butter, Owen teased and sucked while he wormed his other hand under the elastic waistband of his boxers, grabbing hold of his own penis and stroking himself.

Owen then maneuvered his head around and buried his face, licking that particular spot right at the base of Enrico's testicles and stroking him faster.

Suddenly, his balls became taut. "Ahh, I come!" Enrico gasped.

Like a starving man Owen engulfed Enrico's cock to its base. Owen's eyes teared and he barely swallowed before he felt a wave of gooseflesh run up his spine. His balls tightened and Owen shot out the top of his boxers, then collapsed onto the mattress, his chest rising and falling like waves.

"Wow! I really wasn't expecting that." Enrico laughed nervously and quickly pulled his Speedo back up.

"I didn't really plan it either. It just kind of happened." Owen chuckled while he tucked himself back into his shorts. "Thanks for a fantastic last morning." Owen moved in to kiss Enrico on his lips, but Enrico turned his head sideways and Owen ended up kissing his cheek instead.

"We've got to go. Lunch will be ready soon and you have to pack." Enrico quickly pushed himself upright. "Bello, Americano." He patted Owen's cheek, jumped onto the seat and started the engine. The outboard roared, the bow lurched skyward, and they sped back toward the boathouse.

This was not the first time Owen had fooled around with a guy and afterward the guy was cool and distant. Enrico was obviously not as into it as he was. Too bad, because he really liked him. But it was probably for the better. After all, he was leaving in a couple of hours and would never see Enrico again. At least he now had an adventure story of his own to share with Maggie.

CHAPTER THIRTY-THREE

FABRIZIO SWAGGERED into the dining room to find Enrico setting out their grandmother's china plates on the freshly pressed linen. He made a farty-sounding kiss on the back of Enrico's neck and rested his chin on his brother's shoulder

Enrico swiveled around. "I asked Tata to make risotto with gorgonzola, and I've opened a bottle of Barbaresco," he said. "I have to admit it, you were right. We just might be able to make this B&B work."

"Of course I was right. So, what's with Grandmother's good dishes?"

"I just want to make their last lunch a little special." Enrico curled his hands in against his chest as if to sign, *why, what's the problem*?

"You've got the hots for him, don't you?"

"No!" Enrico said.

"Enrico's got a crush on Owen." Fabrizio sang out the words like a taunting schoolkid.

"Shut up! Okay, maybe just a little. But it doesn't matter because he's leaving today."

"Well, he certainly likes you." Fabrizio did a little dancing gesture, pointing his fingers at Enrico.

"How do you know?" Enrico beamed and his dimples showed.

"Because he told me so out on the boat." Fabrizio patted his pockets and took out a pack of cigarettes.

"He told you?" Enrico dropped one eyebrow.

"Yeah. You were out running an errand for Tata, and he asked to go out in the boat one last time." He flicked the pack twice and a cigarette popped out. "He thought I was you."

"What did he say?"

"Well, he didn't actually say anything." Fabrizio pulled a cigarette out and placed it on his waiting lip. "His mouth was full at the time." He bobbed his eyebrows.

"What are you talking about?" Enrico's tone became suspicious.

"Well, it's not like I encouraged him, but the next thing I knew, his hand was down the front of my Speedo. Hey, normally I don't go for guys, but since he thought I was you, all I could do was play along."

"You had sex with him?"

"He gave me a *pompino* out on the boat, That's not the same as having sex with him." Fabrizio held out his hand and wiggled his thumb signaling for a light. "Hey, but I could tell by the way he did it, he's really hot for you!"

"Ahh!" Enrico had that expression of disbelief on his face he always wore when Fabrizio had crossed the line. "Did Tata drop you on your head when we were babies?" Enrico clasped his face with his hands.

"Come on, guys fool around together all the time. It's not like I let him kiss me or anything." The cigarette hung from Fabrizio's lip.

"I should have known," Enrico growled and shook his head.

"What's the big deal?" Fabrizio had a blank expression on his face. "What about you and Luigi?"

"That's different."

"How's that different?" Fabrizio said.

"Because you're my brother." Enrico sneered.

"And Maria is your friend." Fabrizio held out his hands and shrugged. "I don't see the difference."

"Look, there are some things we can't share."

"But we share everything?" Fabrizio rolled his head. "Like, when I pulled Grazia. She said she wouldn't mind if you wanted to give her a poke too." Fabrizio held out his palms. "And it wouldn't bother me, either. You know what they say, a boner makes his own friends."

"I don't want to have sex with Grazia or any of your *troiottole!*" Enrico barked.

"That's because you like dick, not *fica*." Fabrizio snorted out a laugh.

"That's because we're not the same person!" Enrico jabbed his finger at Fabrizio. "I want something that's my own!" Enrico stormed out of the room.

The sun coming through the window cast a square patch of light onto the wooden floor in front of him. Fabrizio stood with the unlit cigarette stuck to his lower lip. It was as if something had just been severed from his heart. For the first time in his life, he felt alone, and it terrified him. "What did I do wrong? I was only trying to help," he mumbled.

Chapter Thirty-Four

"WHERE ARE the guys? I thought they were going to join us," Maggie said as Tata placed the plates of *risotto al gorgonzola* in front of them.

"They said they had something to do, but you should start because your taxi will be here in an hour. Now eat before it gets cold." Tata hurried off back into the kitchen.

Maggie looked disappointed as she lifted her glass.

"You heard what the lady said, eat!" Owen picked up his fork.

"Okay, I can't keep it a secret any longer." Maggie put down her glass.

"You're holding out on me? We share all our secrets. How dare you!" Owen laughed. "Besides, I've got a secret of my own to share."

"No fair. Mine first. For once in my life I have a better story than you do."

"Oh, honey." Owen patted the back of Maggie's hand. "You could never have a better story than me."

"Oh yeah, take this!" Maggie said.

"I love it when you talk tough to me. Spill, girl. Then I'll follow up with mine and we'll decide later who's got the better tale to tell."

"Well, last night, just as I was ready to climb into bed, I heard a knock on my door. I thought it was you, so I answered the door wearing nothing but my new bra and panties."

"Oh, don't stop. I'm getting all sweaty." Owen fanned himself.

Maggie swatted him. "Listen up, you fool. You'll never guess who was standing there holding a plate of tiramisu."

"Tata?"

"No!" Maggie looked around, then held her hand against her mouth as if she were about to reveal a great secret even though they were alone. "Fabrizio," she whispered.

Owen snickered. "And?"

"And, I invited him in and well…."

"No, no, girl! It's too late to fade to black now. I want details."

"Well, let's just say that we didn't use a fork to eat our tiramisu."

"I'm so proud of you." Owen reached over and put his arm around Maggie. "It's about time you left the memories of high school in the dust and went back down on the pony."

"Isn't it supposed to be, get back up on the pony?"

"All depends on what you're doing to him at the time. But enough about you and your midnight snack. I just licked the bowl clean myself, so to speak."

"No! When!"

"This morning, out on the boat. I gave that Italian boy a tip I'm sure he won't soon forget."

Maggie shook her head. "Okay, it's confirmed. You're a pig."

"Oh, look who's talking. From what I heard coming through the bedroom wall last night you really *do* like tiramisu."

"Ahhh! You heard?"

"Of course I heard!" Owen threw both hands up in the air. "Oh, Fabrizio," he said in a mockingly effeminate voice. "I'm on a diet."

Maggie covered her face with her hands. "You definitely are the most horrible person I know."

"I know I am, but you love me just the same." Owen pulled Maggie over and kissed her cheek.

"Forget that I haven't had sex in, like, forever. The problem is, I could really fall for Fabrizio. He's kind and funny, and most of all he makes me feel, well, beautiful."

"You are beautiful. But I know what you mean. I'm not the man you need to hear that from. Just be careful with your heartstrings; you know this is only the first stop on our vacation."

"I know. It's so unfair. Why can't I ever find a guy like him back home?"

"Hey, look at that plastic club kid, Lane, or whatever his name was. Why can't I find a real guy like Enrico?"

"Of course, let's not overlook the fact that Fabrizio is possibly the sexiest man I've ever seen much less been with," Maggie continued as if she were not really listening to Owen.

"How can you say Fabrizio is sexier than Enrico? They're identical."

"They're not identical. Fabrizio has that scar above his eyebrow that makes him look like a swordsman, like one of the three musketeers."

"What are you talking about? Enrico's the one with the scar. I just noticed it this morning on the boat." Owen paused. "Oh shit!" He slapped his head.

"What?"

"That explains why he wouldn't kiss me."

Maggie turned white. "You didn't?"

"I think I did."

Maggie stood up and her serviette fell to the floor. "It's always about you, isn't it? My one big moment and it's all about you again." She turned. "I'm not hungry."

Owen stood up as Maggie walked out of the room. "I'm sorry," he called after her. "I didn't know."

CHAPTER THIRTY-FIVE

FABRIZIO TROTTED up and opened the gate. The taxi rolled in and stopped at the front door. Owen handed his bag to the driver who loaded it into the trunk as Fabrizio came back down the drive.

"Can I use the toilet?" the taxi driver said to Fabrizio.

"Of course, just go in, first door on the left." Fabrizio sauntered over to Owen. "Is Miss Maggie ready?"

"She's in the kitchen saying goodbye to Tata."

"I suppose she knows what happened?" Fabrizio said.

"Yes. I accidently spilled the beans during lunch."

"I'm really sorry." Fabrizio looked at Owen with an expression of genuine remorse.

"You should have told me before I made a move." Owen scowled.

"I know. It happened so fast. I was only trying to help my brother out and things got a little out of hand. Are you angry at me?"

"Well." Owen smirked. "You're not the first straight boy I've blown." Owen shook his head. "But I really wish it had been Enrico and not you."

"I do too." Fabrizio had a concerned expression. "Is Maggie angry at me?"

"I think you could say she's angry at you and disappointed with me." Owen shoveled the gravel with his foot. "I suppose Enrico knows too?"

"Oh yes. And he isn't too happy with me, either."

"Why do I always end up with the wrong guy?" Owen said as if he were speaking to himself.

"Ha," Fabrizio scoffed. "Don't ask me. I'm the world's expert on doing things wrong." Fabrizio scratched the back of his head. "Especially where my brother is concerned."

"Well, I guess what's done is done," Owen said with a tone of regret.

"Wait." Fabrizio darted up the steps and disappeared inside.

Owen opened the rear door and threw his carry-on onto the seat, then stood there leaning on the open door, looking out toward the lake. Everything had been so perfect, except for one mistake—one big mistake!

Fabrizio reappeared. "After you leave, please give her this and tell her how sorry I am." He handed Owen a red paper bag that was taped closed.

"What's this?"

"Oh, nothing, just a half kilo of cocaine," Fabrizio said with a flat expression.

Owen flinched.

"Ahh, Americano," Fabrizio jibed.

Owen rolled his eyes. "Italiano. Why couldn't you have been your brother?" Owen put out his hand to shake.

"That would have been better for both of us." Fabrizio ignored his hand, embraced him, and kissed him on either cheek.

"It's probably best you stay out of sight until we're gone," Owen said as Fabrizio released him.

"I understand." Fabrizio turned and started to walk away, then stopped. "Oh, by the way, thank you for the blow job." He continued on, leaving Owen standing by the taxi shaking his head.

"Tata, I just wanted to say thank you for everything." Maggie was standing in the kitchen doorway.

"Nothing, child." Tata came over and embraced her. "I hope you will not forget us and come back and visit us again someday."

"Well, maybe." Maggie looked down.

Tata took her chin. "I don't know any of the details, and I don't want to, but I do know that when a man does something stupid, his dick is usually involved."

Maggie tried to force a smile and nodded.

"Men!" Tata threw her hands up and blew out a puff of air. "They're all little boys, really." She patted Maggie's cheek softly.

"As you said, that's why we love them, isn't it?" Maggie said.

"When you get home, find some man, make him a bowl of carbonara, and make love to him until he begs for mercy." Tata blew her a kiss, turned, and opened the fridge.

Maggie left the kitchen and climbed back up the stairs to get her carry-on.

Coming out of the room, she jumped when she almost ran headlong into Enrico, who was standing in the doorway.

"Please don't hate my brother," he said.

"I don't." Maggie shook her head slowly. "I just wish things had turned out differently."

"So do I," Enrico said softly. "Fabrizio has a heart of gold and would never hurt anyone deliberately. It's just that he never thinks about consequences." Enrico looked to the floor. "I guess it's always been my job to protect him from himself."

"He's lucky to have a brother like you."

"I hope he finds a woman almost as wonderful as you someday."

They embraced and kissed. Enrico bent over and picked up her bag, and Maggie followed him down the stairs and out to the taxi.

Enrico held the gate open as the taxi drove up the lane. Owen's face was pressed against his window, and as they passed, Enrico held up his hand and made a little sorrowful wave.

They drove down the winding lakeside road and through the gallery to Laveno. Two minutes later, as the taxi slowed for the curve past the Bar Milano, Owen sat up and turned to Maggie. "Here." He handed her the red paper bag. "Fabrizio wanted you to have this."

Maggie examined the bag, rolling it over in her hands.

"Well, are you going to open it?"

Maggie looked back at Owen and smiled sardonically. "Not right now." She held out her hand to Owen. "Here."

Owen held out his hand. "What is it?"

"Enrico wanted you to have this." Maggie dropped something into Owen's palm that felt like a stone.

Owen looked down at a tiny lump of colored glass. "Oh shit!" He closed his hand tightly around it.

Maggie was silent for a moment. "It wasn't really your fault, you know. They do look almost identical."

Owen breathed in deeply. "Listen, if it's any condolence, Fabrizio didn't intend it to go that far, either. I kind of pounced on him."

"I don't know why you feel the need to defend him. He acted like an idiot."

"I know, but I guess in his own stupid way, he just wanted me and Enrico to get together."

"Well, it's not the end of the world, and I'm certainly not going to let one blow job ruin my trip. So let's just drop the whole incident," Maggie said with a definitive tone.

They bounced over the railway, leaving Laveno and Lago Maggiore behind as they drove down the provincial road toward the highway and Milan.

An hour after they had boarded the train to Venice, Owen fell asleep. Maggie stared out the window and watched the flat plane of the Po River Valley as they raced by. She reached down to her pack at her feet and took out the red paper bag. Inside was a small worn cookbook titled *La Cuccina Italiana*. She opened it. A note was written on the front page.

> *Dear Miss Maggie,*
> *Whenever I eat tiramisu I will think of you.*
> *I'm so sorry for what happened.*
> *Forever, Fabrizio*

She shook her head and rolled her eyes. Last night had truly been magic. She clutched the book to her chest. Why did he have to spoil it?

PART THREE

CHAPTER THIRTY-SIX

"HEY! WE have our first review on Trip Advisor," Fabrizio called out to Enrico, who was lying on the bed reading.

Enrico flopped his book down on his lap. "I'm afraid to know what they wrote after the fiasco."

"Do you want me to read it or not?"

"Go ahead," Enrico moaned.

"Okay, here goes."

On my recent trip to Italy I went shopping for shoes in Milan, floated down the canals of Venice in a gondola, rode a horse-drawn carriage around the coliseum in Rome, marveled at a 30-foot marble statue of a 400-year old boy and was serenaded by a mandolin in Napoli. The hotels, food, and wine and sites were marvelous.

"Good, there's nothing about us," Enrico said.

"Hold on a minute." Fabrizio continued to read.

All the same, the whole flight home all I could think about was Lago B&B (even if it didn't quite match its description or the photos on the website). The house is a gorgeous but somewhat dilapidated, eighteenth-century villa set on a hill overlooking Lago Maggiore. I had a room in the tower with a view of the lake and mountains that fulfilled all my fantasies about a room with a view. Tata, the best cook I've ever met, taught me to make pasta that is guaranteed to turn any man into my slave. Most of all, the twins with their hospitality, humor, and sincere desire to please, introduced me to an Italy that I didn't know existed and made me feel like I had found some place truly special.

Book now, while you still can.

"Man! Are you a *cretino*!" Enrico gasped. "How could you let a woman like that escape?"

"It wasn't my fault, you know." Fabrizio sulked.

"You made love to the woman, then let her best friend give you a blow job the next day. How is that not your fault?"

"Wait, we've got another review."

"Let me see." Enrico pushed his brother out of the way and read.

It's not posh or elegant. All the same Lago B&B has stolen my heart.

Enrico smiled.

"Now, I'll bet you're glad I let him give me a blow job," Fabrizio said.

"Why would I be glad he blew you!"

"Because he's thinking, I've had a taste of Fabrizio's big salami, and I'm sure Enrico's is almost as good!"

"Ahhh!" Enrico pounced on top of his brother, throwing him onto the floor and batting him with his open hands.

"Well it's true," Fabrizio taunted as he shoved the pillow in Enrico's face. "You'll never be as good a lover as me."

Just then the computer made a *bing* sound.

"Wait, wait," Fabrizio said as he wriggled out from under his brother and pushed himself up to where he could reach the keyboard. "We've got a booking! A couple from Germany for five days. They'll be here next week."

CHAPTER THIRTY-SEVEN

OWEN SNIFFED. Why did all community center rooms smell the same? It was as if there was a deodorizer specifically scented to smell like chlorine, dust, and dirty feet. A woman at the front of the room with a nasal voice was going on about how she used to hide bottles of gin in her garage. *Substance Dependency Support Group*. Why was he here? It's not like he was a real cokehead. He had just gotten a little carried away, that's all. That nosebleed he got the night of Pride didn't really count. He was the kid in school who always got nosebleeds. It was just… well, when the blood started trickling down his lip, it really scared him. But it wasn't like he was addicted or anything. Then he recalled his father taking another cigarette out of his pack, sticking it in his mouth, lighting it and saying he could quit smoking whenever he wanted to. If that were true, his father wouldn't still be smoking, would he? Besides, Maggie had made such a big deal of it, it was the only way to get her off his back.

Owen gazed out at the drizzle streaking down the window. It didn't really seem fair. Canada made all that cool air and blew it south across the lake where it picked up as much moisture as it could, then dumped it on Syracuse, Rochester, and Buffalo. Summer in Upstate New York had definitely come to an end. He wondered if it was still warm in Italy, but then he thought about the time difference. It would be the middle of the night over there. An image of Enrico lying in bed, naked with the sheet loosely covering his backside, flashed through his mind.

Suddenly someone said his name and Owen looked up. It was his turn. He might as well get it over with. He stood up, walked to the front of the room. A bleached-blond woman in a purple sweatshirt, an enormous man with a tattoo on his neck, a bored-looking young woman chewing gum, and a collection of other people slumped on stackable chairs looked back at him.

This didn't feel at all like when he'd given the valedictorian speech in high school. Owen's palms were wet. He cleared his throat. "Hello, my name is Owen."

"Welcome, Owen," the group said in unison. Owen cringed as he remembered *the welcoming* they always used to do at his mother's church, those pious faces with their forced smiles and limp handshakes.

"And I have a problem with coke," he continued.

"We hear you, Owen," the woman in the purple sweatshirt called out as if she were at a bible reunion.

"Actually, I was never a heavy user," Owen quickly added.

"Excuses, Owen," the mountain of a man yelled out.

"Judgmental, Owen. It's not a competition. We're all dependent on something here," sneered the woman chewing gum.

Owen took a deep breath. "Let me start again. I'm a cokehead and I haven't snorted for forty-two days."

The woman in the purple sweatshirt called out again, "Good for you, Owen." The group clapped.

After the meeting, as Owen was pouring himself a cup of coffee at the back of the room, a heavy hand patted him on the shoulder, causing him to spill some of his coffee.

Owen looked up at a tower of flesh standing in front of him.

"Hey, how's it going?" the mountain of a man said as if they were old friends.

Owen furrowed his brow. How could he forget someone like that?

"Big Eddy! You know, the door guy from the disco night at Skate-O-Rama?" He reached out and took Owen's hand, which disappeared inside his beefy grip.

Suddenly it dawned on Owen. "Sergeant Eddy! Two tours in Iraq, right?" Owen felt his tense muscles loosen.

"Yes, sir, that's me." Big Eddy was beaming.

Owen didn't know what else to say, so he just kept nodding and smiling.

Big Eddy broke the silence. "It's one step at a time, huh?"

That was exactly the platitude Owen expected to hear. But Owen didn't feel like he had made a step at all. He felt more like he was sinking in wet concrete.

"By the way, I never got the chance to thank you," Big Eddy said.

"Thank me? For what?" Owen squinted.

"When I walked in off the street and asked you for a job. You took one look at me and said you're hired."

"Oh, it was nothing." The last thing Owen wanted was for Big Eddy to feel indebted to him.

"Nothing? Are you kidding me?" Eddy's face was like steel.

Every muscle in Owen's body went tense again.

"After the army, you were the only person to ever take a chance on me. I asked myself, what the hell did that little fairy boy see in a big loser like me?"

"We needed a doorman, that's all," Owen said.

"Do you believe in karma?"

"No, not really," Owen said, not wanting to challenge or offend a man as big as Big Eddy.

"Don't matter. Now it's my turn to return the favor." Big Eddy smiled, showing a missing front tooth. "You got a sponsor, yet?"

"No. I'm okay on my own." Owen took a sip of his coffee.

"You wouldn't be here if that was true. Get out your phone, copy my number, and give me yours?"

Owen did as Big Eddy instructed hoping that this would appease him and he would either go away or let him go.

"There. You just got yourself a sponsor. You call me. Day or night. It don't matter. You hear me?"

"Yes." Owen nodded, "I hear you. Um, thanks, Big Eddy, but I have to go now. My Italian night class is about to begin." Owen threw his paper cup in the bin and hurried toward the door.

"Day or night, you little motherfucker," Big Eddy called after Owen as he rushed out the door and down the hall.

He darted into the classroom and claimed an empty desk in the back. He sank low in his chair and punched in Lago B&B. At the front the teacher was explaining something about the reflexive form of the verb *piacé*—to please—but he wasn't really listening. The Lago B&B website popped up and he scrolled down and gazed at the photos, just like he had done numerous times before.

CHAPTER THIRTY-EIGHT

"WE HAVE a registered letter," Fabrizio said as he shook off the umbrella and put it in the stand by the door.

"Well, open it and see who it's from," Enrico said.

Fabrizio ripped open the envelope, pulled out the letter, and unfolded it. "It's from Francesca's lawyer."

"It's probably just a copy of that document Francesca and Pietro wanted us to sign," Enrico said.

Fabrizio mumbled as he read the letter to himself. "It says that Francesca's apartment was given to her before our grandmother died, so it's not included in the inheritance."

Enrico shrugged. "See I told you, it's just a formal separation of the properties."

"Wait a minute!" Fabrizio held up his finger. "It also says that she is entitled to one-third the market value of our house!" Fabrizio put his finger on the line of text.

"There must be some kind of mistake. Let me see that." Enrico took the letter and read it.

"And that we either pay her or the property will be sold and the money divided into three parts," Fabrizio continued reading over Enrico's shoulder.

"One-third? But that's got to be about five hundred thousand euro!" Enrico waved his hands erratically.

"Does it say anything about the money our grandmother left us in the trust fund?" Fabrizio leaned over his brother's shoulder and scanned the page.

"Nothing," Enrico said. He handed the letter back to Fabrizio. "There's got to be some kind of mistake. I'll call her." Enrico took out his phone and dialed. "The phone is ringing, but she doesn't answer."

"Leave a message," Fabrizio said. "She'll call back."

"Why don't I try calling Pietro?" Enrico said and dialed.

"*Pronto*," Pietro responded.

"Hi, Pietro. It's Enrico." Enrico tried to control the nervous jitter in his voice. "How are you?"

"Fine, thank you." Pietro's voice was professional and cold.

"Just a second. Fabrizio is here with me, so I'm putting you on speakerphone." Enrico touched his screen, then held out the phone. "Listen, we just received a letter from Francesca's lawyer." Enrico paused, not knowing what else to say.

Pietro made a forced chuckle. "Oh, it's nothing to be alarmed about. Just a formality, I assure you."

"But it says we owe Francesca for one-third of the house," Fabrizio piped in.

"You know the way legal language is," Pietro said with a flat paternalistic tone.

"And what about the money Grandmother left us?" Fabrizio added.

Enrico shook his head back and forth and waved his hand.

"You'll have to talk with Francesca about that," Pietro said.

"Is she there?" Enrico said. "Can you put her on?"

Pause.

"She's meditating right now. You know all this business about her grandmother and her mother has been very upsetting for her." Pietro cleared his throat loudly into the phone. "Don't worry, you'll be contacted." And he hung up the phone.

Enrico looked at his phone and wrinkled up his face like he had just eaten a bad peanut.

"What does that mean, 'We'll be contacted'?" Fabrizio said, cupping his hands and bobbing them.

CHAPTER THIRTY-NINE

IMMERSED IN her first-level chef's course, Maggie had hardly noticed autumn's frosty greeting. In fact, other than her cooking course, she had trouble concentrating on anything. She placed the old recipe book Fabrizio had given her on the coffee table, got up from the sofa, and went into the kitchen, where Owen had tossed the mail on the table. In among the flyers and bills was a small letter with a handwritten address and an Italian stamp. Owen hadn't said anything. He mustn't have bothered to check. She made a growl in the back of her throat. Ever since they had gotten back from Italy, that boy's head had been in the clouds. Clutching it, she tossed the rest of the mail on the table and returned to the sofa where she examined the letter, turning it over. Some writing was scrawled on the back of the envelope. *I carry this letter inside my shirt to the post and that is the reason why it is all wrinkled.*

Maggie shook her head. She knew who the letter was from. Her hand was shaking as she tore it open, pulled out a single folded page, unfolded it, and read.

> *Dear Miss Maggie,*
> *I am Fabrizio. The reason I send to you this letter is because everybody knows the internet is a bullshit. In fact, Tata tells me I am an idiot and so does my brother. I want to tell you how sorry I am for what I did and how much I miss you.*
> *Please don't hate me.*
> *Sincerely Fabrizio*

Maggie held the letter to her nose, closed her eyes, and sniffed; the faint odor of his perspiration mixed with cologne went straight to her brain and transported her back to that night when he came to her room and they made love. She clutched the letter to her breasts.

An hour later Owen walked into the living room and looked at Maggie still sitting on the sofa, staring into space. "Ever since we got back from Italy your head's been in the clouds, girl."

"Me!"

"Yeah, you. You're not still angry over what happened on the boat, are you?"

"No." Maggie sat upright and casually tucked the letter into her recipe book. "As Tata said, when a man does something stupid, it usually involves his dick." She paused. "It's just...." Maggie sucked air in through her teeth.

"Talk to me."

"I know, I'm acting like a silly schoolgirl, but...." Maggie covered her face with her hands.

"But what?"

"But I can't get Fabrizio out of my mind!"

Owen flopped down on the sofa beside her and put his arm over her shoulder. "I can't stop thinking about Enrico, either."

"Man! Are we pathetic or what? Our first vacation ever and we both fall in love with two guys who run a B&B somewhere on a lake in northern Italy."

"It's ridiculous," Owen said. "We hardly even know them."

"We're like those desperate lonely people who go on vacation and think they fall in love on the beach only to find their fantasy washing out to sea with low tide."

"We really don't know anything about them," Owen said. "Maybe they're mass murderers or something."

"Are you kidding me?" Maggie threw Owen an incredulous glare. "Those two are the sweetest guys on the fucking planet!" She slid forward and got up. *Even if Fabrizio did act like an idiot*, she thought as she went to the kitchen. A few minutes later she came back with two glasses of prosecco and handed one to Owen.

"I read on the internet that it only takes four minutes to fall in love," Owen said as he took the glass.

"Well, as Fabrizio says, the internet is a bullshit." Maggie sat down next to him.

"I remember that first time I saw Jessy back in fifth grade." Owen stared at his glass. "I was in love with him at first sight."

Maggie patted Owen's knee. She didn't add that the first day when Jessy and Owen paraded into homeroom, while all eyes were trained on Jessy, it was Owen who had held her gaze and captured her heart.

She took a sip of wine. "You know, my mom and dad got engaged over the phone. They met for the first time at the airport. And look at them. Thirty years later they're still like a couple of teenagers in love."

Owen also took a sip. "Um, nice." He put his glass on the coffee table. "Think about all the people who married soldiers they hardly even knew and came here and they could barely speak American?"

Maggie sighed. "Whatever happened to the happily-ever-afters?" She took a drink.

"I don't know, maybe the internet killed romance." Owen leaned over and picked up his glass.

"What do you mean?" Maggie said.

Owen was just about to take a drink, but he paused. "We don't trust anyone anymore. We want a no-risk, money-back guarantee on our happiness!" He took a large swig.

Maggie rolled her eyes. "Well, I had to go all the way to Italy to realize that I've been stuck in liminality ever since high school?"

"What's liminality?"

"Ah, it's a word Tata used to describe when you can't move forward because you're neither here nor there. You get trapped somewhere in between."

"Ha! I guess that makes me the world expert on liminality."

Maggie just shrugged. She didn't need to explain to Owen that it was him who had trapped her.

"When you made love to Fabrizio, did you still feel like you were stuck in liminality?"

With that the tears came rolling down Maggie's cheeks. Why could Owen always see what was in her heart? She sniffled loudly and wiped her face with her sleeve. "It was like I'd found a door I'd missed," Maggie whispered. "When I stepped through it, Fabrizio was standing there on the other side waiting for me." She leaned over and buried her face in Owen's neck. "What am I going to do?"

Owen cradled her. "I'll tell you what we're going to do," Owen said tenderly. "We're going to stop pining like lovesick puppies over guys we can never have and get out there and meet somebody who we can."

Chapter Forty

"What are those men doing with that telescope and those measuring tapes?" Tata said as she stood on the terrace staring out into the garden.

"They're land surveyors. Francesca sent them to do a property estimate," Fabrizio said.

"A property estimate? What business is it of hers how much your property is worth? She's got that two-million-euro apartment in downtown Milan."

"There's something you should read." Enrico went into the house and came back with the registered letter and handed it to Tata.

"Read it for me. I don't have my glasses."

Tata held her expression flat as Enrico read the letter. When he finished, she took the letter from Enrico's hand, calmly pulled her reading glasses from the pocket in her apron, and examined it. "Mmmm" was all she said, but her heart was pounding.

"Well, our first step is to go through all those old documents and letters and see if we can find your grandmother's will," she said as if it were nothing more important or urgent than a misplaced umbrella or a lost photograph. "I'll take a look. Nothing to worry about, I'm sure."

As soon as Enrico left and went back into the house, Tata growled, "If that Milanese *putana* wants war, this Sicilian *strega* is going to give it to her." She strode back into her kitchen.

CHAPTER FORTY-ONE

"I HOPE you're not still thinking about that guy you met in Italy," Becky said. "Wait till you meet Hal. He's perfect! You'll love each other at first sight." She had insisted so much that Owen finally agreed to meet her and her friend Hal for lunch.

Becky always exaggerated and only spoke in superlatives—that's what made her a good promoter—but this time her description was pretty accurate. Hal was tall and handsome, in his early forties. He had short blond hair, meticulously styled, with high cheekbones and a strong chin. Even his polo shirt and jeans were pressed, and not just an antiwrinkle cloth out of the dryer. He smelled of expensive cologne, like the stuff they spray at you when you walk past the perfume counter in the shopping mall. Owen couldn't help but notice his teeth were unnaturally white, but that was a nice change from the tobacco-stained teeth of the guy he'd linked up with last week through Grindr.

"Let's all have the sushi platter," Becky suggested as she threw back a cup of sake, then ordered without waiting for a response.

The waiter arrived with the large platter of assorted rolls of raw fish, seaweed, and rice. While Owen and Becky picked up their chopsticks, Hal looked up at the waiter and said, "A fork please."

"Oh, try the chopsticks, honey," Becky said. "It's more authentic that way."

Hal shook his head. "No, they're not sanitary."

The waiter came back with a fork.

"*Buon appetito*," Owen said, using a new phrase he'd learned in his Italian class. He picked up a piece of salmon sushi from the platter, dipped it into his little bowl of soya and wasabi, and popped it into his mouth. As he did so, he caught sight of Hal wiping the fork clean with his napkin. Hal then selected one of each of the different pieces of sushi from the platter and carefully placed them on his plate.

Becky looked over at him. "Oh, don't worry, it's all you can eat, so we can order another platter if you're still hungry."

"No, I prefer to eat off my own plate, thank you. My ex-boyfriend always used to eat french fries from my plate. It's one of the reasons we broke up." He stabbed a tuna roll with his fork and cautiously bit into it.

"Ha! My ex used to lick chocolate syrup from my belly button." Becky laughed. "I think it's the main reason I kept him for so long."

Owen laughed along with her while Hal grimaced. For the rest of the lunch Becky orchestrated the conversation, asking questions and answering them. "Tell Owen about what you do at the law firm."

Hal swallowed. "Mostly contract law, but I focus on intellectual property and copyright."

"Copyright?" He had caught Owen's attention. "You mean like books and music?"

"Yes, sometimes, but most of it's not so artsy—business designs and industrial processes, that sort of thing."

"Oh, tell Hal about the wonderful wedding you put together for Tim Dally and Neil Burman at the Landmark Theater."

Owen chewed and swallowed.

"It was fabulous!" Becky continued. "When Tim and Neil finished their vows, twenty singers broke into that chorus from *Cats*, or was it that musical about Argentina!"

"That must have cost a lot," Hal said.

Owen nodded.

"It cost a fortune!" Becky said. "But it was worth every penny, don't you think?"

Owen blushed and chuckled. "It was lots of fun."

"Fun!" Becky poured herself another sake. "Everybody was talking about it for weeks."

Becky popped a piece of salmon sushi into her mouth and chewed. "Oh, tell Hal about your trip to Italy this summer."

"Italy?" Hal said.

"Oh yes." Owen grinned. "My friend Maggie and I did a two-week tour in July, you know the usual thing, Rome, Venice and Florence." Owen paused and furrowed his brow. "Funny, the part I liked most was the three days we spent hanging out at the lake," he said as if he were speaking to himself.

"Well of course half of Hollywood has a place on Lake Como, and I guess after that car scene in the Bond movie it's crawling with tourists,"

Hal said and stabbed another piece of sushi, sniffed it, then carefully put it in his mouth.

"No actually, we went to a tiny spot on Lago Maggiore." Suddenly, hidden behind the smell of sushi, tempura, and Hal's cologne, Owen thought he detected another scent—the smell of Enrico's neck as he clung on to him on Angelina. He imagined his arms wrapped around Enrico's waist and his thighs squeezing him tighter with every sway and swerve. Owen shivered and swallowed.

"Oh!" Becky said, "Watch out for that wasabi. It's really spicy. Look, honey, you're even sweating." She leaned forward and dabbed Owen's forehead with her napkin.

After lunch, as they stood outside the restaurant and said goodbye, at Becky's suggestion, Hal and Owen exchanged phone numbers.

CHAPTER FORTY-TWO

ENRICO AND Fabrizio waited at the foot of the terrace steps as Grazia marched down the gravel drive as if she were on a military a mission, her best friend Maria trailing behind.

"Ciao, Grazia, Maria." Enrico kissed each of the women on their cheeks.

"Ciao, Enrico," Grazia said sweetly.

"Ciao, Maria. Ciao, Grazia." Fabrizio kissed Maria's cheek, then leaned forward and kissed Grazia's cheek, but she held her head firm.

"Fabrizio," she said with a flat tone.

"You'll stay for lunch, won't you?" Fabrizio said. "I'll tell Tata you're here. She's making a big pot of *risotto al funghi*."

"No, we can't stay," Grazia snapped.

Maria, who was normally the talkative one, remained strangely silent.

"How's Luigi?" Fabrizio asked Maria.

"Fine," Maria mumbled. "He's home."

Enrico could feel the tension in the air. Something was definitely wrong. He thought about the last time he had met Luigi after the bar closed and they had fooled around in the alleyway. Had someone seen them and said something to Maria? A drip of sweat ran down from Enrico's armpit. But lots of guys fooled around, and nobody ever talked about it. Enrico bit his lip.

"What's going on? What's wrong?" Fabrizio said.

"Isn't it obvious!" Grazia's face was like stone.

Maria dropped her head and looked to the ground.

"No, what's happened?" Fabrizio said.

"I'm pregnant!" Grazia spit out the words.

"No!" both boys said with their mouths hanging open as they stared at Grazia.

"Yes, and guess who the father is?" Grazia glared at Fabrizio.

Enrico looked at his brother, who turned white and staggered backward, reaching for the cement banister to support himself.

"I thought you should know before everybody in the area finds out." Then her voice changed from bitter to sweet. "I would never pressure you into something you didn't want to do, but…." She brought her hand to her mouth and lightly bit her knuckle. "If you won't take responsibility," she sniffled, "I can always raise our baby on my own."

"No, no," Fabrizio mumbled. "I can, I mean we can…."

Enrico stepped in front of him and took Grazia in his arms. "Please, Grazia, this is a big shock. I know you must be very frightened."

"I'm ruined for marriage, you know!" she said as tears came streaming down her face.

Enrico knew that wasn't quite true, but now was hardly the time to discuss it. "It will be okay. Just give us a little time to digest all of this."

Maria, who had remained tight-lipped, suddenly spoke up. "Let's go." She took Grazia's hand and led her back to her car parked outside the gate, leaving Enrico standing beside his brother.

Chapter Forty-Three

"Sure, dinner at eight sounds great," Owen said. "Okay, I'll come by your place at seven for a glass of wine first."

Owen hung up the phone. Even if that sushi lunch with Becky had been a little awkward, Hal had actually called him. Finally, he was doing things the proper, mature way. Sure, a hookup on Grindr was fast and easy, like the drive-through window at McDonald's. But this was a real date with a complete sit-down meal. In fact, this would be his first real date ever.

All the way up in the shiny glass-and-steel elevator Owen repeated to himself, "I'm not going to talk about Italy. I'm not going to talk about Italy or Enrico." He felt the cramps in his stomach, and his hands were shaking. Just a little snort would take away all of that nervousness. The elevator stopped and the door slid open.

Hal was standing in his open doorway waiting. He was wearing a beautifully tailored light blue button-down shirt and deep blue slacks. His blue eyes sparkled, and the front of his blond hair was gelled back in a tiny wave.

"Good to see you," Hal said and leaned forward.

Owen leaned forward, too, thinking Hal was going to kiss him on the cheek but instead he kissed him on the lips. Owen flinched.

"Oh, you're a shy one," Hal said with a smile as white as the steps to the courthouse. "I like that."

Owen felt his groin twinge. He hadn't had sex for a couple of days, and he was horny. Maybe they would fool around before dinner?

"Oh, you can leave your shoes here at the door," Hal said as he gestured for Owen to come in.

Owen slipped off his loafers and held out the bottle of Valpolicella he was carrying. "I bought this in Italy this summer. It's from a small vineyard near Lake Garda in the north. Not too heavy with a fruity aftertaste." Owen made a nervous laugh.

"Ah, yes it's quite common," Hal said.

"The truth is I don't know anything about wine. I'm just repeating what Enrico told me." Oh no, he thought as the words left his mouth, he was hardly in the apartment and was talking about Italy again.

"Enrico?" Hal took the bottle and held it like one might hold a bottle of Coca-Cola or a Big Gulp.

"Oh, he's the owner of the B&B we stayed at in Italy."

"That's good to know. For a moment I thought I might have some competition." Hal had a smug look on his face.

"No, no, he's nobody, really." Owen felt his face go flushed. "I'm totally unattached." He held up both hands.

"Well don't just stand there." Hal placed the bottle of Valpolicella on the edge of the bookshelf near the door. "Come in." He turned and walked into the living room.

Owen followed and surveyed the room. It was carpeted with wall-to-wall white pile. The walls were papered cream with a delicate gold paisley design, or was it off-white? Owen could never really tell the difference. The coffee table and side tables were smoked beige glass with gold metal legs. The sofa and easy chair were also cream, and the dining room table was covered with a matching tablecloth. A large portrait of a pickle-faced woman hung in a gold Baroque frame over the sofa. Against the picture window was an artificial white Christmas tree with gold decorations.

"Wow, you're certainly ready early," Owen said.

"What do you mean?" Hal said.

"For Christmas, I mean." Owen pointed to the tree.

"Oh that," Hal said as if he'd forgotten about the tinseled tree in front of his window. "My mother and I have a competition every year for who has the best Christmas decorations." Hal touched his chest. "I always win, of course. And you? What do you do for Christmas?"

"I don't." Owen frowned.

"C'mon, everybody celebrates Christmas. Even the Jewish guy at the office gets dressed up as Santa every year." Hal paused and furrowed his brow. "You're not Jewish, are you?"

"No, I'm what you might call a recovering Christian." As Owen spoke he could almost smell the musty basement of his mother's church where he had spent every Sunday of his childhood.

"Surely a party organizer does Christmas," Hal said.

Owen looked at Hal. He couldn't understand if Hal's expression reflected disgust or bewilderment. "For my clients, but not for myself."

"We'll just have to change all that, won't we?" Hal turned toward a side table and poured two glasses of wine.

Owen braced himself. He needed to be forthright and tell Hal about his problem with coke and his support group. But not right now. Maybe during dinner, after they had gotten to know each other a little better.

Hal turned back and handed Owen a glass. "This is a chardonnay I purchased directly from the famous Larkmead Winery when I did a wine tour of the Napa Valley in September." He held up the glass and looked at it as if he were reading a message floating inside. "I'm really into California and French wines, you know." Hal looked back at Owen. "Have you been to California?" he said brightly.

Owen shook his head. "Actually, other than a school trip to Niagara Falls and that trip to Italy in July, I've never been outside New York State." Owen shrugged.

"Well then, it should be fun educating you in some of the finer things of life," Hal said.

Owen glanced down at his feet. His sock had a hole in it.

"Here." Hal raised his glass. "To new horizons." He clanked his glass against Owen's.

Owen smiled but felt his lip quiver. "To new horizons." He lifted his glass to take a drink.

"No, no, no." Hal said. "First you must swirl the wine and observe its color in the light and the way it runs down the sides of the glass. Then you sniff it like this."

Owen attempted to mimic what Hal had just done. "Like this?"

"More or less." Hal took a sip of his wine and Owen followed.

"I'm sure this is a much finer quality of wine than you were used to drinking in Italy."

Owen felt the muscles in the back of his neck tighten.

"After all, they squish the grapes with their feet, don't they?" Hal laughed.

Owen stared into his wineglass.

"Relax, I'm just joking," Hal said.

"Excuse me, I need to use your bathroom."

"My bathroom?" Hal looked uneasy.

"Yes, whenever I get nervous, I have to pee," Owen said.

Hal furrowed his brow. "Can't you wait until we get to the restaurant?"

"No. I really have to go." Owen tensed his butt and groin muscles.

"Oh, yes, of course. It's just down the corridor, first door to the left."

"Thanks," Owen said through clamped teeth as he darted down the hall.

"Use the blue guest towels, not the white ones," Hal called after him. "And I would appreciate it if you sat to pee and be sure to flush and leave the seat down, please."

"What? Does he think I was born in a barn?" Owen mumbled to himself as he stood in front of the bowl, peed, and flushed. He went over to the sink. There on the wall was a gold-framed photo of that same ratty-faced old woman. Owen looked in the mirror. The vein on his temple was bulging out, and the corner of his eye was twitching. He washed his hands carefully so as not to splash any water around, wiped the sink dry with a piece of toilet paper, and tossed it into the bowl. Then he moved to lower the seat but stopped. With a sudden flick of his wet hands he sent a splatter of water flying onto the seat and floor. He grabbed the end of the white towel hanging on the rack, wiped his hands, and left. Owen walked down the hall directly to the door, where he bent over and slipped on his shoes.

Hal was still in the living room pouring himself another glass of wine. When he heard Owen at the door he looked over and said, "What's wrong? Where are you going?"

Owen forced a smile. "I'm afraid your wine doesn't agree with me." Owen grabbed his bottle off the bookshelf and walked out the door, leaving Hal standing in the center of his living room holding a glass of fine California chardonnay.

Owen was trembling as he stood in the elevator. The doors opened, and he darted out onto the street and pulled out his cell phone. Maggie had invited a guy from her cooking course over for dinner that evening. It was her first real date and he couldn't disturb her. He scrolled down the list. There was Big Eddy's name and number.

"You call me, you little motherfucker, the minute you have a craving, and I'll be there day or night," the mountain of a man had repeated to him last evening at group. Apart from the fact that he scared the living daylights out of him, Owen knew, despite his menacing appearance, Big Eddy was someone who cared and who he could count on. Owen pressed Dial.

"Wha'chu want, motherfucker?" said a harsh voice on the other end of the line.

"You said I could call anytime," Owen stuttered.

"Where are you now?"

"Armory Square."

"Hang on! I'm in my car. I'll be there in ten," Big Eddy barked.

Big Eddy came walking up and chest-bumped Owen, causing him to stagger backward, almost dropping his bottle of wine.

"Well, if you brought that bottle for me you've just wasted your money. I'm an abstainer. Nothing stronger that coffee and tea."

"No, I brought it for my date, but it seems my taste in wine wasn't up to his standards."

Big Eddy laughed. "C'mon, there's a coffee shop just around the corner."

Owen hurried to keep step as Big Eddy marched off down West Fayette Street like he was on maneuvers in Iraq.

"Hey, can we get a couple of coffees?" Big Eddy called to the tired-looking woman behind the bar as they walked over to a small table by the dingy window, pulled out the chairs, and sat down.

"So, your date must have been a big flop, otherwise you wouldn't have called me," Eddy barked.

"I wasn't there for more than twenty minutes before he tried to train me like I was his French poodle. So I left." Owen tried to control the jitter in his voice.

Big Eddy bellowed out a laugh.

"Hey, what's that you got in your pocket?" Every muscle in Big Eddy's face tensed as he pointed to the small bulge in Owen's breast pocket. "That ain't a chunk of rock, is it?"

"No!" Owen jerked back in his chair. "It's that piece of glass I told you about at group. You know, that guy from Italy gave it to me." Owen reached into his breast pocket, pulled out the little lump, and held it up for Big Eddy to see.

"Why you carrying it around with you?"

"I don't know." Owen shrugged. "For luck, I guess. I want to put it on a chain so I can wear it round my neck."

"Well, I know a guy who makes silver jewelry. He could do it for you. Wouldn't cost a lot."

Big Eddy took the glass from Owen, held it up in the light, and examined it with one eye closed. "So if I got the story straight, this guy in Italy gave you this chunk of red glass and told you it's a piece of his heart, even though you blew his brother." Big Eddy snorted out a laugh.

"Yeah." Owen nodded. "That's the story, more or less."

"So, what're you going to do now?"

"What do you mean?"

"I mean, what're you going to do about this Italian guy?"

"Nothing. I live here and he lives on the other side of the ocean."

"So this piece of glass ain't nothing more than some cheap shit souvenir?"

Owen had a pained look on his face. "No, it has meaning."

"Man, I really don't get you queers." Big Eddy shook his head. "You wanna put this guy's heart on a chain around your neck, but you ain't gonna do nothing more 'bout it."

"C'mon, I hardly know the guy. It's not like some kind of cheap romance story. Life doesn't work that way."

"Listen, motherfucker," Big Eddy said with a tone so deep it made Owen shiver. "I'm a forty-six-year-old veteran who lost his home and his family snorting coke and smoking crack. Don't tell *me* how life works."

CHAPTER FORTY-FOUR

"BUT I don't understand! I only had sex with her once and that was three months ago. I was careful. I used a condom." Fabrizio lay on his bed holding his pillow over his head.

"I don't understand either." Enrico sat down on the edge of the bed. "But like it or not, there is a baby on the way." He put his hand on Fabrizio's shoulder. "And you, big brother, are the most likely candidate for father."

"But I don't want to marry Grazia. I don't love her," Fabrizio pleaded. "Wait!" He lifted the pillow off his head. "I have an idea!"

"What?" Enrico knew his brother's unique perspective on the world all too well, and he dreaded what was about to flow forth.

"Before you throw something at me, just listen," Fabrizio said. "Why don't you marry Grazia?"

"Me!" Enrico shoved him and stood up. "Are you insane? Why should I marry Grazia? Are you forgetting I'm gay?" Fabrizio had surpassed himself this time.

"No!" Fabrizio swung his feet around and sat upright. "Just listen to me. How many openly married gay couples do we know?"

"Antonello and Giorgio." Enrico shrugged.

"Exactly. One. And how many homosexual men married to women do we know?"

"Too many." Enrico scowled.

"Look at your fuck buddy, that asshole architect with his designer purse wife and their ugly brat." Fabrizio spit.

"Why are you attacking me!" Enrico yelled. "I'm not the one whose dick got him into trouble."

"I'm not attacking you. I'm angry. But you know as well as I do. Even if we have civil unions in Italy now, and Pride marches in every town from north to south, the church still hasn't changed and neither have people's minds." Fabrizio stood up and wrapped his arms around his brother as if he were trying to shield him from arrows. "You've already been fired from the hotel for being gay. You'll never have the same chances as me for a good job or a promotion. You won't even get respect in the street."

Enrico remained still, not knowing how to react.

"It kills me to see my little brother, the man I care for most in this world, gossiped about and sneered at behind his back, expected to stand at the end of the line and to take second best and be thankful for it." Fabrizio was trembling as he released Enrico.

"I know what you're saying." Enrico's tone was soft. "But even if I'm expected to be a *bravo ragazzo* and pretend like I'm straight and marry a woman and have kids." Enrico scowled. "I refuse to live a lie."

Fabrizio swallowed. "You know, when our egg split." He sniffled. "You got all the courage and brains and I got the crap that was left over."

Chapter Forty-Five

"This is a bottle of Barbaresco I bought when I was in Italy this summer," Maggie said as she poured the deep burgundy wine into Tony's glass, then poured one for herself. "I don't know much about wine, but Fabrizio and Enrico told me that it goes well with grilled steak, risotto with porcini mushrooms, and mild cheese." Maggie sat down on the sofa beside Tony with her ankles crossed.

"Fabrizio and Enrico?" Tony repositioned himself slightly closer to Maggie.

"Oh, sorry. They were the co-owners of this little B&B we stayed at on Lago Maggiore."

"I guess even in Italy most of the B&B's are run by gay couples, aren't they?"

Maggie frowned for a second, then forced a smile. "Yes, I guess so." She clinked her glass against Tony's and they drank.

"Oh, that's very nice, very nice indeed. I can taste it going with a cream-based pasta."

Maggie beamed. "I'm glad you like it."

"So have you decided what pasta dish you're going to present for our final?" Tony said.

Maggie took in a breath. "I'm not sure if I should go with something traditional, like a *pasta e fagioli* or maybe something a little more unusual."

"I'm going to play it safe and present a classic lasagna," Tony said. "I think I have the *besciamelle* down pat. My grandmother would be proud."

"You absolutely do." Maggie clinked Tony's glass again. "You make the best *besciamelle* in the class."

Tony gazed into her eyes. She felt her face become warm. Tony continued to stare at her, and she took another drink trying to avert his gaze.

"So what's your reason for taking this course?" Maggie said.

"To seduce women." Tony grinned wickedly and laughed.

"Touché," Maggie chuckled.

"No seriously." Tony's tone shifted. "I haven't said anything in class, but my family has a small Italian restaurant near the waterfront."

Tony paused. "Quite frankly other than the family name, garlic bread, and spaghetti with meatballs, pizza is about as Italian as we get. With the new waterfront development, I figure everything will go upscale, and I'm trying to convert us into a proper Italian bistro and wine bar." Tony took a sip. "By the way, I've taken note of this little number." He held up his glass and swirled it. "It's perfect." He took another sip "And you?"

"I work with a friend of mine doing special events, but when I was in Italy, I kind of fell in love with the place and the culture, and…." Maggie paused as the image of Fabrizio flashed through her mind.

"And?"

"And the cuisine, of course. I guess it's now my passion." She felt the tiny hairs on her nape tingle, the way they had when Fabrizio softly blew on the back of her neck before he nibbled on her earlobes. "Oh my." Maggie fanned herself. "It's warm in here." She placed her glass on the side table next to the bottle.

Tony placed his glass on the coffee table and leaned in closer. He looked directly into her eyes and held her gaze. "You know, Maggie, there's something about you. I don't know, mysterious. You're not like the other women I know."

Even if this was Maggie's first real date, she knew a come-on line when she heard one.

He placed his fingers gently under her chin and kissed her lightly on her lips. His lips weren't as full as Fabrizio's, but they were soft and welcoming. He leaned forward to kiss her again, but this time Maggie pressed her hand against his chest and he stopped abruptly. "What's wrong?"

"Nothing," Maggie said. "Everything is fine. It's just…." She shifted away.

Tony looked confused.

"I want to take this slowly."

"Why, what's the problem? You got a crazy ex-husband, a kid asleep in the next room? No, I got it. You're a lesbian?" Tony jested.

"Sorry to disappoint you. I'm not a lesbian." Maggie inhaled deeply and braced herself. "It's just I've been in love with my roommate for years…." Maggie scrunched up her face.

Tony sat back and held up his hands.

Maggie waved her hand. "Don't worry, he's gay."

"Ah." Tony snorted out a laugh. "Well, what you need is a real man, then."

Maggie felt all the blood drain from her face as he moved in close to kiss her again, this time reaching for her breast, but he bumped the table with his foot and knocked his glass over. The rich burgundy liquid ran across the table and trickled onto the floor.

Maggie shifted away, leaned forward, and set it upright. "You know," she said flatly and stood up, "I don't think this is going to work."

Tony frowned. "If you don't want to have sex, why did you bother to invite me over in the first place!" He stood up. "Man, I don't get you fag hags." He stomped to the door and grabbed his coat from the hook. "See you in class," he blurted out as he left.

Maggie swallowed, hardened herself, rose, and walked calmly to the door. She looked out and secured the lock. Then she returned to the sofa and sat down again, reached over, took the bottle, and poured herself another glass. Her hand was trembling as she slowly raised it to her lips. She stopped, placed the glass on the coffee table, flopped over, and buried her face in the pillow.

Chapter Forty-Six

ENRICO LOOKED over at his brother curled up in his bed. He hadn't left the room in days. Enrico wished there were something he could do or say that would make things better, but an unexpected baby had the power to change everyone's life. He pictured Grazia standing defiantly in the driveway. She was understandably mad, but there was also something else in her attitude, something insincere or contrived. He pictured Maria cowering behind Grazia. Strange, Maria was usually the gregarious one, but she seemed to be in shock. And when Fabrizio had asked about Luigi, Maria looked as if she were about to burst into tears. There was definitely more to the story, and somehow Maria and Luigi were involved. It was Friday night and Maria would be at the bar, as usual, waiting for Luigi to finish his shift.

"I can't sleep. I'm going to the Old Milano. Be back in a few hours," Enrico said as he got up out of bed. Fabrizio just made a moan of acknowledgment but said nothing. Enrico slipped on a pair of jeans, grabbed the keys to Angelina, and left the room.

Twenty minutes later Enrico walked up to Maria, who was sitting alone in a dark corner of the patio typing on her cell phone with an empty cocktail glass beside her. "Here, after the big news I thought we could both use a drink." He placed a large pink cocktail next to her.

"What's this?" She looked up from her phone. Her eyes were red as if she'd been crying.

"Sex on the beach." Enrico grimaced. "Oh, maybe that wasn't the best choice, was it?"

"No." Maria scowled. "It's perfect. Absolutely perfect!" She spit out the words.

"Here's to mistakes," Enrico said and clinked his glass against hers.

Maria scoffed, grabbed the straws and tossed them on the patio pavement. "Mistakes." She threw back half the cocktail.

"Fabrizio is my brother, and Grazia has been your best friend forever." Maria snorted and drained her glass.

Enrico took a long draw on his straw. "How long has she known?"

Maria looked back at Enrico with the expression of someone whose dreams had just been shattered and replaced with disillusion.

"Maria, we've known each other since grade school. Talk to me," Enrico said.

"All I ever wanted to do was marry Luigi and have some babies. Is that too much to ask for?" She took out a cigarette and lit it, then leaned back in her chair and blew out a stream of smoke. "Four months. She's four months pregnant."

Enrico raised one eyebrow. "And so?"

"And so, Fabrizio's not the father." Her face was like stone. "Is that what you wanted to hear?"

"The father is...."

"Luigi!" Maria bent forward, hiding her face in her hands.

Enrico stood up, took the cigarette from her fingers.

"But what can I do?" she sobbed. "I still love him."

Enrico put his arm around her shoulders. "Come on. I'll walk you home."

After dropping Maria off, Enrico hurried back to the bar where he'd parked Angelina. He was sorry for Maria, and for Grazia, too, but Fabrizio would be more than relieved to hear that Luigi was the father, not him. As Enrico straddled the bike his phone beeped. He whipped it out. It was a message from his architect fuck buddy.

I need my ass pounded.

Where and when? Enrico typed.

Usual spot in ten minutes.

Enrico revved Angelina's engine and swerved out onto the lakeshore road. Just a quickie on the way home. Why not? But he could come up with a lot of reasons why not. He emerged out of the gallery tunnel, at the small parking area alongside the roadway, where he spotted the familiar blue Lancia in the far corner. Enrico let off on the gas and glided up behind the car. The passage door swung open. Just as he was about to climb off Angelina, Enrico paused. He thought about sitting next to Owen on the dock that first morning and how he'd longed to kiss him. Enrico was horny, but the guy sitting there in the car wasn't who he was horny for.

Enrico gunned the gas, sending a spray of gravel out behind the back wheel, veered around, and sped off down the lakeshore road toward Castelveccana and home. From now on, the architect would just have to find someone else to pound his ass.

Chapter Forty-Seven

"I KNOW I can run off at the mouth a little bit, but isn't that what you're supposed to do on a date? Talk." Ian ran his hand through his hair.

Owen smiled and nodded as he sat perched on the barstool nursing his beer at Wolf's Den.

"Anyway, as I was telling you," Ian continued. "My ex is an English professor at the university. He's thirty-nine, a good ten years older than me." Ian seemed to want to emphasize their age difference.

"One weekend, after we'd been together for almost three years, he invited me to come with him to Chicago to meet his parents. Only he failed to mention that the reason we were going to his parents' that weekend was because it was his sister's wedding. Even worse." Ian took a slurp of his drink from the straw and swallowed quickly as if he were afraid his story might be interrupted. "He hadn't told them he was gay! Can you imagine their reaction when I showed up at the door?"

"It sure sounds like a recipe for disaster." Owen shook his head.

"Well, he introduced me as—" Ian made quotation marks in the air. "—his friend!"

Owen took his cue and curled his lip disapprovingly.

"That evening, when it came time for the wedding rehearsal, John said he had a migraine and that I could stand in for him. So off I went with his mom and dad, sister, and his old grandmother while he stayed at the house."

There was something suspiciously familiar about this story, Owen thought.

"Now, of course I wasn't there, but it seems as if, while we were all out at the rehearsal, John went upstairs and put on his sister's wedding dress, veil, and shoes—I don't know how he fit into her shoes other than his sister has these enormous feet—anyway, I guess he was prancing around in the outfit and the heel of the shoe must have caught on the hem of the dress and John went tumbling down the stairs and hit his head."

Yes, he had heard this story many times before. Usually the teller claimed it happened to a close friend or even a cousin.

"So, when we came back and his parents opened the front door, they found John lying spread-eagle at the foot of the stairs, unconscious, with a gash to his head and the wedding dress up around his tits."

Owen laughed and took a sip of his beer.

"And you can't imagine what happened next."

On the contrary, Owen knew exactly what happened next.

"His sister took one look at her brother lying there in her wedding dress and screamed, 'You've ruined everything!'" Ian said with a high-pitched squeal in his voice. "And she leapt over John and ran hysterically up the stairs with her mother chasing after her." Ian took a quick draw on his straw and continued, "His father dropped to his knees beside John to check if he was still breathing. Then he turned to me and said, 'We better get him to the emergency room. Help me carry him to the car, would you?' Can you believe it?"

Of course, Owen couldn't believe it, but he nodded approval anyway.

"But wait, this is the best part. John's father then told John's grandmother to go upstairs and help calm the women down. Well, that old lady just looked back at him and said, 'There's no way I'm missing this. I'm coming to emergency with you!' I could have died!"

Owen laughed along with Ian. Even if the story was an old urban myth, Ian told it with such enthusiasm that it was easy to believe it might have really happened to him.

"Needless to say, I broke up with him in the car on the way back to Syracuse." Ian took another sip from his drink. "So what about you? What about your last disaster?"

Owen immediately thought about that fateful boat trip with Fabrizio. "Well, he wasn't my boyfriend, but I made a big mistake."

"Why? What happened?" Ian leaned in close with a look of conspiratorial curiosity pasted on his long skinny face.

Owen sucked in air through his teeth. "I blew his brother."

"Ohhh!" Ian pulled back and made a sour face like he'd just smelled a fart. "That's not good." He shook his head disapprovingly. There was an uneasy silence. "Listen, I should tell you about what happened to my other boyfriend before him…."

While Owen drank his second beer Ian recounted a nightmarish tale of the year he lived with his bisexual lover and his lover's wife in the same house in suburbia. By midnight Owen had drained his glass. He slid off his barstool, leaned over, kissed Ian on the cheek, and offered him the usual excuse. "It was nice to meet you, but unfortunately I have an early morning."

Owen really did intend on going home, but he got sidetracked. It was still early, and he was horny. Why not pop into the Clinton Street Spa and get a little action in the sauna?

As Owen walked in through the front door, there wedged against the corner by the reception desk was a five-foot-high plastic copy of Michelangelo's *David*. He'd never realized how much faux Italian stuff there was in Syracuse. Even the city was named after Tata's home in Sicily! Owen groaned, turned, and hurried back out the door toward home.

A half hour later, Owen lay in bed with his cell phone in his hand scrolling down the icons on his screen.

Grindr? Delete.

Tinder? Delete.

Then he went to his telephone lists.

Hal? Definitely delete.

Ian? Well, maybe not. He was a nice guy even if he talked incessantly.

Big Eddy? No, Big Eddy would break his legs if he deleted him.

Suddenly, an old address popped up. *Lago B&B*. He was just about to hit Delete when he paused and sent a happy face emoji, instead.

"Shit! Why did I do that?" he said out loud.

Within seconds a wave emoji popped up.

Owen's hand was shaking. He typed, *Enrico or Fabrizio?*

Less than a minute later a message appeared. *The one without the scar.*

Owen turned his head and looked over at his night table. There, sitting next to his alarm clock was the lump of red glass on a silver chain. He held it up in the light that was coming through his bedroom window from the streetlight outside. Its ruby color was so deep that the light could barely penetrate it. What could he possibly say to Enrico?

CHAPTER FORTY-EIGHT

"GOOD. SO, are you going to pay Francesca the money you owe her, or will we have to sell the house?" Pietro's tone was curt.

"Sell the house?" Fabrizio's voice rose. "We can't sell the house! Where will we live?"

"That's not your sister's concern. According to the law, Francesca has the right to one-third of her grandmother's entire estate," Pietro said as if he were giving a lecture on Italian inheritance law.

"But Grandmother left the apartment to Francesca and the house to us," Fabrizio pleaded.

"She left Francesca the apartment long before she died, so it's not part of the inheritance," Pietro insisted.

"And what about the bank account that Grandmother left us?" Fabrizio shot back.

"What bank account?" Pietro's tone had gone from curt to belligerent. "I don't recall any bank account."

Fabrizio took in a deep breath. "Just let me speak with Francesca and I'm sure we can get this all straightened out."

"She's not in Milan. She's spending the next two weeks at the spa in San Moritz." Pietro's voice dripped with theatrical tragedy.

"Can I phone her there?" Fabrizio's voice was trembling.

"I think you've already caused her enough emotional stress with your ugly attempt to cheat her out of her birthright."

"But...."

"You'll hear from her lawyer. Goodbye." Pietro hung up.

As Fabrizio lay in bed, what Pietro had said kept rolling over and over again in his mind. Surely there must be some kind of misunderstanding. If only they could talk to Francesca, they could straighten everything out.

CHAPTER FORTY-NINE

STRANGE, I can't find that pair of underwear I lent you last summer, the message read.

A wicked smile spread across Owen's face as he stretched out on the bed like a cat. *I'm wearing them*, he typed.

Send them back!

No way! I'm keeping them. Owen ran his hand down his abdomen and over his crotch. *I'll send you a pair of mine if you want?* He chuckled.

Yes! But don't wash them!

With a surge, Owen's penis became hard, peeking out from the top of the underwear. *Are you alone?*

Not exactly. Fabrizio is asleep in the other bed. How about you?

I'm in my room. Owen was so horny he was shaking. *Maggie's not back from her cooking classes yet, and….*

And?

I have a little problem. Owen rubbed his hand across his chest.

What?

I have some uncomfortable swelling. And you're the cause. Owen caressed his stomach.

And so, what's the problem?

I'm right-handed. Owen's hand trembled.

Type with your left hand.

Couldn't we just Skype? Owen pictured Enrico naked on his bed.

It's not the same. Besides….

Besides what? Owen wondered if maybe he'd gone a little too far.

I want you to suffer. Close your eyes and imagine me touching you.

Oh, yes! Owen reached into his underwear and grabbed his hard cock. *I'm suffering now.*

Good boy. So am I.

Ohhhhh. Owen pumped.

I'm rolling my tongue over your swollen head and running my lips down your shaft.

Yes, yes, I'm going crazy! Don't stop! It was as if Enrico were really there with him.

Now I'm licking your big hairy balls.

He could almost feel Enrico's tongue. *Oh, oh, I'm coming.*

So am I! ahhh$%)?....

What was that? Owen was barely able to strike the letters.

I dropped the phone.

Opps! I got a little on my screen. Owen smirked and wiped his screen with the corner of his sheet.

Oh no! Fabrizio just rolled over.

Owen shook his head.

He says hello.

Say hi to Fabrizio for me. Owen rolled his eyes.

Fabrizio says to give Maggie a kiss from him.

Owen chuckled. *Tell the heteros to do their own sex chat!!!*

CHAPTER FIFTY

"WHERE'S TATA?" Enrico said as he came down to the kitchen and found his brother standing in front of the stove making coffee.

"I don't know. She left early this morning. Said she had something important to do." Fabrizio took the Moka pot off the burner and poured the coffee into two tiny cups. "Listen, I talked to Pietro yesterday and…."

"And what?" Enrico said.

"And it looks like we're going to lose the house…."

TATA WALKED up the steep hill and past the cemetery and the church with a large brown envelope firmly clutched in her hand. She turned right and walked up the street past the grand villas that had recently been restored. She held her back straight, her shoulders relaxed, and her head high— dignified and self-assured without any suggestion of arrogance or conceit— the way the boys' mother used to, even in the final days of her pregnancy with Francesca. At the end of the street stood the grandest villa of all, not so much for its architecture but for its sweeping gardens, positioned on the peak of the hill overlooking the bay of Castelveccana.

She approached the gate. Dott. *Gaetano Pozzi, Notaio*, was printed above the buzzer. Tata knew the family well. Old man Pozzi had been a notary, and so it was only natural that his son, Gaetano, followed in his footsteps. She smoothed her dress and pressed the buzzer. The gate clicked open. After all, she was expected. She walked in and along the gravel lane lined with northern palms, toward the house.

Gaetano and Tata had met when they were only seventeen. But what could a boy from the best family on this side of the lake possibly have seen in a domestic servant girl from Sicily? After that summer of first love, Gaetano went to university in Milan, and Tata, of course, remained at the lake looking after the old woman. Eventually Gaetano's family introduced him to his wife-to-be, a beautiful woman from a respectable Milanese family.

Years later, on a breezy summer's afternoon, much like the one when they first met, Tata stood at the foot of the steps of the church bouncing baby Enrico and baby Fabrizio in their pram and watching as Gaetano and his bride emerged from the church to a hailstorm of rice. He was so handsome in his black tuxedo and she was so lovely in her white gown with her veil flowing behind her.

Then baby Enrico began to fuss, and Tata bent over and put the chew-chew back in his mouth and tucked the blanket in around baby Fabrizio's neck. By the time she looked up again, the bride was standing in front of the open door of a black Mercedes decorated with flowers. She launched her bouquet in the air and a small horde of desperate-looking single women pounced upon it like a pride of lionesses on a gazelle. Tata smiled, turned, and wheeled the pram around and back down the steep street toward home. It was feeding, changing, and nap time.

His wife's funeral was the last time she had seen Gaetano. After that, while Tata had been busy raising two boys and looking after their aging grandmother, Gaetano buried himself in work. Maybe those were just excuses they used to protect themselves from a story that could never be. But that was such a long time ago.

Gaetano was now bald and had a paunch, but his eyes were still as blue as she remembered. After an hour, Tata left the grand house with the taste of coffee still on her tongue. In her hand she held a copy of the original document she had left behind with him. As she walked down the hill toward home, her feet felt much lighter than they had walking there. She entered the kitchen, where she found the boys hunched over at the kitchen table.

"Here." She placed the envelope in front of them.

"What's this?" Enrico looked up.

"It's a registered copy of your grandmother's will and testament."

"Where did you find it?" Fabrizio said.

"In that old trunk in the back. It's still full of your grandmother's stuff."

Enrico opened the envelope and extracted the pages. Fabrizio pressed up against his shoulder.

Enrico smoothed it flat and they began to read. "It says clearly that the apartment in Milan goes to Francesca."

"And the house goes to us," Fabrizio added.

Tata pointed to the bottom of the page. "It's signed by your grandmother and witnessed by old Giusseppe Trota. He was the village mayor at the time." Tata tapped her finger on the signature.

"But look here," Enrico said. "It also says that since the market value of the apartment is more than twice the value of the house, Grandmother left us the difference in a bank account."

"But…," Fabrizio started.

"Francesca claims there was no money?" Enrico finished.

"Well, now it's time to talk with a lawyer." Not since she had marched up to the church to confront that priest who had insisted Enrico make private confession in his study had she been so angry, but outwardly, Tata remained calm and composed. Francesca was their sister, if only by half.

"First I need to change into something more practical and prepare some lunch," Tata said in a casual tone.

While the two boys remained at the table examining the document, she walked out of the kitchen and went to her room. They didn't see her crack her knuckles or hear her mutter, "Nobody messes with my boys." Then she stopped in her tracks and pressed her finger to her lips. "Hmmm," she said to herself. "I wonder if the revenue police would be interested in knowing about Francesca and Pietro's frequent trips back and forth to Switzerland."

CHAPTER FIFTY-ONE

CHEF NERI put the fork of spaghetti alla bolognese in his mouth and chewed. Then paused, put a serviette to his lips, and spat into it. The young man standing behind the bowl of pasta had a terrified look on his face.

Chef Neri dropped the wad of serviette onto the table in front of him. "A glass of water please, so I can wash the taste out of my mouth."

The instructor handed Chef Neri a glass of sparkling water. He took a large swig, swished, and spit it back into the glass. "When you start with canned ingredients you end up with canned spaghetti."

He stepped over to Tony, who was standing behind a plate of lasagna.

Chef Neri examined the dish. Then he bent over and sniffed. "Heavy on the garlic."

"I only used…." Tony trailed off as he caught the instructor waving his hand vigorously behind Chef Neri's back.

Chef Neri took a fork and tapped the surface of the cheese. "Is this real Parmigiano-Reggiano?"

"Yes, sir," Tony said.

Chef Neri dipped the fork in and lifted out a small slice. He put it in his mouth, stared at the ceiling, and chewed slowly. "The pasta is slightly overdone, but the béchamel is smooth and creamy."

He looked directly at Tony. "What wine do you recommend with this?"

"Wine?"

"Yes, wine, or perhaps you recommend Pepsi Cola?" he barked.

"No, er, wine, yes. What about a bottle of Barbaresco?"

Chef Neri said nothing. He walked over to Maggie, examined her dish, then looked at her. "*Pasta all'arrabiata*? Are you angry about something, my dear?"

"Yes, a little." Maggie nodded.

"Well, let's just see how angry your angry pasta really is." He picked up the fork and flicked the pasta lightly, then he bent down over the dish and sniffed. "Hmm, basil, peppers." He squinted, cocked his head sideways, and looked back at Maggie again. "Do I smell mint?"

"Yes, sir, just a sprig."

He picked up a piece of pasta, examined it closely, then put it in his mouth and closed his eyes and chewed. He swallowed and breathed in deeply.

"Mmm! And for the main course what do you suggest?"

"Eye of pork chop, dressed with a slice of baked apple," Maggie said without hesitation.

"Why?"

"Because the pork is robust enough to balance the *rabbia* of the pasta, and the apple is sweet enough to calm the fire."

Chef Neri raised one eyebrow.

"And for wine?"

Maggie drew in a deep breath. "I'd recommend an aromatic wine, like a dry Riesling or a possibly a semi-aromatic wine like sauvignon blanc."

"Why?" His tone was clipped.

Maggie swallowed. "Because the fruitiness works well with spicy foods, sir."

Chef Neri turned and faced the other candidates. "Any half-decent pizza cook with a timer, a pot of boiling water, and salt can cook pasta." Then he turned back toward Maggie. "But you, my dear woman, understand the emotion of the food." He cupped his hands. "Which, of course, is the essence of Italian cuisine."

"Yes, sir." Maggie nodded.

"What restaurant are you with?"

"None, sir."

"Good! Be at my restaurant tomorrow, 10:00 a.m. sharp."

"What for?" Maggie squeaked out.

"You're my new chef in training." He picked up the bowl of pasta, walked over to the central table, and sat down. "Now somebody get me a glass of Riesling to accompany this fine dish."

CHAPTER FIFTY-TWO

Dear Mr. Tun,
I am Fabrizio. I have twenty-four years and I have
no diseases and no police records. I am very pleased
to tell you that I have recently discovered I have not
fathered any children (although I believe I am fertile).
I am a good man and I can work hard. I love your
daughter Maggie and I am writing for your permission to
ask her to marry me.
Sincerely, Fabrizio.

"Are you mentally damaged?" Enrico said as he read the screen over his brother's shoulder.

"What?" Fabrizio said. "Stop criticizing and check my English for me."

"Okay, now I'm convinced Tata dropped you on your head."

"Now that I don't have to marry Grazia, I want to tell Maggie that I love her and want to marry her." Fabrizio reached up and scratched his head nervously. "But I don't know how I'm supposed to do that!"

"Do you think we live in the 1800s or something? Get on the phone and call her!" Enrico held out his phone.

"And what do I say?" He didn't move to take the phone from his brother's hand.

"Tell her how you feel."

"And what if she says no?"

Enrico grabbed the arm of the chair and spun Fabrizio around to face him. "And what if she says yes?" Enrico batted his brother's shoulder. "Look, you hardly even know her."

"So you're telling me to forget her?"

Enrico immediately thought about Owen and felt a twinge in his stomach and a ping in his loins. "No, all I'm saying is slow down a bit. Give it time."

"You know, everybody thinks I'm a cool guy with the women."

"Trust me, nobody thinks that!" Enrico said.

Fabrizio ignored his brother. "But the truth is, other than a few quickies and that time with Grazia, I've never been good with women."

"What are you telling me that I don't already know?" Enrico said.

"Then there was that night with Maggie. It was the only time I've ever really felt like I was making love."

"Look, she's an intelligent woman and I'm sure she knows what a great guy you are." Enrico waved the phone in front of his brother's face. "Even if you are a *cretino*."

Fabrizio sat there staring at the screen, chewing his lip. "I'm scared."

CHAPTER FIFTY-THREE

YOU COULD come to Syracuse? Owen's hands were sweaty.

Maybe for a short visit someday, Enrico wrote.

No, I mean forever! We could be together. His hand was now quivering as it hovered over the Send button. Not since he had confessed his love for Jessy had he been so direct and honest about his feelings. He pressed Send.

I can't leave Tata and Papà? Enrico replied almost instantly.

Fabrizio is there with them.

Fabrizio is the adventurer, not me. I'm just a simple lake boy.

We have lots of beautiful lakes in America. I live just south of Lake Ontario!

There was a pause. Owen waited. After about a minute a message appeared.

It's hard to explain. You're from a big, sophisticated American city, but I was born in the tiny town of Castelveccana. Lago Maggiore is more than my home, it's who I am.

Owen jabbed at the keys. *But I want to be with you! I want us to be together. I want to try!*

Remember that silly story I told you about the princess in the tower?

Yes. Owen felt his throat grow tight.

Please don't ask me to leave. My heart would shatter like glass.

Owen stared at the message, not knowing how to respond.

A moment later a message followed. *Good night, sweet prince.*

Owen placed his phone on the nightstand and tried to swallow the lump in his throat.

Two minutes later Owen's phone beeped. He snatched it up off the table. Maybe Enrico had changed his mind. Owen punched the WhatsApp icon.

Jessy?

He opened the message.

Hey buddy, sorry for not answering back, but California is like a black widow. She makes love to you, then eats you whole. We've been working day and night on the script and it's a go! I've decided to transfer here permanently. You'd love it! California has it all, except for one thing. You. And I miss you like my runaway shadow. Come out here and move in with me? The Jessy-Owen duo forever!

IT WAS well after midnight when Big Eddy and Owen walked into the all-night coffee shop on West Fayette Street. "Hey, are you hungry? They got some muffins and cakes and things."

"Yeah, maybe I'll have some tiramisu," Owen said.

"Make that two and two coffees," Big Eddy said to the tired-looking woman behind the counter.

They went over and sat down at the table in front of the window that looked out onto the street.

"So, you're wearing a piece of the Italian guy's heart around your neck and this other guy in California wants you to be his shadow, right?" Big Eddy sat down.

"Yeah, that's more or less it," Owen said as he sat down across from Big Eddy.

"Now that's what I call karma. Let me see that chunk of glass again."

Owen slipped the chain over his head and handed it to Big Eddy. "You don't really believe life works like that, do you?" Owen said.

"Listen, motherfucker, for most of my life I believed in nothing and no one. And that's exactly what life gave me. Nothing!" Big Eddy held the blob of glass up to the light and stared at it like it had magical powers. "Then one day I looked at myself lying there, dirty and miserable and I said, Big Eddy, with nothing, you got nothing else to lose. So—Allah, God, Fate, and Karma—call it what you want." Big Eddy handed the pendant back to Owen. "Why not believe in it all?"

The woman came over and placed two cups of coffee and two bowls of tiramisu on the table.

Owen looked at the dessert.

"What's wrong?" Big Eddy hunched over his bowl and shoveled a spoonful into his mouth.

"Whipped cream with a cherry on top?"

"Eat up. It's good."

Owen pushed aside the whipped cream until he could see a piece of sponge cake buried below. He raised his spoon to his mouth and tasted it cautiously. "Yuck! Instant coffee." He made a sour face and put his spoon down.

"Tastes good to me," Big Eddy said as he shoveled the last spoonful into his mouth, then looked over at Owen's bowl. "Hey, if you ain't gonna eat that, give it to me."

"Be my guest." Owen slid the bowl over to Big Eddy.

Big Eddy dug his spoon in and shoveled a mound of whipped cream into his mouth. "In the army you learn to take what they give you," he said as he swallowed.

"It's just, once you've had a taste of the real thing." Owen shrugged. "It kind of ruins you for the rest."

Big Eddy looked up from his bowl. "Are we still taking about the dessert or something else, here?"

Owen let out a breath. "I don't know."

"Listen up." Big Eddy licked the last of the whipped cream off his spoon. "I got a question for you. What kind of gambling man are you?"

Owen frowned. "What do you mean?"

"I mean are you the type of man who goes with the odds, pulls the arm of that same old slot machine one more time, and heads out to California, or do you change games, risk it all, and go over to Italy and see if you can hit the jackpot?"

"I've never even been to a casino," Owen said.

"Oh, but wait! There's a third game." Big Eddy held his fat finger in the air.

"What's that?"

"Do nothing." Big Eddy swept his hand. "Look around you. Your happily-ever-after is right here with me and the rest of us fools who are too frightened to ever gamble on the real thing."

Owen glanced back at the woman behind the bar, the man in the old trench coat holding his cup with both hands, and the boy sitting in the booth peeling the label off his bottle of Bud. "I'm not much of a gambling man," Owen said.

"Sure you are." Big Eddy nodded. "That white powder you so happily sucked up your nose was probably smuggled into the country inside someone's butthole, then cut with baking soda and maybe some laundry soap and who knows what else." Big Eddy hunched his massive shoulders. "So you've already proven you like to gamble against the odds, haven't you?"

"I thought you were supposed to be helping me?"

"Look, motherfucker, I got way too much hair on my back to be your fairy godmother, so you're gonna have to figure this one out on your own."

With the pendant held tightly in his fist, Owen looked out the grungy window onto the dark empty street. The full moon painted the pavement and buildings with a silvery hue. He opened his fist and stared down at the piece of glass. Suddenly his face burst into a smile. "Give me a ride to the airport?" Owen didn't wait for an answer as he sprang to his feet. "Got to stop by the house and pick up my stuff first." Owen paused and looked at Big Eddy. "How did you get so wise?"

"In the army."

"The army?"

"Yeah, after the shit I saw in Iraq…." Big Eddy stood up, scraping his chair loudly against the floor. "If you're not already brain-dead, the army will eventually wise you up."

CHAPTER FIFTY-FOUR

"CIAO, LITTLE brother," that familiar voice dripped over the line.

"Ciao, Francesca." Fabrizio's tone was steady and guarded. "How are you?"

"Not good, not good at all." Francesca's voice was heavy and throaty. "I suppose you've heard the awful news."

"That depends on what you're referring to." Fabrizio tried to hold back any tone of anger from his voice.

"Oh, yes. I'm sure you have enough worries of your own without concerning yourselves about me."

Fabrizio said nothing.

"Well, I just wanted to call. I haven't heard from you in so long." Francesca paused. "How is Tata and your papà?"

"Everyone is fine, thank you," Fabrizio said coldly.

Francesca took in a large breath of air. "Listen, dear brother, do you remember when you and Enrico asked to borrow money from me?" She made a nervous little laugh. "Well, it seems that Pietro and I have run into a little financial problem and, well…." She paused again. "I need to ask you for a small loan," she said, rushing out the words. "Fifty thousand should be fine."

"Ahhh," Fabrizio started. "Francesca, you are the only sister we have—"

"Just a short-term loan," she interrupted.

"Of course, we would help you if—"

She cut him off again. "Oh, I knew I could count on you, little brother."

"But we don't have any money either. Right now, we are living off Papà's pension and hopefully in the spring, the B&B will get going."

"Well, what about me!" She slurred out the words like she'd been drinking.

"I'm really sorry, Francesca," Fabrizio said.

Suddenly Francesca's voice became hostile. "That *cretino*, Pietro, got caught for trying to hide money in Switzerland. The revenue police have frozen our bank accounts and repossessed the

BMW." She made a little gasp. "I don't even have enough money to pay the condominium fees!"

"I wish we could help, but as you know our bank account has been frozen, too, until the revenue police have finished their investigation, so as I said we only have Papà's pension and...."

"This is all your fault!" she screeched. "You and your brother and your *frocio* father killed my mother!" The phone went dead.

CHAPTER FIFTY-FIVE

OWEN STORMED into the house. "Maggie!" he hollered.

"What's wrong!" Maggie burst out of her bedroom.

"Nothing." He scooped her up in his arms and swung her around.

"Put me down." Maggie's tone was serious. "Before you say anything more, there's something you need to see first."

Owen lowered Maggie to the floor. He furrowed his brow. "What's happened? What's wrong?"

"Come with me." She took his hand and led him into her bedroom.

"Read this," she said, pointing to her screen.

"What is it?"

Maggie's hand trembled as she scrolled down her email page. "I need to know what you think."

A feeling of dread swept over Owen as he pulled out the chair, sat down, and read.

> *Dear Maggie,*
> *We do not know each other for a long time but I can't stop thinking about you and I want you to come to Italy and marry with me. My brother told me to phone you and tell you how I feel but I'm too frightened you will say no, so I write you an email, instead.*
> *Love Fabrizio*
> *P.S. This is not a bullshit. I want to be your man.*

"Oh, honey." Owen voice was filled with tenderness. He looked up at Maggie and smiled. "So, are you going to go to Italy?"

"I can't! I just started my apprenticeship with Chef Neri. I'll never get a chance like this again as long as I live!" She looked as if she were on the edge of tears.

"And you'll never find a man like Fabrizio as long as you live."

"What am I going to do?" She broke into sobs.

Owen lifted her chin and looked her directly in the eyes. "Easy, you're going to write him back and tell him to get a visa, hop on the next flight, and come here."

Maggie's chest heaved and she sniffled. "You really think he'd do that?"

"If he's smart enough to know how lucky he is, he will."

Maggie nodded and continued to sniffle.

"Now dry your eyes and blow your nose. Big Eddy's waiting outside in the car. I just came home to get my toothbrush and a change of socks and underwear."

Maggie eyed Owen suspiciously. "You're not going to do what I think you're going to do, are you?"

"Do you remember that twenty-foot diving tower at the pool where Jessy used to lifeguard?"

"Yeah, of course. Norman Elgin pushed me off. I did a massive belly flop and was red for a week after."

"Well, I can't tell you the number of times I stood on the end of that board with Jessy coaxing me to dive off, and when I finally did, I almost drowned myself." Owen nodded.

"And?"

"Massive belly flop or not, I'm about to dive off the end of that tower headfirst, once again!" Now Owen was having trouble holding back the tears.

"So, you still haven't told me, is that tower facing west toward California or east toward Italy?"

"Honey, do you really need to ask?" Owen beamed.

Maggie smiled back at him. "You know," she said. "You're the only person who's ever made me wonder what it would be like if I had been a gay guy."

"And you're the only person who's ever made me regret I wasn't born straight." He wrapped her in his arms and held her tight against his chest.

CHAPTER FIFTY-SIX

"THEY'RE HERE!" Enrico ran up to open the gate.

A red Fiat 500 ran over the stone at the edge of the garden, flattening the hydrangea as it pulled in and drove down the lane. It jerked to a halt and stalled. Fabrizio got out of the driver's side and stood leaning against his open door, with a smile as wide as the lake. Enrico ran down the lane and the two boys embraced.

The passenger door flew open and Maggie stepped out. She was wearing a knee-length khaki skirt, tan pumps, and a beige cotton blouse. Her black hair glistened down to her shoulders.

"Who is that breathtaking woman standing in our driveway?" Owen called out as he ran up, wrapped his arms around her, and swung her in the air. "Sous-chef. Wow! Big promotion. Congratulations."

"What happened?" Enrico said as he held his brother back and looked him up and down. Fabrizio was wearing a pair of Levis, cowboy boots, and a Ralph Lauren plaid shirt. "Were you kidnapped by cowboys?"

"Hey, it's American style." Fabrizio held up his thumbs. "I start business school at Syracuse U as soon as we get back, and I want to make a good impression."

"Oh, my heavens!" Maggie said. "The house looks gorgeous! Even better than the photos!"

"Ahh, we've still got a mountain of work to do, but just wait till you see the tower," Owen said as he took Maggie's hands in his. "Hey, you better be careful or you'll dislocate your shoulder wearing a rock like that on your finger." He held up her hand and examined her engagement ring.

"Oh, by the way, Big Eddy sends his love," Maggie said. "We went to his graduation just before we left. Top of his class at Law Enforcement and Security Guard College." Maggie shook her head. "You know, that was the first time I've heard a valedictorian speech start out with the phrase, 'Listen up, motherfuckers.'"

"Oh, I heard from Jessy!" Owen said. "They've just finished a script treatment and they're pitching it to George at his place on Lake Como, so Jessy will be spending a few days with us afterwards."

On the other side of the car it was as if Enrico and Fabrizio had never parted. "What about Grazia's baby?"

"Well it turns out Maria is unable to have children of her own, and so she and Luigi have adopted Grazia's baby. Funny how things work out, eh?"

Fabrizio's face became serious. "What about Papà?"

Enrico shrugged and nodded. "He's the same. He asks about you. You were always his favorite boy, you know."

Fabrizio held Enrico's face in his hands, and they touched foreheads the way they always used to do. "And you will always be my favorite boy, little brother."

"I know." Enrico shot a glance over at Owen and winked. "Just don't tell my husband. Now c'mon, there's a little old Sicilian lady in the kitchen whose been cooking for three days straight, and she's dying to see you."

A long-distance romance never works, so some say. It will rob you of your sanity and drain you of your money. In 1997, MARK DAVID CAMPBELL met Piero Salvioni on a rock in Mykonos, where they spent less than forty-eight hours together but stayed in touch. After a four-year long-distance relationship between Toronto and Milan, Mark finally moved to Italy, and more than twenty years later, they are still together, dividing their time between their apartment in Milan and the house at Lago Maggiore.

Also from Dreamspinner Press

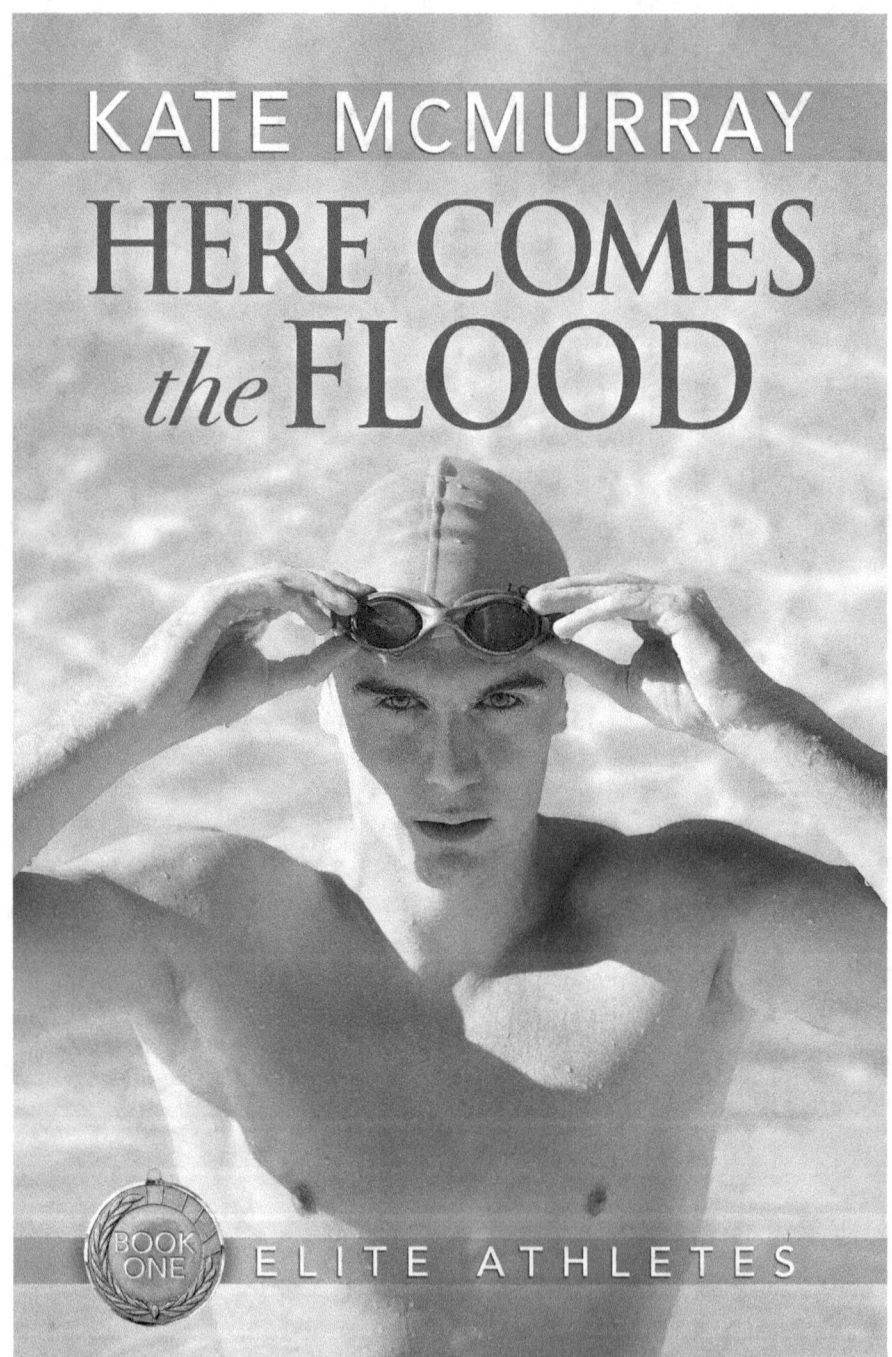

KATE McMURRAY

HERE COMES
the FLOOD

BOOK ONE — ELITE ATHLETES

www.dreamspinnerpress.com

www.ingramcontent.com/pod-product-compliance
Lightning Source LLC
Chambersburg PA
CBHW070116260626
47160CB00004B/1488